ALSO BY WILL LAWRENCE

Williams, Deputy Marshal

Williams, Broken Star

The King: Excerpts from the Chronicles of Agan

Dead Quiet

Dead Tired

Dead Ahead (October 2023)

The Land of Kole—Inoveh

The Kand of Kole—The Beginning

COLLECTED SHORTS

COLLECTED SHORTS

Will Lawrence

ISBN: 978-0-578-37926-5
Independently published

The cover:
Background Photo - Wirestock Creators/Shutterstock
Design - The author

w-lawrence.com
will@w-lawrence.com

For Hiram. Miss you, bud.

Table of Contents

Preface

W hen you're long enough in the tooth to have read, watched, and seen a lot, it's sometimes difficult to know if the brilliant thought that pops into your gourd at three in the morning is uniquely your own.

Humans have been around for thousands of years so I don't think anyone can lay exclusive claim to anything. (Excepting, maybe, the Einsteins of the world.)

I owe debts of gratitude to the artists who've given me inspiration and ideas. If I've missed someone or something obvious, it's because I've Alzed it out or back-brained the whatever decades ago. I welcome all notifications of my omissions.

A big Star Wars fan, I couldn't resist the temptation in "Truck Stop."

"The Bidsim Mods" pays homage to Philip K. Dick for his *Do Androids Dream of Electric Sheep?* and Ridley Scott's 1982 film adaptation "Blade Runner." And even greater honor to Isaac Asimov.

"The Sealed Thingie" was my submission to a short story competition with word count capped at fifteen hundred. I added a teeny bit more detail but tried to stay true to the original lean flavor. This story owes its existence to my ongoing disgust with the predations and machinations of the medical-insurance-big pharma industrial complex and its government enablers. Oh, and a small tip of the hat to the movie "The American President."

"A Perfect Life" was written aboard the cruise ship *Caribbean Princess*, on which guests were subjected to continued reruns of *The Love Boat*. Selected characters from that show make their momentary appearances in this story. There's also a touch of

Gilligan's Island and a hint of the film *Pretty Woman*. Ned Land of Jules Verne's *Twenty Thousand Leagues Under the Seas* stops in for a moment, as does Melville's Moby Dick.

"Reset" owes Sir Francis Galton a nod for his development of eugenics. (Although sadly perverted by the forces of evil and intolerance, it's a concept that bears rational reconsideration.)

Some say it's an urban myth, but seeing what homo sapiens is capable of, I bet that locking a living monkey's head into a vise, cutting the top of its scalp off, and spooning out the brains is a delicacy somewhere on this planet. "The Lord's Table" leans on the notion originally presented in the Twilight Zone episode "To Serve Man": It reduces humanity to happy livestock (think Kobi beef) on its home planet. After all, to me it makes perfect economic sense to minimize shipping and handling costs.

"Dead Ahead" builds on my previous work in *Dead Quiet* and *Dead Tired*. Theresa asked me to put something together in which she was a character. I tried to oblige.

Daniel Defoe's *A Journal of the Plague Year* was the inspiration for "Night Shift." If you ever want to be depressed (anew, I hope) by the recurring human failure to learn anything from history, I highly recommend reading this book and comparing it to the stupidities we saw (and continue to see, as of this writing) during the Covid-19 pandemic that began in 2020. Samuel L. Jackson and *Pulp Fiction* butted in for a second.

For those who profess to be horrified by the antics of the Taliban or the Islamic State, I invite your attention to Catherine Nixey's *The Darkening Age*. The real Saint Shenoute was the inspiration for the character of the same name in "Divine Retribution."

Finally, I continue to owe an extraordinary debt of gratitude to everyone at The Willcox. They keep the Old Thinky flowing. Most of this collection was written there. If you're ever in Aiken, stop in; I'll likely be in a buying mood. Bring a copy of this book with you and the first round will definitely be on me.

Will Lawrence
7 November 2021

Truck Stop

A lan Tyler's subcutaneous implant vibrated and buzzed in his ear. Engrossed with his telescope, a brand-new 350 millimeter Mak-Newt astrograph, he instinctively brushed the side of his head, as if waving away an insect.

"Sir?"

Tyler sighed. "What is it, Stop?" replying to the facility's managing artificial intelligence, Station.

"A vehicle with assisted operation is scheduled to arrive in twenty-one minutes."

The old man groaned as he straightened. He affixed the protective cap onto the objective lens of his pride-and-joy Finished, he stretched and rubbed his lower back. "What's the ride?" he asked.

"A mega-hauler outbound from Detroit with an onboard update to its autonomous response functions."

"I expect it has an escort."

"Yes," Station answered.

"Shit." Tyler looked upward. It had to happen on a perfect night for some great shots of the Eagle Nebulae. "I guess we ought to fire up the kitchen."

"Full operational capability is in four minutes, sir."

The man chuckled. "Don't miss a truck, do you?"

If Station had a face, it would have smiled. "Perhaps, sir, you meant 'trick.'"

"Piss off, Stop."

"Yes, sir." A second passed. "The range reports readiness. Shall I preheat?"

The man sighed. "Who's the backup driver?" he asked.

"Robert Carson"

The man stopped abruptly. "No shit."

Station was accustomed to the ways of the human with which it worked. "None."

"Damn. Thought he was dead," the man muttered.

Station said nothing.

"Hell. Are there any steaks in the fridge?"

"Three ribeyes remain from the last delivery. There is a package on the shelf beneath that I estimate to be—"

"Venison. Yeah. Meat anyway." The man rubbed his chin and snicked his teeth. "Get the steaks started. Ditto potatoes: baked. I'll do the salad."

"Do you wish to have the meat broiled to your preference?"

Alan Tyler snicked his teeth. "Did you ask Carson?"

"Mr. Carson is asleep according to Vehicle."

"Oh Lord," Tyler groaned. "Is the op registered?"

"It is, sir."

"Damn fool." Department of Transportation regulations still required a human at the controls of an autonomous vehicle when running in 'assisted' mode, especially when the trip was registered. Violations could result in loss of all driving privileges for the offender, not to mention the hefty fines DOT loved slapping on anyone breaking their rules. Oh, and jail time, if the AV was involved in an accident. "Do those steaks my way. Bastard can eat grass if he doesn't like medium rare."

Tyler, seventy-eight and the owner of what was still officially known as "Tyler's Fuel and Feed", glanced at the sky, disappointed his viewing session had been interrupted.

He shivered. The night was cooling off; dew was in the air. He remembered when the seventeen acres of blacktop and concrete his daddy had built into one of the most popular stops on the interstate held the day's heat all night. His dad swore astronauts could see the the truck stop while they spun in orbit, the place had been so lit up.

Tyler covered the telescope as the roof of his observatory slid closed with a barely audible *sush*, and as the viewing platform descended to ground level. He stepped outside, locked the door, and made his way to the sole structure that remained after the highway went autonomous and the people stopped coming. The building, once a palace of blinding fluorescence and greasy floors, crammed full of schlock souvenirs, junk food, and (so very long ago) shelves of skin magazines and cheap porno paperbacks, was now dark and silent. *Brooding*, Tyler thought on his darker and lonelier nights.

Chip-based lifeforms don't need any of that crap.

Tyler stopped and watched as a rig slid into one of the twelve induction charging bays. It was black and barely visible, even in the glowing bright of the stars. If he was Station or another rig, he'd be about blinded by the hash the freight hauler was no doubt broadcasting: infrared and ultraviolet running lights; ultra- and very high frequency proximity signals; and scanning with lidar and sonar. Even, sometimes, visible lights if the area was dense with humans.

"What just came in?" Tyler asked Station.

"A Department of Defense contract vehicle. The cargo is classified."

Tyler blinked. "Escorts?"

"None reported or manifested."

"Ah." Tyler shook his head. Government bastards classified anything they could get their hands on, he knew. There were no human escorts or guards so the load was probably toilet paper or something else equally vital to the national defense. He hawked a loogie into the rose bushes he'd planted a few years ago, back when he could get his hands on some grant money the federal assholes were eager to pass out.

It was the second of five Technology Adjustment and Transition Acts that provided Tyler the cash to convert what once had been a fossil fuel- and meat-lover's snarling, fume-filled wet dream into the hushed computer-controlled and monitored destination it had become. The building that once was the center of the truck stop was now Tyler's home. *Saved by the TATAs!*

Station ran the place. Tyler snorted as he stepped through the plate-glass doors that opened before him. *Hell. All I got to do anymore is sleep and shit.* "You take care of everything, don't you, Stop," he muttered ruefully. A little grudgingly. Perhaps a tad mournfully.

"Sir?" Station replied.

"Nuthin'. How's the steak doin'?"

"Thawing."

"Yeah?"

"Yes," Station confirmed. "Mister Carson will be arriving in thirteen minutes."

"Okay. Let's give him some time to stretch and pee." Tyler scratched the back of his head. "How soon does he need to be back on the road?"

"Forty-five minutes after arrival."

"Is he awake yet?"

"Yes. He has acknowledged the stop and has requested human services."

Tyler snorted derisively. "Like what?"

"His request is limited to use of sanitation facilities and refreshments."

Tyler shook his head. "Plan on serving fifteen minutes after he arrives."

"Yes, sir."

Tyler went inside and began to put together a tossed salad. "Hell. We're outta cucumber."

"My apologies, sir. Cucumber is already on tomorrow's delivery order." A millisecond pause. "Mister Carson has arrived."

"No worries on the cukes, Stop. Damn things make me want to fart."

"You always were a stinky sonofabitch."

Tyler whirled and crouched, his favorite twelve-inch chef's knife held low and flat by the side of his thigh. "Who the hell let you in?" he snarled.

Bob Carson smiled and pointed to the ceiling. "It did."

"I did," Station confirmed.

Tyler's eyes narrowed. "You pee yet?"

"Nope. I was in a rush to see my old friend. Don't suppose you've seen him around? Good lookin' fella, sort of rotund, and real soggy in the ass. And not a whole lot of hair." Carson squinted. "You kinda look like him, I gotta admit. I'm bettin' it's a good thing this place don't draw much human traffic. The gay Bay boys would be lusting after that youthful ass and them broad shoulders. Not to mention wantin' to twine their fingers in those golden locks."

"Carson, you're still an asshole. And you're still the fat-ass dickhead I remember. Good to see you, anyway." Tyler stepped over to the sink and rinsed the blade. "Steaks in the broiler, if'n you're interested."

Carson sniffed. "I am. Got time for a 10-100?"

Tyler shrugged. "Station? How long before the steaks are ready?"

"Four and half minutes, sir."

"Well, Carson, as long as you ain't planning on a reading marathon, yeah, you got time. Stop, light up the way."

"Yes, sir," Station answered as a holographic crimson ball formed before Carson. "If you'd follow the guide, sir."

"Will do. Thanks. Uh, Station, right?"

"Yes, sir," Station confirmed.

"Got it. Thanks again, Station. Lead on, if you would."

"Carson?"

"Yeah, Tyler?"

"Be sure to wash your hands."

"Always do."

"Bullshit. That'd be a first," Tyler replied with a sneer.

Carson laughed. "Kiss my ass. Things change. Hell. You learned to grow hair. Why should I be any different?"

Tyler sent his friend off with a double bird and began to set their places. He was studying the wine rack when Carson returned a few moments later. "Feel better?" he asked.

"Oh yeah. And I washed my hands, Didn't I, Station."

"Yes, sir."

"Good to see you, Bob," Tyler offered. "Think you can handle a glass of wine? I've a decent Malbec I think you'd enjoy."

"It's good to see you, as well," Carson answered as they shook hands. He grimaced. "I probably shouldn't."

"Hell, boy. You're already toast," Tyler replied.

"Eh? How's that?"

"Stop told—"

"Stop?"

"Nickname for my friendly AI, Station." Tyler answered. "Anyway. Stop told me you were doin' some snoozin'. You're toast when the feds find out."

Carson chuckled. "They ain't gonna. I know—"

"Station! Privacy," Tyler barked.

Carson blinked and frowned. "What?"

"I thought you were going to say something stupid. Something like you know someone who'd hacked the real-time data stream so your malfeasance wasn't being transmitted to the government assholes. You *were*, weren't you." The broiler chimed; the steaks were ready. "I'm not going down for aiding and abetting a moving violation," he said as he slid his hand into a hot pad.

Carson looked sheepish. "It was nothin' like that. Really. No, Tyler. I mean it. It was..."

Tyler stared quizzically. "It was what?" he asked quietly.

"It's my last run," Carson offered softly after a moment. He shrugged. "Don't matter what I do this time. I'm never driving again."

Tyler nodded. "The wine?"

Carson shrugged. "The doc says I shouldn't."

Tyler plated the flash-baked potatoes. "Doc?"

Carson looked embarrassed. "Booze ain't good for the diabetes," he answered, softly matter-of-fact.

Tyler was stunned. "But that's been cured. Damn. I got fixed."

Carson grimaced. "I happen to be one of goddamn few that can't." He shrugged. "What the hell. I'll try some. One won't hurt."

Tyler poured a sample and passed the glass to his friend. "What do you think?"

Carson sniffed. He took a small sip, his lips parted to take in a small bit of air. "Not bad. Chocolate. Cherry. Hm. A hint of violets, as well. Starts easy on the tongue but swells as it moves onward. Good." He pushed the glass toward Tyler. "If you would be so kind."

Tyler chuckled. "Where the hell did you learn that? You sounded almost educated."

"I took some wine appreciation classes before the doc...well, anyway. I picked up some things." Carson raised an eyebrow. "How'd I do?"

"Good. Cheers."

"Cheers."

They enjoyed their wine for a moment.

"Damn."

"What, Carson?" Tyler asked as he loaded their plates with the steaks.

"I remember when this place was lit up. Full of people. All day and all night." Carson closed his eyes. "I remember how this place smelled. Funny, huh?" He draped his napkin in his lap. "Thanks." He cut into his steak. "Medium rare." He took a bite. "Perfect."

Tyler finished his first bite. "What smell?"

Carson shrugged. "It was a...it was grilled meat. Your daddy did some mean steaks back then. And it was diesel. Not so much that you thought you were outside fueling up, but enough to let you know where you were. Funny, ain't it."

Tyler slowly worked his way through his potato. "Butter? No? Okay." He thought about it as he dolloped butter onto his spud. "No. Not funny. I guess I never noticed it. I grew up here." He frowned. "Was it that bad?"

"Not at all," Carson answered. "It was a home smell, one of those you get as a kid and can't forget. You know: bacon; toast; popcorn; chocolate chip cookies. I ain't ever gonna forget the smell here." He shrugged. "Looks like you're doing all right, anyway."

"Okay, I guess," Tyler agreed. He waved his fork. "TATA Two got me a chunk of change to convert from carbon to induction. The cash for replacing the lot lights and the asphalt came from Four."

Carson leered. "Skim some of those government bucks for the hair and the bod?"

"Didn't have to. All that was Universal Care money after I was diagnosed...Anyway. I agreed to sign up for a stem cell trial." Tyler patted the side of his head. "Worked, yeah?"

Carson laughed. "Wouldn't know. You aren't my type."

"Thank God. Want some more wine?"

Tyler's friend pursed his lips. "I shouldn't. Screw it. A splash, enough to cover the bottom of the glass. Maybe a bit more. That's good. Thanks."

The two said nothing as they finished their steaks and potatoes.

Carson belched. "Good."

Tyler stood and began to clear dinner plates. "Salad?"

"Thought that came first."

Tyler snorted. "Only in America, you low-class heathen. Well?"

"Nah," Carson answered, his pinky working a piece of gristle out of his teeth. "My colon wouldn't know what to do with the roughage," he observed nonchalantly.

"Yeah? Well, mine *does* know," Tyler replied as he tonged a heaping portion of mixed greens into the chilled bowl he'd taken from the freezer.

"Shit, Tyler. You're just trying to keep that ass of yours from swelling anew."

"Sure. Why not?" Tyler shrugged. "It was a long time coming. I'm doing what I can to keep it." He leaned across the table. "Unlike you. Guess you like that extra cushion." He winked. "Adds a bit of comfort on all those long miles, I suppose."

Carson reached across the table for the wine. "Ain't so many of those anymore," he replied tersely as he poured for himself some more wine.

Tyler said nothing as he watched his friend fill his glass to the brim. He watched as his friend gulped a half-glass of the wine. "Should I open another bottle?" he asked quietly.

"So. What do you do for fun these days?" Carson asked, ignoring the question.

"Keep an eye on things, mostly. When I'm finished, I have a small gym out in what was the bunkhouse." He paused for a second. "Silicon shit is why you're retiring?" he asked quietly, delicately.

Carson's emotionless response was confirmation. "Some. Mostly. I guess. Things ain't the same." He sighed. "Damn computers." He muttered as he crossed his arms. "Why'd you decide on the cosmetic makeover? You're still the same cheesedick I knew."

Tyler flipped him off.

"There's a story there, bud."

Tyler went for another bottle of wine. "It wasn't anything," he muttered as he twisted off the screwcap. "Ready?"

"No, thanks. I'm good. And bullshit: It was something. Woman?"

"Damn it. Yes," Tyler admitted.

Carson leaned back in his chair. "Thought so. Let's hear it."

Tyler slumped into his chair. "She was a babe. A software engineer, she said, riding one of the first AVs, right after the Government converted the slow lane on the interstate to autonomous only." He sighed. "Her rig pulled in, straight onto the induction pad like it was supposed to. She came inside and ordered some lunch." He grimaced. "This was back when DOT's rules for humans were still in force." He shrugged. "She was here for awhile: mandatory rest stop."

"You tried to move on her, I bet" Carson speculated.

Tyler chewed his lip. "Yep."

"What happened?"

"She told me she'd rather have sex with Jabba the Hut," Tyler quietly recollected.

Carson guffawed. "You *were* a lard-ass back then."

"Fuck off," Tyler told Carson wearily. "It was a good thing. I guess." He gestured at himself. "I'm now healthy as shit and a fine figure of a man, thanks to modern medical science. And, I gotta admit, thanks to one smart-ass bitch."

Carson smiled. "What was her name?"

"Janet."

"Ever see her again?" Carson asked.

"No. Didn't—don't—want to."

"Well, what do you do around here in the evening?" Carson asked as he looked around. "Got yourself one of them 'hypoallergenic surrogates' Health Services is pushing?"

"Fuck that," Tyler protested. "I have a stable of blow-up dolls in all shapes and sizes. With those, I don't have to worry about telemetry getting back to the Government."

"No shit? Can I borrow one?" Carson asked.

Tyler snorted. "I'd let you use my toothbrush before that. Besides, you have everything you need at the end of your arms."

"Yeah. But I was looking for some variety."

"Use your toes."

Carson grinned. "Tried. The knees don't bend like they use to." He glanced outside. "Guess you don't need good knees these days around here."

Tyler sipped wine. "Not really, no." He shrugged. "To tell the truth, the silicon pretty much runs itself. An hour, maybe two, in the morning, to wander around the place. Hell. That's not necessary; Station does all the real work, don't you, Stop."

"Your oversight is required by law, Mister Tyler. I am happy to assist in any way I can," Stop replied.

Tyler rolled his eyes.

Carson grinned. "So. Aside from pumpin' iron and slippin' your rod into latex love-dolls, what else do you do to keep busy?"

"Got some grant money and built a small observatory out back," Tyler answered. "I'm one of the space agency's citizen data harvesters," he declared proudly. "I was outside with my new rig when you showed. Wanna see it?"

Carson blinked as he unconsciously touched an ear. "Like to but can't. Truck just said I gotta go in five minutes. Anyway. Science ain't my gig." He stood. Stretched.

Tyler, too, stood. "Good to see you, man."

"Thanks. And thanks for the grub. Are you sure you can't—"

"Thank Stop. It did all the work," Carson quickly deflected.

"Ah. Right. Okay. Thanks, Stop," Tyler offered sadly. "Well. I better git before the rig leaves without me."

"No. You don't want that to happen. Feds would be all over your ass," Tyler agreed as he led his friend to the door. Station dimmed the interior lights a few seconds before they stepped into the chilly night.

"Brr. Cold," Carson shivered. "Fuck the feds. I'm sick of their shit." The gull-wing door on his rig opened silently, the interior lit by dim red night-lights. "Home. Sweet fuckin' home." He held out his hand. "Take care, you old sunabitch."

Tyler took Carson's hand. "You bet. Stop by again." He winced, embarrassed, unable to go back in time to retract the absurdity.

"Sure. Soon. Right after the guvmint lets us drive on the big road again." Carson declared sardonically. He tossed a two-fingered salute and shuffled to the dark monster waiting for him.

Tyler waved as the rig gently hissed off the induction stand.

Carson raised a hand in reply.

Tyler watched as the AV disappeared from sight. "What time is it, Stop?"

"Zero two thirty-eight."

"How's the weather holding?" he asked.

"Viewing conditions remain optimal. JPL confirms receipt of your earlier data," Station answered.

"Yeah? Let's see if I can't send 'em some more. Open her up."

"I already have, sir."

"Damn, Stop. You think of everything."

Station verified the rig who carried the human Tyler was no longer capable of transmitting telemetry.

"Yes, sir. I do try to help."

The Bidsim Mods

Product Quality Control Monitoring, Rytell Corporation

O ne of two duty technicians kicked her coworker's chair. "Hey, Smith! Wake up, asshole. We got a deader."

Smith snapped out of his doze. "Bullshit. It's only just past," he glanced at the digital timer mounted above the status boards mounted on the front wall of the control room, "23 hour. You're just messing with me." He flipped her off and closed his eyes. He snapped them open when he heard her make the call.

"Corp," she snapped. "Activate the emergency duty roster. Priority," she studied her console for a few seconds, "contact to Corporate Legal."

"The duty roster has been activated, Technician Bradford. Attorney Hudson is standing by," Corporation confirmed.

"Shit," Technician Smith muttered, now fully awake. He scanned the alert displayed on his console:

Client ID 209 (Vanderbilt, C.). Deceased.
Model Romeo.
Product ID Romeo Hotel 99.
Click, Tap, or Speak for Mods Listing.

"Display product mods," Smith ordered, hoping for the best, expecting the worst.

The worst it was.

"Double shit." Smith saw Bradford was on a sealed comm. He checked the incident status; yes, she was briefing the lawyer. "Corp, get me a priority connect to the duty factory rep."

"Factory Representative Derrick is holding, Technician. Sealed or open?"

"Sealed. Hey, Derrick. This is Smith in Monitoring."

"What's the flap?" Derrick asked.

"A dead client."

"Indeed. That's why I'm standing here dripping semen on the floor when it should be merrily conveying my spermatozoa to its greater glory," Derrick replied. "Who was it?"

"Vanderbilt. Cecil Vanderbilt. Domicile is—"

"Empire Towers, Penthouse Thirteen," Derrick interrupted. "How'd we find out?"

"The unit commed Corporate."

"The Romeo?"

"Yes," Smith confirmed. "There are no other products at that customer location."

Derrick already had the answer but asked anyway: "Any unit telemetry available?" He knew the standard specifications and available options by heart. Especially for the Romeo line. Especially for the Hotel models.

"Factory recovery only," Smith confirmed.

"I expect the Constabulary has been notified. What about a lawyer?" Derrick asked.

"Corp passed the alert on to the Constabulary per protocol. Bradford's on the comm now with Attorney Hudson; did you want to speak to her?"

"No. Zip up the legal bullshit and make sure it's downloaded to me. I'm heading to the scene now."

Empire Towers

Derrick's car slowed and began to turn. The gate before him rose and the vehicle made its way down into the sub-basement garage.

As Car looked for its assigned parking spot, Derrick checked his mobile comp and confirmed the documentation—production history, test validations, behavior analyses, purchase contract, and the oh-so-important releases from liability—had been downloaded.

Car eased its way into a space and stopped. "Technician Smith wishes to speak with you, sir," it said.

"What do you want, Smith?" Derrick asked after he authorized the incoming comm.

"Car reports your arrival at the scene. Attorney Hudson is expected to arrive in seven minutes. Corp says the download was completed."

"I have it," Derrick said. "When's Corporate Communications expected to arrive?"

"In about an hour," Smith answered. "Representative Rockwell's flight home was hung up in Atlanta; tornados shut down the airport."

"No backup?" Derrick wondered dryly.

"Sandler's assigned but we've been unable to comm him. Hold on. Yep, Director Farmer is on her way. Her car says she's approximately ten minutes out." A pause. "And Representative Sandler's employment has been terminated."

"Tell the good Director that KMBA is already on the scene." Derrick had ordered Car to circle the building before they parked.

"She's gonna shit," Smith observed. KMBA was a shill for Rytell's only real competitor, Natural Love Technologies. NLT paid well to ensure the news station used every possible opportunity to embarrass Rytell Corporation.

"Indeed!" Derrick agreed cheerily. "Am I good to go?"

"Yes. Towers confirms receipt of your credentials and has given you temporary access to the residential lifts. The on-scene Constabulary commander also confirms."

"Got it. Clear." Derrick stepped out of the car. His implant chimed, announcing an incoming comm.

"Welcome, Representative, to Empire Towers. The amber lights will guide you to the residential lift."

Empire Towers, Penthouse Thirteen

Derrick stepped out of the lift. "I'm—"

"Factory Representative Derrick. Rytell Corporation," the visored constable standing in the hall finished. "I'll escort you inside."

Derrick couldn't tell if the cop was a man or woman, or even human. The voice was flattened by the helmet's speaker. The gold finish of the visor's anti-laser coating obscured the individual's features. Breasts, if any, were smashed by body armor and an equipment harness.

And no matter how nice a person's ass might be, the black flame-resistant cop-suits made all butts look big.

Derrick followed the policeman into the penthouse. Despite it being his third visit, he was still impressed. Residents had to have—and maintain—seven figure incomes and six figure portfolios. They were free to decorate their homes however they wished once they closed the sale. Vanderbilt had opted for a surprisingly tasteful Italian Renaissance look that was all creamy marble and lots of indirect lighting. The furniture was functionally elegant. The chairs and divans inviting and comfortable whether it was a white-tie dinner party or scumming around on Saturday morning in one's underwear, scanning the news or snoozing in front of the fire.

Derrick knew the paintings and sketches on the walls were originals. Appraisals were part of the financial statements Rytell required customers to provide before it would send a top-of-the-line model into the field. He also knew Vanderbilt was a human pig which made his taste in furnishings surprisingly incongruous;

psychological profiles of prospective customers were also required.

The cop led Derrick into the master bedroom. One man, frazzled and tired looking, wearing a pair of faded blue jeans and a tatty corduroy jacket, watched as a pair of white-suited crime scene personnel took pictures and gathered evidence. They'd save the largest piece, the corpse sprawled face-up across the bed, for the coroner.

Jacket man looked up when Derrick walked into the room. "You're the factory rep."

"Yes. Name's Derrick."

"I'm Detective Watts. I thought you people built better."

Derrick said nothing. Consumer and client product issues were best handled by the corporate attorneys and, when necessary, the public relations flacks. *Farmer's gonna have her hands full with this one,* Derrick thought. The deceased was prominent in the local community, someone with the pretensions of leadership that come from having too much money.

"What do you think?" Watts asked as he pointed at the bed.

"Well. It's a dead body," Derrick noted blandly. Vanderbilt's lifeless eyes bulged from his face and his tongue protruded stiffly from his mouth. And there was no mistaking the smell of feces, voided from the gelatinous blob when it died.

"Right. Be an asshole," Watts snarled.

"Sorry, Detective," Derrick held his hands up in apology. "I was hoping I wouldn't have to work tonight." He shrugged. "Hands and feet cuffed to the bed posts and a silk scarf around the neck. No surprise. Where's the unit?"

"In the study down the hall. I have a couple of uniforms watching it. I need you to put it in safe mode so I can take it downtown."

Derrick was perplexed. "Downtown? For what?"

"Are you serious? I got me a homicide here."

Attorney Hudson stepped into the room. "Homicide, by definition, is an act between humans." She glanced around the room. "So, we'll retrieve the unit and leave you to your work."

"Bullshit," a red-faced Watts spat.

Hudson nodded agreeably. "That may be. But the fact of the matter is title reverted back to Rytell when the customer became deceased. You may have unlawfully taken possession of a corporate asset. Your continued possession of said asset will result in Rytell Corporation suing you, the Constabulary, and the city for theft."

"Residence streamed the suite security video for us when we arrived. Besides, it—your *unit*—said it was strangling the man."

"And that means what?"

"It means there's a dead fat white guy on the bed. Killed by your unit," Watts answered sourly.

"Detective. I'm glad you said that in the privacy of this room. Otherwise, I'd have to sue for slander." Hudson crossed her arms. "But it's late and I'm sure we're either tired or wishing we were doing something a bit more pleasant." She coughed. "Can we step into the hall and away from this?"

"No."

Hudson smiled at the detective's peevishness. "As you wish, Detective. First. Any statement made by a synthetic not made in the presence of a registered psychorobiticist is inadmissible. Are you one? Was there one present at the time? No, I didn't think so. Second. If the unit did in fact cause the man's death, this is a product liability concern of the Rytell Corporation. Which, in this particular case, is not a concern at all. But even if it were, it would be a matter of civil law, *not* of criminal law. And, then, third. There is no evidence that the man died by strangulation. That is merely conjecture on your part. Unless the medical examiner has made her determination as to the cause of death?" Hudson smiled. "She and I were at the same opera. I left during intermission to come here. She, on the other hand, appeared to be interested only in her wine. And the second half. So I expect no formal determination has yet been made."

Watts glared. "The law says history and data extracted from the unit *is* admissible. I'm sure that in the spirit of cooperation, you'll download the data before you take your property away."

"That's not possible," Derrick interjected.

The detective crossed his arms. "Tell me why" he ordered, his anger a soft flutter beneath the syllables.

"The Romeo line—"

Watts snorted derisively. "What's down the hall isn't any Romeo. Juliet, maybe."

"We use the phonetic alphabet internally to label the various lines. As I was saying," Derrick continued, "there's no external interface; data extraction for this production series has to be performed at the factory as it requires some delicate microsurgery."

"You're naturally free to observe the extraction," Hudson offered. "In addition, I believe the data stream can be replicated in real time directly into a receiving storage unit you may provide."

"That's true," Derrick confirmed. "Provided it has a compatible interface."

Hudson went on: "Regardless of whether the Constabulary chooses to observe, the extraction will be recorded and a copy of that record provided with a copy of the data."

"How'd you get away with that?" Watts asked.

Derrick chanced a quick glance at Hudson.

"I think we can rely on the detective's sense of discretion," she answered the unspoken question. "And if it proves otherwise, why, we're all aware of the remedies available to Rytell. Detective, what we're about to share with you is considered corporate proprietary. Do you agree to keep it confidential and for your information only?"

"I suppose you're recording," Watts observed sarcastically.

"Since I arrived, Detective. As have you," Hudson replied with a raised eyebrow, seemingly surprised by a statement of the blindingly obvious.

Watts gave a small nod and conceded the point to Hudson. "Yes. I agree."

"The Romeo series original design specifications were developed to satisfy a government requirement for a unit able to pass for human under all but the most intrusive inspections," Derrick said as he scratched the back of his head. "Those specs posed some interesting design challenges that took time to overcome. Rytell incurred some significant contract penalties because of the delay," Derrick recalled ruefully. "But overcome the challenges were. One of the contract conditions was that Rytell would be able take commercial advantage of the capabilities of the Romeos. The federal agency involved agreed to facilitate the granting of the appropriate exceptions with the Justice Department."

"We can share those exceptions with the Constabulary, provided those with access have the appropriate clearances," Hudson interjected.

"We'll see," Watts replied. "Can you tell me something about what makes these units so special?"

"Feel free, Derrick," Hudson said. "It's published, after all."

Derrick nodded as he continued. "When we, Rytell, fully understood the likely operational use cases for the Romeos, we were able to translate those into some significant selling points."

"Those would be?" Watts wondered.

"The almost total elimination of the more awkward mechanical aspects associated with simulating human bodily functions for starters." Derrick thumbed a wave at the corpse. "More importantly, customers like Vanderbilt are willing to pay nicely for being able to touch a unit and not run a finger or a tongue over an interface, whether subcutaneous or implemented in an externally accessible orifice." Derrick snicked his teeth. "'Romeo' is phonetic for 'Real', Detective Watts. Some of my more humorous colleagues call the Hotel models 'Real Human'."

"Let's not forget the provisions for client privacy," Hudson reminded Derrick.

"Ah, right. One of our premium options is the ability for the customer to deactivate the standard situational recording; no audio or video. Nor is there any telemetry transmission to the factory." Derrick sighed. "Since that makes remote diagnostics impossible, it also makes remote bioware updates equally impossible."

"Must be expensive," Watts observed snidely.

"It is. It requires a degree of human interaction and intervention virtually unheard of anymore," Derrick agreed. "That's what brought me here a few months back. I had to escort the Romeo back to Service for a diagnostic check and software update."

Watts shook his head. "You know, the notion of having sex with a thing makes me queasy. I prefer the old fashioned Rosy method." He glared. "But the unit down the hall has me questioning my preferences," Watts muttered with disgust. "I wish you'd call it something else. Romeo in my mind does not have long honey-blonde hair, great breasts, or a killer ass."

"The factory assigned name is Rachel," Derrick softly replied. "I believe the customer preferred 'Slut'. During the day, anyway.

"Okay. Now what the hell does *that* mean?" Watts asked.

Derrick glanced at the cadaver and chose to answer indirectly. "However, when Customer Vanderbilt decided to play, he preferred Miriam."

"Play?"

"What you see here, Detective," Hudson answered.

"You mean the bondage."

"And the strangulation. Yes," Derrick replied. "Vanderbilt had an unusually complex set of requirements, well beyond our usual options." He sighed. "Even for this."

"You're serious," Watts said tersely. "You have 'options' for *this* kind of crap?"

"Rytell doesn't advertise them. It's up to a perspective customer to inquire as to their availability," Derrick answered. "We call them the Bidsim mods."

"Who's Bidsim?"

"Not a who, a what: Bidsim. Bondage. Domination. Sadism. Masochism. In addition to the physical modifications necessary to simulate things such as bruising and erythema, the—"

"Era what?" Watts wondered.

"Erythema. When the skin turns red after being slapped."

"Oh."

Derrick went on: "The mods require relaxing the standard Asimov Laws in the unit, particularly—no, *especially*—the First Law; that's Alpha One. In Vanderbilt's case, we had to notch that setting down to the absolute legal minimum and crank up Alpha Two, the Second Law, to enable the strangulation. But Rytell decided these had to be temporary setting changes; the unit would revert back to the installation defaults when commanded to do so by Vanderbilt." He rubbed his chin wearily. "We also had to clock down Alpha Three to be on the safe side."

"Why?"

"Vanderbilt was erratic and abrupt in his transitions between dom and sub. Either way, he was extremely abusive." Derrick looked sick. "The first two units we placed here were scrapped after they were damaged beyond economical repair. I argued against selling a third."

Hudson shrugged. "Because of that history, Rytell charged heavily for the additional service and options. Given the nature of those options and the sensitive nature of the Alpha adjustments, we also demanded he place in trust ten million credits which would immediately become Rytell's if he or anyone associated with him attempted to sue the corporation. An insurance fund, so to speak, to help discourage any precipitate legal action, and thus helping to ensure Rytell would be free of any liability in the event of untoward consequences resulting from the installation of those behavior modifications."

"Ten million? He agreed to that?" Watts asked, dumbfounded.

"His lawyer was adamantly against it. However, Vanderbilt willingly signed." Hudson smiled. "He fired his attorney as soon as the contract was finalized. In any case, the interest on the escrow account was his and his alone. For all intents and purposes, it was simply another investment for him," Hudson answered with a disinterested shrug.

Watts shook his head. "Wait a minute. The behavior parameters are fixed by law," Watts said.

"What humans can fix, humans can unfix," Hudson replied with a small smile. "Or adjust to accommodate the circumstances."

"Let me guess: your special federal friends leaned on Justice for this bullshit, as well."

"Perhaps," Hudson agreed. "I have no specific knowledge of that. But the fact is we do have a Justice Department exception." She chuckled. "Based upon what I've observed over the years, there's a surprising number of powerful and politically influential people who enjoy this sort of activity. I can imagine how our federal friends would find it useful to know who those might be. Domestically or diplomatically."

Watts looked ready to spit in Hudson's face. "I always figured you shits were nothing more than pimps."

"We didn't invent humanity, Detective," Hudson replied, brushing off the insult. "We simply provide it the services it demands."

"Yeah? Tell me: Do you have a Justice Department exception that allows you to sell kid lookalikes? What do you call those, hm? Toys?" He sneered at Derrick. "Sorry. I should have said Tango Hotels, shouldn't I've?"

"We leave that segment of the market to our competitors on the other side of the Pacific, Detective." Hudson took a breath. "As we seem to have digressed from the reason why we're here, I suggest Mr. Derrick retrieve the unit so he can get it to the factory."

A uniformed constable stepped into the room. "The coroner's team has arrived, Detective."

"Get 'em up here," Watts ordered sourly. He faced Hudson. "And I'm not releasing the unit into your custody. It's going downtown with me."

"You have no legal basis, Detective. The provisions of the Synthetic Intelligence Protection Act alone prevent you from doing so." Hudson reminded him flatly.

Watts snorted and sneered. "SIPA's corporate bullshit."

"Perhaps," Hudson agreed, "but irrelevant. Prevent Mr. Derrick from doing his job and I'll see to it that you are sued into penury. And I can guarantee you'll never work in law enforcement again. Anywhere."

"Are you threatening me?" Watts asked with a small, dangerous laugh

"Not in the least. Merely acquainting you with the facts of life as they apply to this situation." Hudson yawned. "Excuse me. Look, Detective Watts. You wouldn't arrest a ground car that had wrapped around a tree killing the drunk at the controls. Nor would you incarcerate the knife some poor unfortunate used to slit her wrists. The Romeo, Rachel, is a thing, Detective, as is the ground car and the knife. That she looks like a person and can act like a person doesn't make her more than the thing she is."

"The car would go into impound and the knife into the evidence locker, ma'am," Watts riposted.

Hudson nodded. "True. But then in this case you wouldn't have the data you seek."

The detective reddened and glared. "How long before I have the data extract?" Watts finally asked, the angry flush faded.

"The procedure takes approximately two hours," Derrick answered as he looked at his watch. "We can stream the data to the Constabulary sometime around 0300."

"If I don't have it by 0400, I'll come looking for you both and bust your asses for obstruction of justice before I take possession of the unit. Now, take your *thing* and get the fuck out of here."

The Sealed Thingy

A young girl stepped into a room dominated by the hospital bed and medical apparatus that seemed to imprison the old man in the middle of it all. "They're talking about who's going to kill you." She sat.

"Damn," Grandpa coughed and closed his eyes. "I wish they'd be quieter about it."

Madison stretched from her grandfather's easy chair and pushed the bedroom door closed.

Grandpa wheezed. "Thanks, Maddie."

"I hate when you call me that."

Despite the cannula connecting the old man to his oxygen, he managed a cheery grin. "I know," he cackled evilly. That led to a racking cough.

Maddie stood and walked to the side of the bed. She wiped his mouth and nose. "No."

"No? No, what?"

"I'm not going to wipe your butt, Grandfather."

He chuckled toothlessly. He quit bothering with dentures when they brought him home to die. It didn't matter: All his nourishment came from the IV drips hanging from the head of his bed. "You aren't going to let me forget that, are you?"

She crossed her arms. "Nope."

He chuckled again. "You can be a bitch, Maddie."

"Probably. Does it matter? You like it."

"And a smart ass, as well. Just like your mother." He sobered as he pushed his head into his pillow. "What's her take on this?"

Maddie hooked her thumb toward the IV pole that stood in a distant corner of her grandfather's bedroom. "That?"

"Yeah."

She shrugged. "She seems to understand." She frowned.

Her grandfather noticed. "What?"

"I don't know why it's so hard," she answered a moment later. "I mean, I get it."

William Pierce, eighty-seven, retired lawyer, and current—dying—cancer patient, fumbled the bed control.

"Can I help?"

"I can do it. I'm not totally helpless."

Madison, fourteen, currently a student, chuckled. "Oh? Really?"

William gave Maddie the finger, wincing as the IV needle grated inside his flesh at the abrupt and extreme movement. He ignored Madison's raised eyebrow as the head of the bed elevated enough so he could sit upright. "Yes. Damn it. 'Oh. Really.'" He paused for a few breaths. "Jesus."

"Are you okay, Grandpa?" she asked softly.

His eyes were scrunched shut. "Lord, girl. I'm dying. How can I be more okay than that?" He opened his eyes, once a deep azure, but now a washed-out, murky gray, the color of sun-bleached asphalt. William thought she looked like she might cry. He huffed and straightened. "But that isn't news, right? Right?" He didn't wait for an answer. "What about your aunt?"

"Which one?" Maddie asked as she answered a text message.

"The one with the lunch-tray ass, four tits, and a horn growing out of her forehead."

Her head snapped upwards. "What?" Maddie asked incredulously.

"I was wondering if you were paying attention. Why do you have your head in that thing all the time?"

Madison rolled her eyes and ignored the question. "*Which* aunt?"

"Your mother's sister."

Maddie's eyes went wide before they rolled around their sockets. "They're both her sisters. Have you gone mental?"

He sniggered. "Got you to pull your head out of the whatever-it-is, didn't I? Do you ever read a book? You know, something made of paper?" he asked sarcastically. He took a breath. "Adelaide," he answered Maddie's original question.

Madison shook her head. "She's worse than mom. I can't believe they're sisters."

William managed to quirk an eyebrow slightly. "Oh? How's that?" He coughed a little.

She managed to look embarrassed.

William noticed. "Tell me."

Maddie shrugged. "I, um, call her Aunt Addled. Not to her face, though."

He snorted so hard the cannula flew out of his nose. "'Addled!' I love it!" It took only a few seconds before his chortles became a weak, racking cough. "Damn," he wheezed tiredly. "I love it."

Maddie wiped pink froth from his mouth. "Grandpa?"

"What?"

"What's a lunch-tray ass?"

William slapped the bed weakly and gasped.

Madison flushed when she realized he was laughing. "Well?" she demanded.

He spread his arms, careful not to wrench the needles stuck into his forearm and his hand. "It's a butt this wide. It sticks this far out; big enough you can set your lunch tray on it while you decide which dessert you're going to have. I learned that when I started going for chemo."

Maddie giggled. "Aunt Adelaide—"

"Addled works for me."

They sniggered together.

"Aunt Addled's butt is not that big, Grandpa."

His eyes glittered. "I know. Like I said: I got your attention."

Madison tossed the tissue into the wastebasket. "The last time I was in the kitchen, she was saying she'd have nothing to do with it."

William's face settled. "Doesn't surprise me. She always was a dipshit."

"Grandpa!"

"What?"

"She's your daughter."

He shrugged a small, bedridden shrug. "Just makes it easier to judge. Sydney, at least, has brains and a good head on her shoulders." He shook his head.

"What?"

"For a smart girl, your mom married a real dip."

Maddie giggled. "He's not bad. I think it's kinda cute: Sydney and Wade. Sounds like a movie."

"What was he doing, the last time you were out there?"

"Listening, mostly."

"Yeah?"

"Yes. I heard him tell them it wasn't really his to say, but if mom or the others couldn't make a decision, he'd—"

William chanced ripped veins and shot upright. "No!" he spat. "Not him," he managed before another coughing spasm. "Someone I love. Not him." He gasped. "You make sure they know that."

"I will, Grandpa."

"Good." He took a breath. "What about the other one, uh . . ."

"Alice."

"Yes."

"Don't know. She didn't saying anything when I was around."

He sighed. "She never did have much to say. Don't know where that came from. Probably the milkman."

"What's a milkman?"

"Usually a bad joke."

"I don't understand."

"You will. One day."

Madison watched him fall asleep. She fiddled with her device for a few moments. She stood and walked into the distant corner. She split her attention between the appliance there and the content streaming on her tablet.

"What're you doing?"

"Looking," Madison answered. "You want anything?"

"I want them to pull their heads out of their asses." His eyes watered. "It hurts. I want this done."

"*No! I won't!*" A door slammed, a muted thud to William and Madison.

William groaned. "What the hell are those idiots *doing*?"

Madison stepped to the window and pulled the curtain aside. "It's Aunt Addie. She's outside; yep, crying." She shook her head. "Want me to go find out what's going on?"

"No. I know what's going on. They got down to picking straws. Addie won. But the girl doesn't have any balls."

Madison giggled. "None of them do, Grandpa."

"You know what I meant, Maddie." He groaned and shifted the pillow. "I guess it's not their fault."

"What?"

"The difficulty."

She pointed. "That? Why?"

"Most of my life, someone who wanted to take the easy way out shot himself, or jumped off a bridge. For my girls? Well, it started out the same. Then people started talking about it; then some started doing it. It was illegal for a long time."

"What happened?"

The old man's smile was wan. "The government and the insurance companies finally realized it was cheaper. That was enough to make it legal, moral, even, when they bought the bible-thumpers off. You grew up with that. My girls didn't."

"Oh." She stared across the room. "Grandpa?"

"What?"

"I'd do it for you."

His toothless smile was bright. "I know." He paused. "You're a minor. Next year, maybe, with my permission, the government would let you." He sniffed. "I'd wait a year for the honor and privilege of having you see me off." He blinked a few times. "I don't have a year. I don't *want* a year."

Madison sniffed. "I understand."

"Anyway, you don't know how to work the thing."

"Bullshit."

"Maddie!"

She ignored the feeble rebuke. "I could. Here." She held up the tablet and tapped an icon.

They watched together for a moment.

"That's it?" he asked tremulously.

"Yep."

"Show me."

Maddie wheeled the termination unit to the side of the bed. She started pointing: "The needle cap comes off. The needle goes into the catheter. The seal gets popped." She took a breath. "This thingy gets twisted." She shrugged. "Easy."

Another muted thud.

"What now?" he wondered wearily.

Madison went to the window. "Mom and Alice are talking to Addie."

"Crying? Hollering?"

"Crying, yes. No one's yelling."

"I wish I still had a pistol," he rasped and closed his eyes. He began to snore.

Madison started to doze off herself.

"Are they still outside?" he asked softly a few moments later.

Madison woke up and looked. "Yeah."

"Jesus." William studied Madison, illumined by the afternoon sun as she watched out the window. "You're a beautiful girl. You're going to break hearts."

She blushed. "That's more bullshit."

"It's not. Show me again."

She did. "Easy, right?"

"Yes, it is easy. Madison?"

"Grandpa?"

"I'm glad it's you. I don't give a shit what the government says. Not now."

Madison frowned. "Are you sure?"

"More than you know. Go on."
She popped the seal a few seconds later.
"I love you, Madison."
She twisted the thingy. "I love *you*, Grandpa."

A Perfect Life

R ichard arrived on Earth with more than the standard share of Perfection alloted to a new human.

The proto-spirit destined to become Doctor Richard Ellsworth Conrad was next in line at the Perfection Distribution Point, patiently awaiting its receipt of its allocation of Perfection. But the Perfection Distribution Device coughed and died after the spirit in front of Doctor Conrad-to-be received its measure of Perfection.

The Proto-Spirit Assembly Line screeched to a halt in a dignified and spiritual manner. The Duty Apprentice responsible for ensuring the Perfection Distribution Device was kept filled with Perfection was nowhere to be seen for he was off playing with his Harp.

The gruff grey-haired Chief Spirit in charge of Perfection Distribution thundered and stormed. He threatened the shame-faced Duty Apprentice—when he finally appeared—with permanent reassignment to the House of Representatives. The Duty Apprentice shuddered with horror; he did not yet know the Chief Spirit lacked the authority to condemn anyone to Eternal Damnation in the Lowest Circle of Perdition. (Nor did the Duty Apprentice know the threat was hollow: The House already overflowed with Clowns and the wait list for occupancy was completely filled for at least the next few Earthly Decades.)

The Duty Apprentice sheepishly tucked his Harp into his robes and hastened to refill the Device.

Happy the delay had not been inordinate and pleased the Line was ready to restart, the Chief Spirit failed to notice the Duty Apprentice had forgotten to properly clear and reset the Perfection Dispenser.

Perfection, as we all know, is toxic in excessive quantities.

Massive over-allocations of Perfection are rare but not unheard of. Should one occur, the spirit will be removed from the Line and purged of the excess, if possible, and discarded if not.

It is quite easy to identify a massive over-allocation: the spirit swells so much that it plugs the line. If the massive over-allocation is the result of a Maintenance Failure, the entire Staff of Perfection Distribution is reassigned to the Sewers of Spirit Disposal for a millenia or three.

Critical over-allocations are, unfortunately, more common and, unless a keen eye is affixed to the Perfection Distribution process, virtually impossible to detect during Manufacturing.

It is only after Delivery that a critical over-allocation can be identified. The victims—known as Coans in Spirit parlance— quickly develop an incurable rash on the brain. As the rash grows, the brain swells, forcing intellection from the Coan's ears. Drivel flows unceasingly from lips that have become pursed, their corners twisted downward. (Biting into a Perfect Lemon can produce a similar effect.) Clouded vision makes it difficult to discern others and then only from the bottom of the eyes, yet perversely sharpens visual acuity in the presence of reflective surfaces. And Coans are quite prone to hallucinations and delusions, with the belief that they are the Center of the Universe the most common.

It is with Heavenly Irony that secondary and tertiary symptoms present in those within proximity of a swollen-headed Coan. Rolling eyeballs, frequent unnecessary visits to the closest Waste Flushing Facility, or activation of those areas of the brain set aside for the planning of homicide, are sure indicators of the presence of a Coan.

As are the pleas for Divine Intervention. The Very Big Kahuna smiles and points to the Small Print, reminding the beggars that proper installation and maintenance was and is their responsibility. If that fails to convince, why then, VBK trots out the Cosmic No Deposit-No Return Policy, thereby placing the onus of dealing with the Failure squarely on the shoulders of those who wail and moan the loudest. (And absolving Himself of any future responsibility and liability, to boot.)

Fortunately, the spirit-who-would-be-Richard received only a small extra measure of Perfection, the tiny dribble that always remained in the dispenser tube, no matter how well calibrated the Perfection Distribution Device. Neither the Chief Spirit or the Duty Apprentice realized what had happened.

The Line restarted, the Chief Spirit sternly admonished the Apprentice for playing with his harp whilst on duty. If found doing so again, the Chief Spirit would turn the Apprentice Blind. (This threat was real as it was well within the Chief Spirit's Limits of Authority, along with other sanctions such as Hairy Palms and Tuneless Harps.)

The Duty Apprentice cringed as he suffered the Rebuke of the Chief Spirit.

The Conrad proto-spirit glided ethereally to the next station and on to the end of the Line without further incident.

* * *

Richard Ellsworth Conrad was the Perfect Delivery at the Perfect Time, this after nine months of Perfect Gestation, and that after the Perfect Climax to a Perfect Evening.

Richard courteously announced his desire to see a bit more of the world with a gentle tap-tap of his toes against the wall of his Room.

It was the Perfect Time for the Perfect Arrival. His mother was in the hospital visiting a friend who'd broken her leg eventing. His father, home on vacation, a rare break between his frequent trips abroad, was in the Coffee Shoppe next door to the hospital. He was struggling to finish a double latte with a necessary acquaintence who clearly presented the late-stage symptoms of Critical Over-allocation. And so when Richard's mother made The Call, Richard's father was afforded the Perfect Excuse to rush away.

Richard's father's timing was Perfect; he dashed onto the elevator in which Richard's mother was being shown to her maternity room.

Richard's arrival was Perfectly and Quietly Dignified. His mother made no fuss, offered no red-faced rants or screams or moans, threatened no one (not even Richard's father), and issued no demands for opiates. She barely broke a sweat. Nor did she make much muss, less than the usual aftermath, as was noted by some of the attending staff.

(The hospital's accountant was not at all pleased, however. He growled and moaned when he realized Richard's mother had declined to avail herself of the entire range of mechanical and chemical delivery services, the prices for which contributed nicely to the state of the hospital's balance sheet.)

Richard's father stood to one side, paid close attention, beamed proudly, and suffered no ill effects from the Perfect Event to which he bore witness.

Richard himself made his way out of his mother's Perfect Room already bright-eyed and cooing happily. No paddles or swats were needed to jar him awake, no sir! He was Johnny-on-the-Spot from his first moment! He waved to everyone and giggled Perfectly as he was washed and swaddled.

Things went so perfectly that Richard's mother decided to get in a couple of sets of tennis that evening. As she played, Richard's father basked in the adulation of his friends while he described Richard's Perfect Delivery, all the while sipping a rare and extremely expensive Scotch at the Country Club.

Richard did not begrudge his parents their celebrations. He was quite delighted with his new surroundings and spent the rest of the day and that night generally having a gay old time chatting with his neighbors.

* * *

Much to the chagrin of the local retail establishments which profit greatly from the sales of child care items, Richard arrived with a quick wit and a fast appreciation for the benefits of using the loo. His early failures—inconsequential slips and misses, really—were Charmingly Perfect, made even more so by their rarity.

Parents of children less Perfect than Richard shared tedious stories of their offspring's first words, invariably "Goo goo." Richard's parents were pleased to share *their* stories of how Richard had quickly learned to, all by himself, go poo poo.

Richard also learned quickly to walk, so quickly that he trekked with his parents in the nearby forest with a Perfect Little Pack strapped over his shoulders in which he carried his own water and favorite bag of trail mix, while other little not-Richards were strapped to Momma's aching back or carried marsupially in Daddy's chest pouch, their little legs a-kicking in the air and their faces troweled with sunscreen.

And talk! Oh, how Richard could talk! And talk. And talk. And talk. His early tales were the creations of a Perfect Imagination, peopled with dancing cars and cats who went "Vroom!" and fish who could fly to space. Unlike other children of the same age (and unlike many significantly older adults, the Very Big Kahuna was forced to admit when S/He/It was sober), Richard, by the age of two, was able to Perfectly Describe how the beat of a butterfly's wings somewhere on the steppes of Asia would affect the global bond markets in the weeks that followed.

Richard could walk and talk and do his business and use a knife and fork before he turned three. He eschewed coffee but enjoyed herbal tea. He brushed and flossed his Perfect baby teeth in the morning and in the evening before he went to bed.

He took such Perfect Care of his dentition that one night, shortly after his fourth birthday, the Fairies came and took his baby teeth, leaving behind a set of Perfect Pearly Whites that would be the envy of politicians and movie stars. (And that were the scourge of dentists and orthodontists desperately determined to maintain their cash flows so their yachts would float freely.)

His new teeth were so Perfect, his parents garbed him in one of those cute little sailor suits, complete with ascot, pocket handkerchief, and peaked hat with lots of gold braid and a huge anchor sewn onto the front, and took him to the photographer's studio. There he sat for hours as the studio's owner delighted in taking pictures of Richard from all angles and with different backdrops. The owner's single ocean scene was a drab and inadequate setting for a Perfect Little Sailor such as Richard. They settled on a tropical beach background that was all wavy palms and buxom native villagers. (Bare breasts and tall glasses full of brightly colored liquids and garnished with little umbrellas, were airbrushed from the final prints.)

The assistant photographer was kept entertained by Richard's Perfect Knowledge of things such as shutter speeds, focal lengths, and the right sorts of film. (Digital cameras were still CLASSIFIED, then used only in reconnaisance satellites and by Secret Agents.)

The results of the afternoon's film shoot were such a Perfect Success that it cost Richard's parents not a dime. A blizzard of Perfect Prints soon fell on Richard's neighborhood, in the halls and offices of Richard's father's office, and in the locker rooms, restaurants, and bars of Richard's parent's Country Club. So many prints were mailed to Richard's relatives and his parent's distant friends that the United States Postal Service broke even that fiscal quarter.

* * *

During Richard's early years, his parents were the talk of the neighborhood, especially when they weren't around. Their supply of "Richard this" and "Richard that" and "Have a picture!" and "Isn't he Perfectly Adorable!" could not be exhausted, despite the neighbor's (and many strangers) obvious fatigue. Richard's parents, when they noticed, were sure the glassy eyes and blank stares were the consequences of too many martinis and whiskey sours. Spiteful mutters, if heard at all, and hateful glares, if seen at all, were easily dismissed as evidence of the envy that filled the hearts of those with little snots who clearly had not received even the Standard Measure of Perfection when their proto-spirits passed the Perfection Dispensing Device. (Indeed, this was the result of a low-order Manufacturing Process Flaw that had gone unnoticed for Eons. More on this in a future episode.)

But let us return to the day of Richard's first Perfect Photo Shoot.

After reminding his father to put on his seat belt, Richard announced he would welcome the opportunity to learn how to ride a bicycle. So, gleefully sped they to the closest department store. Richard, still in his Perfect sailor suit with his peaked hat, led the way into the Sears and Roebuck. (Yes, there was retail life before Amazon. Google it.)

As the doors swung open, Richard entered the store, the Perfect Image of the Perfect Explorer laying claim to some unknown land; the conquering general, his enemies bleeding in the sands of the beach he'd Perfectly Stormed; Thurston Howell wading ashore of some tropic isle, alone, as all his baggage had been swept away by the Perfect Typhoon.

Straight to the bicycles Richard strode. And without demur or delay, he selected the Perfect Bike, cherry red with a black seat and big rubber tires. Set into the grips, also black, were sparkly, colorful wavy things that Richard knew would Stream Perfectly in the wind as he pedaled down the street.

The salesman was one of the last in Richard's town who had yet to meet the Perfect Boy. He tried and tried and tried to explain that the Perfect Bicycle was only a display model. But there was one in the back just like it and it would take him only a moment to have it taken to Richard's parent's Car. It would be a new-new version of the Perfect Bicycle, did not Richard agree?

No, Richard did not agree. He began to point out to the hapless salesman all the characteristics of the Perfect Bicycle that would be impossible to find in other bicycles, no matter how much they might resemble the Perfect One.

At that time in his life, and then only briefly, Richard's skills in diplomacy were approximately the same as the average traveling adult. That is, when confronted by someone who seemed unable to understand what was being said, Richard—much like your average bermuda-shorted, sandal-wearing, repulsively-flowered shirt-clad adult—said the same thing more slowly and more loudly. Again and Again.

The store manager, berating a cashier in the Ladies Intimates Section, rushed over, the din leading him to quickly surmise something was amiss.

The manager, a member of the same Country Club as Richard's parents, quickly recognized Richard (a framed copy of Richard's First Perfect Photo hung on the wall near the manager's favorite bar stool at the Country Club). The recipient of a Standard Measure of Perfection, he quickly offered to not only let Richard have the Perfect Bicycle but that he would waive the assembly fee, as well.

All was Perfect! Richard led the way from the Sears and Roebuck, the haughty explorer rowing back to his ship to search for new lands to conquer; the steely-eyed general boarding his landing craft, eager to assault another beach; Thurston rowing back to the *Minnow* with Mary Anne, looking for lovey.

But wait! you may cry. The narrative makes no mention about Helmets or Knee Pads or Elbow Pads or the other Protective Impedimentia so dear to the hearts of parents today. Perhaps it does not do so because the Minimum Required Safety Equipment is already at Richard's home, you may speculate.

And you would be wrong. The equipment was not mentioned because virtually all children, even Richard, had no need for the superfluous. You see, this was a time when children were encouraged to play outdoors. Helmets, for example, were reserved for those few whose needs were more special than not.

During those Perfect Days, if children fell off their bicycles, they cried, picked themselves up and dusted themselves off, held the front wheel between their thighs if the handlebars were bent out of alignment, climbed back on, and sped off, only to laugh and cry as they repeated the process a few blocks later.

It was a time when Mother's Spittle was possessed of Miraculous Healing Powers. So when the wounded returned home, a quick rub of a cloth—almost always a smelly kitchen towel—against Mom's tongue, followed by a vigorous scrubbing of the abrasion or cut or bruise, sufficed to heal most injuries, bleeding or not.

Serious wounds, those that resisted multiple doses of Mother's Spittle, led to reluctant albeit speedy trips to the Doctor's office where the wretched victim was harpooned in the buttocks and filled with a loathsome fluid the nurse insisted was Good For You, this after the wound was stitched closed or the severed limb reattached.

But you remain horrified. No doubt you are aghast that parents would have been so callous and uncaring to allow their children to play outside unattended, there to be threatened by any passing Predator. Indeed, that too was another Manufacturing Process Flaw that took ages to rectify. Suffice it to say, then—and even now—the Winner of Bread, or an Uncle, or a Third Cousin, Twice Removed, posed more of a risk to children than some wandering stranger.

Richard wasted no time once he and his parents arrived home. His father wrestled the Perfect Bike from the car and set Richard on his way with a hearty Hey-ho, Boyo! His parents glowed with satisfaction as Richard sped away.

Their glow faded as Richard quickly returned. Without a word, he went into the garage. Out came he with a crescent wrench and a pair of pliers. With a stern yet Perfect Demeanor, he instructed his father to hold the Perfect Bike.

Off came the training wheels a few moments later. Wheels, wrench, pliers, and parents forgotten, Richard rode off Perfectly Balanced and in Perfect Control of the Perfect Bike.

His parents could not have been more pleased.

* * *

Richard quickly mastered the Perfect Bicycle. In no time at all, he had learned to steer one-handed, no-handed, and knee-handed. He ranged far and wide his first week on his Perfect Bike.

Farther, perhaps, than was wise.

He encountered a Gang of Toughs, most older than he and unimpressed by Richard's Perfection. They were, however, most impressed by his Perfect Bike.

It was a matter of a moment, certainly no more than two, for those vicious Imperfects to take possession of the Perfect Bike after administering a Perfectly Painful Change in Ownership.

Richard took it in Perfect Stride. Despite his bleeding lips and swollen tongue and the abrasions on his cheeks (one of the Imperfects had a special talent for rubbing Perfect Faces into the pavement), Richard limped home, pausing now and then to admire the trees and birds and squirrels he had not seen while speeding by on what had once been his Perfect Bike.

His mom gasped when Richard came through the front door. She almost swooned as she became aware of the Perfect Price Richard had paid during the Painful Change of Ownership.

Her Mother's Spittle lacked the Magic to heal his wounds. (It was, perhaps, because it had been diluted by the gin she'd imbibed while Richard was off exploring). And so off to the Doctor they sped.

It was while the Nurse was cleansing Richard's Perfect Wounds when Richard decided to become a Doctor. He was fascinated by the Pieces and Parts colorfully displayed on the Medical Charts that adorned the walls of the examination room. He listened carefully and learned about infections, contusions, abrasions, bone bruises, and possible concussions.

He was familiar with thermometers and took it in Perfect Stride when one was jammed into his mouth. He was, however, somewhat surprised when the Nurse told him to undue his once Perfect Jeans, now torn and bloodied. His Perfect Eyes grew wide as the Nurse tugged his Perfect Whitey Tighties away from his buttocks and swabbed a Perfect Orb with something icey.

The Doctor cried out "Thar she blows!" and thrust the harpoon Ned Land would have used to slay Moby Dick (had Ned not taken a round-the-world trip on the *Nautilus*) into Richard's gluteus maximus.

Most children would yowl and scream after suffering such an egregious assault on their backside. Since Richard was Perfect, after a barely audible yelp, he pulled on his jeans with Great and

Perfect Dignity, after the Doctor said he was finished playing Let's-Kill-the-Whale.

Richard and his mother shared few words on their ride home. She explained what had happened to his father when he returned from work.

He was aghast at the damage inflicted on his Perfect Son and appalled by the loss of the Perfect Bike which had cost more than a Perfectly Pretty Penny. Out of Scotch, he found solace in his wife's gin.

After a Perfect Snort (room temperature, straight from the bottle), Richard's father asked if Richard could wait a bit before they went in search of another Perfect Bicycle.

Richard declined as he would not have the time. He'd decided to become the Perfect Doctor. To be so, he needed to begin studying immediately.

* * *

Richard's Academic Progress was Perfect in all regards. He never made a grade less than A Minus. But only once. He vowed thereafter to never accept anything less than A Pluses.

He was a Perfectly Keen Student, anxious to learn. At the beginning of his first year, his teachers were amazed by his quick wit and perspecacity, his willingness to help with teacher's chores, and his never-ending delight in washing the blackboards.

By the end of his first year, his teachers were frazzled shells of their former selves, drained of knowledge they had either long forgotten or had no idea they held, and crushed by the frequent humiliation of a little boy quick to highlight their errors.

By the end of his second year and those beyond, a collective groan could be heard during Budget Development Time in the School Board's Finance Department. Salaries for teachers priviliged to instruct such a Perfect Boy were at least double those received by their peers. Despite the budget-busting necessity, turnover of Richard's teachers was also higher than average.

It mattered little to Richard. A doctor he had vowed to be and a doctor, a Perfect Doctor, he would be. So, he studied and studied and studied.

He took his books to lunch and to the playground. He sneaked them under his rug at Nap Time. He read them at night with a flashlight. He read so much that his parents began to fear for his eyesight.

But Richard had Perfect Eyes. He could count the hairs on the legs of the bees that buzzed about his mother's flowers. And he could count the tail feathers of the birds that swooped and circled high in the sky.

He studied so hard and so much that the other children, far less Perfect than Richard, teased him incessantly. He endured their taunts and their blows with Perfect Stoicity as he did those from the other Scouts in his Cub Pack and later in his Troop.

For, you see, Richard was the Perfect Cub Scout. He needed to be shown an Indian dance once or hear an Indian War Whoop a single time in order to reproduce either Perfectly. His Official Cub Scout knife was the sharpest of the Pack. His whittling skills were second to none. His Scout Race Cars always took First Place for both looks and speed.

Richard's Cub Scout friends cheered when adults were looking and tied his shoelaces together when they were not. Richard quickly learned to walk Perfectly no matter what had been done to his shoes.

His Den Mother began life as a God-fearing, teetotaling Evangelical, a saintly and sanctimonious pain-in-most-asses prig who took great Christian pride in denying herself all manner of sinful, earthly pleasures. A person whose only apparent joy in life was ensuring everyone knew of her sacrifices. By the time Richard left the Den to become a Boy Scout, she had a discriminating appreciation for vodka. Her copy of the Perfect Boy's picture was set into the base of the ashtray she'd made with the Den when making acrylic geegaws was all the rage. And, to her surprise, her husband, despite his continuing Fear of the Eternal Damnation meted out to all sinners, had grown quite fond of her lash and her handcuffs.

To celebrate Richard's advancement, she went to one of the town's seedier taverns and decided Jack Daniels wasn't all that bad. When she finished her fourth double—straight up and undiluted—she decided to blow her way around a table of sailors who were freshly ashore after months at sea. She finished the evening with a triple shot of Jack (no, not one of the sailors), the extra shot intended purely for antiseptic purposes.

* * *

Richard's Boy Scout Troop Leader was also a member of the Country Club. He blanched when told Richard wished to become a Boy Scout. A real man, the troop leader gritted his less than perfect teeth and made sure Richard earned all his merit badges as quickly as possible.

Richard did so Perfectly and in record time. The purported Perfect and Unprecedented Progress resulted in many eyebrows raised at the Boy Scouts of America Headquarters. Believing fraudulent intent was at work, BSA HQ sent an investigator. He quickly returned with confirmation that everything was above board and shipshape.

Richard's first merit badge was, it should go without saying, in First Aid. He quickly earned his second in Advanced First Aid, followed almost instantaneously with a third in Cardio Pulmonary Resuscitation. Had there been a Merit Badge available for Surgery in the Field with Nothing But Your Pocketknife and a Bic Pen, he would have tackled that next. He went for Lifesaving and Water Sport Safety instead. He was a Perfect Swimmer, after all, and having that background expanded the range of future career opportunities.

A position as Ship's Doctor held a special allure for Richard. He thought Doc Bricker from *The Love Boat* had the Perfect Job. Not only was he the only Doctor on the Ship, but he was in episodic proximity to that stunning beauty of a Cruise Director, Julie.

It was Julie, as a matter of fact, that led to Richard's Discovery of a Wonderful Nature. His Troop had hiked into the woods on a fall Saturday morning, eager to camp that night in some distant glade where they could look at the stars and poke their Fun in each other's eyes.

Richard had a Perfect Academic Understanding of the transformation he and most of his companions were undergoing. Tired after the hike, Richard only wished to sleep. But he was unable to do so as his tent-mates insisted on playing Who-Has-The-Most-Pubes. Weary of having the others' Fun poked in his Perfect Face and anxious to avoid having to play the My-Dingus-is-Biggest game (he would naturally have won handily), Richard dragged his sleeping bag out into the Perfect Night—soft breeze, no clouds, bright moon, and a pleasing absence of biting insects—he dossed down and soon began a Perfect Slumber.

But the Cruise Director leapt into his head just as he began to snore. As she did, Richard was discomfited by the effects of her appearance. He knew all about the biological necessity of erectile tissue. And he'd studied the pictures he'd found in his father's copy of the *Kama Sutra*. And he'd read *Everything You Always Wanted to Know About Sex* from cover to cover and back again.

Richard knew what he was expected to do, historically, biologically, customarily, and typically. And so he did it. Twice.

* * *

It was during the hike back the next day that Richard realized he might be having a Perfect Effect upon girls his own age. He no longer really noticed when he was the recipient of matronly pinches on his Perfect Cheeks, or of the envious appreciation of his Perfect Thick, Dark-brown Curls by those who struggled to achieve the same result from a bottle or a salon. These and other endearing compliments were par for his Perfect Course.

The epiphany struck Richard a Perfect Hammer Blow right in the middle of his Perfect Eyes, with such force that he stopped without warning or the use of brake lights. Yelps and yells shattered the morning peace as a Perfect Trail-blocking Stack of Scouts was formed by those of his companions who followed him.

The Scout Master chose to ignore the use of forbidden and inappropriate language when he saw who was on the receiving end.

Richard Perfectly Ignored the Titty Twisters and the Butt Pinches and the Snuggies from his peeved Scout companions as they passed him.

He realized he'd been misinterpreting events, signs, and signals for some time: the quickly hushed giggles when he walked into a classroom; the wistful stares to which he was subjected in the cafeteria; the knocks and bumps he suffered in the hallway.

After a night of Thinking Hard about the Cruise Director, he thought perhaps the giggles weren't from the addled, or the stares from the blind, or the bumps and knocks from the clumsy. Perhaps those girls (and, unnoticed by him, the Odd Boy) were in their version of the throes of puberty, with, for most, Richard as the Featured Perfect Cruise Director.

Richard vowed that morning to find the Perfect Girl. Not that he was going to throw over the Cruise Director, no ma'am. She was always handy whenever Richard needed her.

* * *

Richard returned to school that Monday with a new awareness of his surroundings and the feminine creatures with which it was populated. He smiled Perfectly at the blushing gigglers; he nodded Perfectly Regally at whomever he caught staring (excepting the somewhat dreamy-eyed Dainty Boys, the same lads always first out when dodgeball was the game of the day in gym class, whether they dressed out or not); and he exercised his Perfect Manners by apologizing whenever he was bumped or knocked.

The metamorphosis was Perfect. The girls of his school entering the Crashing Surf of the Ocean Named Life at the same time as Richard began to pass him their hastily written notes of amour, all arrow-pierced hearts and red roses with blue violets and long strings of X's and O's. The more adventurous of those young ladies wrote Richard to tell him how much they LOVED him. (Some of the less adventurous, including a few of the newer teachers, did so, as well, but with lemon juice for ink.)

A young man allocated the Standard Measure of Perfection would have found it difficult not to suffer a Swelled Head from all the attention. Richard, as we know from the Beginning, had a Measure a bit larger than the Standard and accepted the attention with Perfect Poise and Dignity. Despite his Perfectly Swelled Head.

The rest of that school year, his eighth, passed quickly. His grades were Perfect and Richard, once again, found himself at the head of his class.

But Richard suffered from a Perfect Degree of Melancholy. He had yet to find the Perfect Girl. And he'd hoped to do so before the summer break; he was eager to document the results of first-hand experience, essential background medical data he knew he needed to be the Perfect Doctor.

* * *

Richard had more than his share of unexpected spurts during the early summer, the most significant (and least inconvenient from a laundry perspective) being one of height. By the end of June, he was only a few inches shy of a Perfect Six Feet.

It was that year that Richard's father decided his son could forgo the traditional summer buzz cut and scalping. It helped that his boss's wife expressed a keen interest in Richard's Perfect Wavy Locks, finding herself—perhaps because of the orange juice-tainted vodka she preferred over the lemonade—unable to resist running her fingers through Richard's Perfect Hair the whole time he and his parents were at the Company Memorial Day Picnic. As she told him just how lucky he was to have such Perfect Waves, she also inspected the integrity of Richard's Perfect Back Pockets. From side to side. And up and down. And around and around.

Multiple times.

(The Boss noticed and never forgot how his wife relished her inspections of the rear of Richard's Perfect Jeans. And so, months later, Richard's father's annual bonus took a sizable hit despite his exemplary performance.)

Richard knew that a Perfect Mind had to be borne by a Perfect Body. So he made sure he spent plenty of time outdoors doing all manner of outdoorsy things such as running and walking and hiking.

Alone, as he was no longer a Boy Scout. He'd earned all the merit badges available and in a spasm of hide-bound conservatism common to large organizations, the Boy Scouts of America refused to let Richard start his own Troop, citing nonsense such as liability insurance and minimum age requirements. In response, Richard crafted a Perfectly Worded Release of Liability form. While it failed to sway the BSA, one of its attorneys was so bedazzled by the Perfectly Crisp Prose and Air-tight Language that he filed off the header and made it his firm's own.

When Richard found out what the scum-sucking, ambulance-chasing nogoodnick had done, he added copyright and intellectual property law to his ever-growing list of subjects to be studied.

Hoping he could learn more, he tried to join the Girl Scouts, but the Girl Scouts of America were dramatically more straitlaced than the Boy Scouts, despite the excellent letters of recommendation submitted on his behalf by the ladies of the local Troops to which he'd applied for admission.

And so with all the running, hiking, walking, and (almost forgot) swimming, Richard became the Perfect Summer Boy Icon: tall but not too tall; fit but not Neanderthal; and evenly tanned everywhere he could be tanned in public.

And then *it* happened.

It was a sultry afternoon, the sort of afternoon Richard delighted in spending at the library relishing the opportunity to learn something new. Or to reinforce the knowledge he had gathered on his road to Perfect Doctorhood. It was on that road, specifically while relaxing at the rest area known as Gynecological Essentials (complete with detailed Drawings and Pictures), when he saw Her.

Now, Dear Reader, certain authorities will insist that pronouns such as her and she are only capitalized when the first word of a sentence. Had one of those authorities insisted that Richard himself adhere to such arbitrary twaddle, he would have parried with a Perfect Sneer and laid low the ignoramus with a Perfect Riposte straight into the middle of the cretin's sentence.

But let us return to Richard's story.

Her transit through the periodicals section was stately and regal. Her back was straight, Her head erect. She was the Perfect Princess who moved serenely and confidently about the royal court. Her dark auburn hair swept over her shoulders and fell to the small of her back, to an inch above Her Perfect Derriere.

It was the Derriere of All Derrieres, Richard saw. (So, too, the old lushes and winos who nursed hangovers while pretending to read the day's newspapers. But Richard, his vision blurred by the sudden redistribution of his bodily humours, had eyes only for the Perfect Moons a-crowned atop the Perfect Legs.)

It was then that Richard, always sceptical of Things Supposed to Be Taken on Faith Especially When They Couldn't Be Seen, Heard, or Touched, knew the Very Big Kahuna truly did exist: Such perfection could only be the result of Perfectly Divine Intervention.

The skirt she wore fell just below her knees. As Richard's eyes cleared (as his body adjusted to the diminished flow of blood to all but one of his organs), he admired the subtleties of her calves. He was quite taken by the lace tops of her socks. His breath quickened as he imagined pulling those socks gently off her feet, slowly revealing Perfect Ankles and Perfectly Kissable Toes.

Richard was in Love. And he arrived there without having seen her breasts or her face. He did not care; he truly believed the craftsthing known as VBK would not leave a work of art such as She half-finished or Less Than Perfect.

He squirmed uncomfortably, attempting to accommodate the unfortunate restriction in his trousers but without inappropriately grasping himself to do so. He was considering a quick trip to the men's room, there to temporarily allay the pleasant discomfort he suffered, loathe though he was to tear his eyes away from the Perfect Vision of Beauty, when She stopped.

She turned and set Her books on an empty library table.

The Cruise Director, Julie, fell screaming into the sea, never to be seen or heard from again.

Richard swooned. VBK had indeed wrought a miracle: Titian would have flung *his* Venus into the trash. Rossetti would have tossed *La ghirlandata* into the English Channel for the honor of capturing Her on canvas. Watts would have sent Lillie Langtry packing from his studio. Edward Lewis would have paid much, much more than $3,000.

She was Perfectly Beautiful. Her full lips were a natural rouge, their corners elevated only a teensie bit in preparation for the smiles to come. Her button nose was set Perfectly above those lips, its size a Perfect Complement to Her Perfect Blue Eyes. Intelligence and humor and a love of la dolce vita emanated from those eyes, highlighted by the Perfect Dusting of Magic Freckles the Very Big Kahuna had no doubt subcontracted to Tinker Bell.

Richard was entranced, frozen, speechless, vapor-locked, gobsmacked. So much so that he experienced an emission of a type he knew typically occurred only while asleep.

He was Perfectly Shocked. Despite the protective layer of his briefs, the force of the experience and the volumn of material released resulted in a spot that was embarrassingly visible to anyone who cared to look. (Richard being Richard, most did.) He did not think it appropriate to approach Her looking as if he'd just peed himself.

He briefly considered she might be flattered to know she'd had such an effect on him. After a moment of Perfect Reflection, he assumed she'd just think he was Perfectly Weird or Perfectly Perverted; either way, not a good start to the Perfect Relationship Richard envisioned.

So he gathered his books and his notes into a Perfect Pile on his lap. The untoward evidence of his unintended diurnal discharge thus masked, he stood. His hopes of catching her eye were dashed. She was engrossed in her studies and oblivious to the scrutiny. Richard was temporarily crestfallen. But in a Perfect Display of Stiff Upper Lipness, he smiled and turned to leave. Tomorrow, he knew, she'd be back and so would he. Their's would be the Perfect Introduction to the Perfect First-Time Experience.

* * *

While Richard makes his way from the library, we wonder: Has he found the Perfect Love? Will She be at the library when he returns on the morrow? Can the Perfect Girl love the Perfect Boy despite the years between them? Will She want to be on top? Will he be able to convince his mother he'd simply spilled some Elmer's glue?

For the answers to these questions and so much more, join us for the next installment of A Perfect Life, The Swollen Root.

Reset

A soft chime preceded the announcement: "Citizen Pair Anderson-Cramer to the front desk. Pair Anderson-Cramer to the front desk, please."

A man with dark brown hair stood as the announcement was made. He offered a hand to his Pair, a brunette whose hair was tinged red by the lights of the State Health Center reception area. "Nervous?" he asked.

"A little," she replied. She stood and took his hand.

The couple were indistinguishable from the ten or so others seated throughout the waiting lounge: early to mid-twenties in age; trim, athletic builds; standard two meter height; and lightly tanned. Most of the women were visibly pregnant.

They exchanged a quick, worried glance as they read "Today's State Minimum: 84" displayed on the neon sign above the reception desk.

"Ma'am, we're Pair Anderson-Cramer," the man said.

The receptionist nodded. "Orderly Smith will show you to Examination Room A. The doctor is waiting."

"This way!" Smith said cheerily. "Just follow me. So, Citizens. How are you today? Enjoying the spring? I remember last year: nothing but rain, rain, rain. Have you heard the latest from the Frontier?" Smith chattered on.

The Pair exchanged an amused glance.

"Here we are. Exam A," Smith said as he keyed the entry code into the lock pad. The door snicked open. "After you, Citizens," Smith said, waving them into the office. He followed, pulling the door shut behind him. He stood quietly at the back of the room.

"Come in. Have a seat," the doctor directed. Most of his attention was focused upon his desk display. He nodded to himself and looked up. "Good morning, Citizens."

"Good morning, Doctor," they replied in unison as they sat.

"Well, let's see how we're doing," the doctor temporized. He pretended to read his display for a few seconds. He took a breath and turned back toward them. "Eighty-One," he declared flatly.

Anderson blinked.

"I don't think I understand," Cramer said bemusedly.

The doctor steepled his fingers, the heels of his hands resting on the desktop. "As you recall from your procreation training, Citizen, viability forecasting remains in its infancy." He paused, wincing internally at the unintended pun. "Reliability continues to improve all the time. This datum is important to the State, a datum which will contribute to the improvement of the forecasting model."

Anderson frowned. "If the viability forecast can't be relied upon, then why should we—"

"Forgive me, Citizen," the doctor interrupted. "Please recall your training: while viability forecasting continues to mature, Prenatal Capabilities Analysis is a proven method."

He continued gently. "Understand, Citizen Anderson, you're an Eighty-Three Male. You, Citizen Cramer, are an Eighty-Four Female. These are good, solid ratings." He paused. "They are not, however, guarantees of procreative success."

The doctor gave them a moment. "What have you decided?" he asked.

Anderson glanced at Sheila and reached for her hand. "We, ah, we haven't really made a decision. We didn't think we'd, well, need to," he answered.

She let him take it, where it lay limp and cold inside his. "Reset," she quietly said.

Anderson, shocked, pulled his hand from hers.

The doctor nodded. "Excellent." He gestured to Smith. "Please show Citizen Cramer to Reset." He turned to Anderson. "The procedure will take approximately two hours. Should you choose to wait, you may do so in the comfort area."

Anderson slowly stood. "I was hoping I could be with—"

The doctor shook his head. "That isn't possible, Citizen. Access to the clinical sections is limited to staff and patients," he replied. "Orderly?"

Cramer turned and followed Smith. She didn't look back at Anderson and said nothing as she left the examination room.

"The comfort room is just down the corridor, Citizen Anderson," he said idly as he updated Cramer's record.

Anderson shuffled out of Examination A.

* * *

"May I interrupt?"

Anderson wanted to be alone, but didn't want to be rude to a member of the State Clergy. "Please, Reverend," Anderson answered.

"Thank you." The priest sat. "Ah," he sighed contentedly. "These old bones don't take kindly to standing for too long."

A server approached. "Would you care for anything, Reverend?" she asked.

"Tea, please." He faced Anderson. "Would you care for another, Citizen?"

"Thank you, but no. I need to get back to work as soon as Sheila. . ."

The priest appraised Anderson for a few seconds. "Just the tea, then, if you would," he told the server.

"Yes, Reverend."

He watched her walk to the comfort area's drink station. "Nice," he observed appreciatively.

"Reverend?" Anderson asked.

"My apologies, Citizen," the cleric answered. "I was a bit distracted." He paused. "You look troubled. Unexpected news?" he asked quietly.

Anderson nodded slowly.

"Reset?" the reverend prompted.

"Yes," Anderson answered.

The server placed the tea service on the table.

"Thank you." The reverend took a sip. "This is excellent," he exclaimed.

The plump server dimpled at the praise.

"What's your name, dear? I don't recall having the pleasure before."

"Worth, Reverend," she answered with a little curtsey. "I've only just started this week."

"Worth what, Citizen?"

"Elizabeth, Reverend. Worth, Elizabeth."

"Well, Citizen Worth, Elizabeth. Welcome to the clinic. Thank you for the tea. I look forward to seeing you again soon."

Citizen Worth flushed crimson and curtsied again. "Thank you, Reverend."

The priest and Anderson watched her scuttle to another table, her buttocks swaying playfully beneath her uniform skirt.

"Forgive me, Citizen," the cleric apologized again.

Anderson managed a small chuckle. "No apologies, Reverend. I understand." He paused. "I'm glad you're enjoying the tea."

"Thank you," the priest said as he took another sip. He set the cup into the saucer and settled into his chair. "So, Citizen. This is your first reset."

"Yes," Anderson answered.

"And your pair's name?"

"Cramer, Reverend. Cramer, Sheila."

"How long have you been paired with Citizen Cramer? Do you mind if I call her Sheila?" the priest asked.

Anderson shrugged. "Not at all. We've been paired since Eleven Month last cycle."

The reverend raised his eyebrows. "Only four months on and we find you here. The deities smile upon you, Citizen, to be fruitful so quickly."

"I wish they'd smiled a bit more," Anderson said ruefully. He started. "Ah. Reverend. My apologies," he stammered.

The priest held up his hand. "Peace, Citizen. The gods understand, I believe."

Anderson sat for a moment. "Do they, Reverend? Do you really think so?" he asked timorously.

The reverend stroked his close-cropped beard. "What's your name, Citizen?" he asked.

"Anderson, Howard."

"Howard. A good name. A strong name. Do you know what it means?" he asked.

Anderson shook his head.

"It has many possible meanings. 'Defender' is the one I prefer."

Anderson said nothing.

"Why did you select reset, Howard?"

"I didn't," Anderson answered flatly.

"I see. Sheila made the choice," Reverend Matthews confirmed.

Anderson nodded his agreement.

"As is her right. Why did *she*, then, select a reset?"

Anderson tensed.

The priest leaned forward and touched Anderson's knee gently. "Howard?" he encouraged kindly.

Anderson sighed. "The PCA," he answered flatly.

"Yes," the reverend said as he straightened. He drank off the last of his tea and looked for Citizen Worth.

A gray haired server came to their table. "Would you care for anything else, Reverend? Citizen?" she asked.

"Citizen Worth has finished for the day?" the reverend asked.

The flint in the server's eyes sparked. "No, Reverend. She's taking her afternoon break. I can call her back. If you'd like."

"No, no. That's quite all right. I'd like some more tea. Howard?"

Anderson looked at his watch. "I suppose another would—" He stood when Sheila came into the comfort area. He watched as she minced her way to the table.

The reverend stood as well. "Perhaps in a few moments," he quietly told the server.

"Sheila?" Anderson asked timorously.

"Yes, Howard," she answered as she sat.

"Uh, how are you?"

She closed her eyes for a second. "Fine, Howard. I'm fine. A little tired, I suppose, but that's to be expected they told me."

Anderson looked lost. "Oh. Okay. Good." He started to sit and bolted upright. "Oh, Sheila. This is Reverend, uh, Reverend—"

"Greetings, Citizen Cramer, I'm Reverend Matthews. May I join you for you a few moments?"

"Sure. Please," she answered.

"Thank you, Citizen. May I call you Sheila?" he asked as he sat.

"If you'd like." Sheila, distracted, did not intend to be rude.

"Thank you, Sheila." He paused. "Howard. Sit."

Anderson, numb and rudderless, sat.

"Would you care for something, Sheila?" Matthews asked. "We were about to order another round."

"Um? No. No, thank you," she answered. "I really only wanted to sit a moment. I know Howard needs to get back to work. And, I, um, have a few things to take care of before I go back to the office."

Sheila stood.

Anderson shot to his feet.

The reverend stretched slowly upright. "As you wish," he said.

"Well," Sheila said brightly. "Shall we, Howard?"

"Thank you for your time, Reverend," Anderson said.

"Not at all, Howard, not at all. I think the three of us should meet again. Let's say tomorrow evening at Twenty-Hour."

Anderson glanced at Sheila; she was staring blankly at the butterflies dancing around the flowers growing in the comfort area. "Reverend, I, uh, we, appreciate the invitation, but—"

"I think it's necessary, Citizens," the reverend declared firmly.

"Sheila?" Anderson asked.

"Hm?" she answered distractedly. "Yes. Fine."

"Excellent!" the reverend said. "Tomorrow at Twenty, then. We can meet here."

Citizen Pair Anderson-Cramer turned to leave the clinic. After a few steps, Anderson stopped. "Wait, Sheila, I need to—"

The reverend held up a hand. "Don't worry, Howard, I'll let the staff know you'll take care of your tab tomorrow."

* * *

Orderly Smith's personal comm vibrated as he watched the Anderson-Cramer pair leave the clinic. "Exam A is ready for Pair Rosenberg-Klein" was the message displayed. He glanced at the receptionist. She discreetly pointed out the couple.

Smith walked over. "Citizen Pair Rosenberg-Klein?"

"Yes?" the woman asked.

"My apologies for interrupting. The doctor is ready. May I show you the way?"

The woman stood and smoothed her skirt as her pair put the report he'd been reading into a portfolio. He stood and offered his arm. "Shall we?" he asked.

She chuckled. "Let's," she answered brightly as she hooked her arm through his.

"Lead on," the man, Rosenberg, said to Smith.

"Thank you, Citizen," Smith answered. "The doctor will be seeing you in Examination Room A. If you'd follow me, please?"

They smiled a greeting to the receptionist as Smith escorted them to Exam A.

None of them paid attention to the message displayed above her desk.

The doctor rose from his chair as Smith pushed open the door of the examination room. "Citizens," he greeted. "My pleasure to see you again. Please. Be comfortable. Would you care for any refreshment?" he offered as they sat.

The Pair demurred.

"That will do for now, Smith." The doctor sat at his desk.

The orderly sketched a little bow and pulled the door shut as he left the rooom.

"Let's get started, shall we?" the doctor asked rhetorically as he scanned Klein's record. "Citizen Female Klein, Joanna. Citizen reference. . ." he mumbled to himself as he read the file.

"Yes, Doctor?" she asked wryly.

"My apologies, Citizen. A verbal tic. I'm just an old fashioned doctor. I often find myself a bit lost among all this technology."

She laughed politely. "No apologies, Doctor. This one," she pointed to Rosenberg, "insists upon his reports in hard copy before he reads them. It's hard to believe he's a Ninety-Five," she said as she shook her head in mock sadness.

"Hard copy? Citizen, wouldn't that be considered an extravagant expenditure of State resources?" the doctor deadpanned.

Rosenberg raised an eyebrow. "What can I say, Doctor? Perhaps I'm just an atavistic throwback."

They shared a chuckle.

"Well, Citizen, I can assure you that that is not true," the doctor replied. "In any case, the State acknowledges the necessity of supporting alternative information consumption modalities. Particularly those of its leading citizens. No matter how archaic," he observed with feigned bemusement.

They shared another chuckle.

"But forgive me. I digress," he said as he finished keying up Klein's file.

The Pair waited quietly and calmly.

"Ninety-Six," the doctor told them beamingly. "I cannot tell you how pleased I am with this outcome, Citizens." He stood and extended his hand. "May I offer my congratulations?"

He sat down after shaking hands with each of the Pair. "Now, the nitty gritty. Your follow-up examinations have been scheduled. The dates and times have been downloaded to both your personal and ministry comm accounts, Citizen Klein," the doctor said.

Klein frowned slightly. "Doctor. This is excellent news; happy news. However, this close to the end of the fiscal year. My—"

The doctor raised his hand. "Forgive, please, Citizen, the interruption. But I feel I must remind you that the provisions of the State Prenatal Health Act apply even to staff of the Ministry of Finance."

She sighed. "Yes, Doctor."

"The ministry has been informed, Citizen. It will accommodate any changes in your work hours and duties which may be required. The State expects and encourages each of you to participate fully during the approved pre- and postnatal periods of your term. Neither of you will suffer loss of status, rank, privilege or seniority. This is provided you each maintain the prescribed schedule of examinations, tests and briefings," the doctor concluded.

"Yes, Doctor!" they exclaimed in unison.

"Excellent. I'll get Orderly Smith to show you to—"

A soft knock on the exam room door interrupted the doctor. "Come in," he ordered. "Ah. Reverend Matthews. What can I do for you?"

The Pair stood and turned.

"We just received the news. On behalf of the Church, I wanted to be the first to congratulate the Pair. And I was hoping you'd let me show them to their next appointment."

"Certainly, Reverend. Citizen Klein, may I introduce Reverend Matthews? He's one of the senior clergy with us here at the clinic."

"Reverend," Klein greeted as she held out her hand.

"A pleasure, Citizen. My congratulations."

"Reverend, this is my pair, Rosenberg, Harold," Klein said.

"And congratulations to you, Citizen Rosenberg."

"Well, Doctor?" the reverend asked as they finished their introductions.

The doctor checked his console. "Yes. We're finished here. Unless the Citizens have any questions?"

Klein and Rosenberg exchanged a glance. "None, Doctor," Klein answered.

"Well then. It's been a pleasure, Citizens. And remember: you must adhere to the recommended schedule and regimens," the doctor reminded them sternly.

"Yes, Doctor," the Pair agreed, laughing as they left Examination Room A.

The reverend and the pair exchanged social inconsequentialities as they made their way down the wood-paneled hall.

They stopped at a pair of double-glass doors. "Citizens, if you'd wait a moment," Matthews asked. He pressed a brass button recessed into the wood trim around the door.

"Welcome, Reverend Matthews. May we be of service?" was the soft, disembodied contralto response.

"Please. Myself and Citizen Pair Rosenberg-Klein. They've an appointment."

"Welcome." The lock clicked. Matthews pulled open the door. "Please, Citizens. After you," he said.

A State Church matron stood waiting in the warmly lit, wood paneled lobby. "Citizens, welcome to our branch of Natal Logistics and Support. I'm Matron Dunn, the branch manager."

As introductions and greetings were exchanged, a younger woman entered the lobby.

"Citizens, allow me to introduce your counselor. Citizen Klein, Citizen Rosenberg, this is Matron Alberts. She is chief of our planning and logistics section."

"Thank you, Matron," Alberts said. "Citizens, my office is this way. If you would?"

The Pair made their goodbyes and appreciations to Matthews and Dunn before following Alberts to her office.

On their way, Klein stopped, entranced by the art work displayed in the office hallway. "This is amazing," she said.

"Yes, some of his finer works," Alberts opined. "I enjoy them, as well."

"Reproductions?" Klein asked ruefully.

"Unfortunately. The Church was able to rescue these prints. But we were unable to save the originals." She paused. "The mobs had already torched his gallery by the time the Church arrived. Shall we?" Alberts encouraged gently.

Alberts' assistant stood as they entered the reception area of the office. "Welcome, Citizens. Maylene is waiting in your office, Matron," the assistant said. "Citizens? Would you care for any refreshment?" she asked.

The Pair declined politely.

Alberts led Klein and Rosenberg into her inner office. A young woman with vaguely Asian features nodded politely. Alberts invited the Pair to chairs before taking her seat behind the desk.

"Citizens, this is Maylene." The young woman took a step away from the wall and bowed slightly. "Should you find her acceptable, Citizen Klein, she'll be your personal assistant. Her specific duties are outlined here," she said, handing each of the Pair a leather bound notebook. "Also included is a copy of her recent assistance history, which includes references and recommendations from those Citizens with whom she's worked."

Klein and Rosenberg leafed through the documentation.

"In summary, Maylene will provide whatever assistance and relief you require. Within the scope of her approved duties," she said, glancing briefly at Rosenberg.

The Pair exchanged a look. "Ah, we're sure Maylene is suitable, but we're concerned about the expenditure required." Klein paused. "We've been investing our extra Credits since we received our procreate license. We'd prefer to continue doing so."

Alberts' eyes twinkled. "I apologize for not being clear. The State and the Church provide this service. It is our contribution to ensuring successful delivery of a new, vital, and capable Citizen: there is no expenditure on your part."

Alberts continued. "The State understands and encourages you to remain as productive and as involved as you can be, within the limits of your prenatal care program. Maylene, or one of her associates should you prefer, provide the support and relief you will need during the development period. That support will relieve you from the day-to-day mundane, routine tasks and obligations you would otherwise face. In order for her to provide the best possible assistance, she will, of course, take up residence with you for the duration of her service." She glanced downward. "I believe you've an extra guest room that she may move into. If that's acceptable."

Klein looked at her pair for a moment. She leafed quickly through the notebook. She looked up at Maylene who'd been calmly and quietly observing, the dark brown of her suit helping her blend into the office paneling. Klein glanced again at Rosenberg.

"It's your call, dear," Rosenberg said in response to the unasked question.

Citizen Klein looked at Maylene. "We'll take her," Klein told Alberts.

"She'll arrive at your home tomorrow, Citizen Klein. I hope that's acceptable," said Alberts.

Matthews beamed. "Outstanding! I believe your schedule permits, so we've arranged a small celebration on your behalf, Citizens. Dry, of course, for Citizen Klein. But I think we can find something to tickle the old brain cells for Citizen Rosenberg. Shall we?"

"Yes, Reverend," the Pair happily answered.

* * *

Anderson pulled the casserole from the oven and set it on the counter to cool. "Supper's ready," he called.

Sheila walked into the dining area as he finished setting the table. He pulled out her chair. "Have a seat?" he asked brightly.

She said nothing.

"Are you okay?"

She smiled sadly.

"What?" he asked reluctantly.

She sighed.

"What is it, Sheila?"

She sniffed and turned her head. "I've registered the unpair," she said to the wall of their apartment. "Your copy of the certificate should be in your personal mail."

Anderson blinked. And blinked again. "Why?" he asked.

Sheila turned and faced him, a mild smirk and raised eyebrow her answer.

"Ah," he said.

Anderson looked at his feet for a second as he scratched the back of his head. He then glanced around the dining area.

Sheila waited.

He went to the kitchen and returned with the casserole. "Would you like some supper before you leave?"

* * *

A soft double bell note announced an alert. The duty civil protector set the news mag on her desk. "What is it?" she queried.

"I am monitoring a civil disturbance," replied Protector, the master cyber system of the Civil Protectorate. "Visual on display alpha."

"Nature of the disturbance?" She called up the indicated display.

"Public intoxication, second degree."

"Probability?" the duty CP asked.

"99.9%, based upon Credits expenditure, purchase history, and body mass index."

The CP watched the real time video stream. The individual, a male, didn't appear to lurch or stagger. "Are there other citizens involved? Any altercations?"

"None and none, Citizen," Protector replied.

"Is the Citizen operating a conveyance?"

"No."

"Display his history."

The civil protector grimaced as she scanned the data. "Best estimate of subject's route?" she queried.

"The entertainment establishment where the alleged intoxication occurred is within 2,000 meters of subject's domicile. The probability is high the subject is returning to his residence," Protector replied.

"Show me the locations of the three nearest field officers on duty."

The console display split to accommodate a street map. Three glowing blue diamonds were shown. The closest was approximately 500 meters from the subject. The CP touched that icon. "Connect me," she ordered Protector.

"You are connected to Field Officer Lee, Citizen," Protector said after a moment.

"Hey, Lee," the duty CP said when the connection was complete.

"What's up?" Lee answered.

"Protector is tracking a public intox, second. Coordinates and an identification visual have been streamed to you."

"Yep. Just received the data," Lee confirmed. "You want me to burn him?"

"Unless he does something stateless, no. The guy's had a bum day so I'm cutting him some slack. Besides, it looks like he's heading home. Still, vector his way, just in case."

"Sure thing. Lee clear."

"Protector," the duty CP queued the system. "Continue to track. Alert me if the subject does anything, or if he goes anywhere other than his residence. Send a standby notice to the other field officers displayed," the duty CP ordered.

"Yes, Citizen," Protector answered.

"Anything else cooking?"

"No, Citizen."

"Good." The duty civil protector put her feet back up on her desk and grabbed the news mag.

Protector tracked as ordered until it received confirmation from the subject's building entry control subsystem that the subject had entered his apartment. Protector closed the case, issued a stand-down order to the field officers involved, and updated the duty shift log.

As a matter of routine procedure, a copy of the case file was also transmitted to State Central, which appended it to the life history of Anderson, Howard, Citizen.

* * *

As Anderson settled down at work the next morning he wondered when the meds were going to fix his headache.

"Anderson."

He turned. "Yes, Citizen?"

"Got a minute?" his supervisor asked.

"Sure," Anderson answered. He walked into the closet the electronics installation team laughingly called an office.

Anderson leaned on the wall as his supervisor sat.

"System, log me in. Billings, Davis. Pull up my messages."

"Voice print confirmed, Citizen Billings. Good morning. Your current messages are displayed," Billings' desk system responded.

Billings stalled as he pretended to read. He exhaled softly and leaned back with his hands behind his head. "How ya doing this morning, Anderson?"

"Not bad. A bit of a headache, but not bad. Er, why?"

Billings waved at his system. "Got a message here from the Protectorate. Says you did some partying last night."

Anderson straightened and looked concerned. "I, uh, it wasn't—"

"Time out, Anderson. Take it easy. I also got a message from State Health and another from Civil Registry. Sorry things didn't work out for you and Sheila."

"Yeah. Thanks. Look, am I in trouble here?" he asked bleakly after a moment.

"Nah. Nothing formal; not even a penalty. The Protectorate passed along the notice and recommended a brief discussion. As far as I'm concerned, we've discussed it. Briefly. Stay safe, okay?"

Anderson tucked his hands into his armpits and looked at the floor. "Yeah, sure." He paused. "Was there anything else?"

"Nope. You have a full schedule. Probably should get to work, right?" Billings replied.

Anderson nodded and turned to leave.

"One more thing, Anderson."

"What?"

"State Health wanted me to remind you about your meeting tonight at Twenty-Hour with a Reverend Matthews."

Anderson raised his arms in mild exasperation. "What's the point?" he asked.

Billings shrugged. "Who knows? It's the Church. It's State Health. Go through the motions. We don't need any more discussion recommendations, right? From anywhere. It'll pass, Anderson; you'll be fine. Plenty of pre-pairs out there looking for a handsome stud such as yourself. Stateless, man, I'll pay for the license if you want to have a night on the town. You know, blow off some steam," Billings smirked.

Anderson sighed resignedly. "Tonight. Twenty-Hour. I'll be there."

Billings waved. "Get to work, then."

* * *

Anderson gingerly sipped the fresh cup of tea, his third since he'd arrived at the clinic. Early; he didn't want to be late and he didn't want another lecture from his boss.

It didn't matter. It was well past Twenty-Hour and the reverend still hadn't arrived. Nor had Sheila.

Stateless, Anderson thought. He waved at the comfort center server.

"Yes, Citizen?"

"Could I have my check, please? And, oh, I have something on the tab from yesterday. The name's Anderson. Let me clear that, as well."

"Certainly, Citizen," the server answered.

Anderson finished his tea. The server returned with the tab. Anderson okayed the Credit after giving it a once over. He stood and donned his jacket.

"Citizen Anderson!" Matthews said as he came into the comfort area. "Citizen—Howard—pardon my tardiness. Sit for a moment."

Howard doffed his jacket and sat.

Matthews sat. "I'm sorry, Howard," he started.

The server returned to the table. "Would you like something, Reverend?" he asked.

Matthews ruminated for a moment. "A bourbon, please," he decided.

"How would you like that?"

"Poured gently into a glass," Matthews answered. He turned to Howard. " I noticed you were leaving. You can stay for another, I trust. My treat, a penalty for my being tardy."

"I'll have the same, Reverend," Howard answered.

"Excellent! Two bourbons, if you would. Make them doubles," Matthews ordered.

"Yes, Reverend," the server acknowledged the order and made his way to the bar.

Matthews exhaled a deep breath. "My apologies for being late."

"No problem, Reverend. I hope nothing's wrong," Howard replied.

Matthews sighed. "A Citizen miscarried. The Pair were distraught. We tried to intervene, but to no avail."

Howard waited for the reverend.

Matthews continued after a few seconds: "We were unsuccessful. A loss for the State. Tragic."

The server returned and set their drinks on the table. "Thank you," Matthews said. He raised his glass. "Lehayim."

"Hm?" Anderson asked as they clinked glasses.

"An archaic term I picked it up during my studies. It means 'to life' or something like that," Matthews answered after a healthy sip of his drink. He took another. "So, Citizen. How are you?"

Howard shrugged. "Okay, I guess. Wondering where Sheila is."

Matthews shrugged. "I excused her. Her willingness to move on is an indicator that she's accepted the circumstances." He nodded. "It was quite the day for you yesterday, Howard. You experienced many things, some of which were, perhaps, regrettable?"

Howard thought a moment. He shrugged again and took a drink.

"Will you new-pair?" Matthews asked after a moment.

Howard looked up sharply.

"Civil Registry ensures the Church is kept informed," Matthews said in response.

Howard slumped a little.

Matthews leaned forward. "Howard: Will you?"

Howard gazed into his bourbon. "Probably," he answered.

"Good," Matthews said. "We, the State and the Church, prefer our citizens in Pairs."

Howard watched a song bird dance in its cage. "Can I ask a question, Reverend?"

"Certainly."

"If that's the preference, why is it so easy to unpair?"

Matthews nodded. "An excellent question," he replied. He took a sip of his drink. "Stability, Howard." Matthews answered. "How much do you remember of your State Social History?"

Howard looked embarrassed.

Matthews chuckled. "Don't be too ashamed, Citizen. We've found the level of student interest in Basic Social History to be superficial. At best. Despite our best efforts to enliven the early syllabi." Matthews chuckled some more. "You are in good, well, sizable anyway, company, Howard." The reverend finished his drink and settled into his chair.

"Stability counts a great deal. On a personal level, it leads to contentment. Contented citizens are more productive and healthier. Contented, productive, and healthy citizens maximize revenue potential and help reduce expenditures in the long run.

"Procreate Pairs ensure the continued viability of the citizen base. For the State, this stability facilitates planning and conduces to broader political and social health." Matthews paused.

"The Church and the State do not expect uniform contentment, however. We are all human, Howard. The State and the Church understand circumstances alter, that citizens change. We naturally hope a Pair will grow closer and remain together. Family stability is one of the bedrocks of social stability, after all. But, there are circumstances when it's better for the State to allow some temporary instability from its citizens."

"Like Sheila and me?" Howard asked ruefully.

"Exactly," Matthews replied. "A reset can be troubling, particularly to those who've let their excitement get the better of their judgment. Please, Howard. I meant no offense nor am I suggesting this was—is—true in your case. Tell me: Are you disappointed about the reset?"

Howard chewed his lip. "Some. Yes, I suppose."

"Why?" Matthews asked.

"I, ah, don't know, really," Howard answered.

"Do you feel a sense of failure, Howard?"

"A little," Howard replied after a few seconds.

"That's to be expected," Matthews replied. "Nature has given us an instinct to perpetuate ourselves for the species. The State has given us a need to perpetuate ourselves perfectly, for the good of the State, and, ultimately, our collective good. It's regrettable that you, and others like you and Sheila, may find it difficult at times to reconcile the two."

"How, Reverend, is perfection possible?" Howard asked.

The server approached. "Another, Reverend? Citizen?" he asked.

"Absolutely," Matthews answered. "It's your round, Howard; one more?"

Howard shook his head. "No, not for me."

Matthews answered while he waited for his drink. "Perfection is an ideal. The State uses the PCA as an aid to help ensure the citizen base is perpetuated towards the ideal."

"Why?" Howard murmured.

Matthews ruminated a bit before he answered. "How much higher level history to you want to hear, Citizen?" he asked rhetorically. "Can you conceive of a time when procreate licenses did not exist? When Pairs, even unpaired citizens, were free to indulge in their instincts? What would you think of a world like that, Howard?" Matthews sampled his fresh drink. "It was chaos, Citizen. Chaos."

Howard was startled by the subtle vehemence. "How so?"

"State resources are finite, Howard. They are now and they were more so before the Revolution. I'm reluctant to admit that my spiritual predecessors widely believed procreation was a divine right. There was no apparent thought about the consequences of allowing citizens to exercise that so-called right," Matthews shuddered at the recollection. "Humans were conceived with little regard to their future potential as effective citizens. No attention was paid to the ability of the parents to shape and mold their procreative results into useful human beings. The actual and potential level of success—educationally, financially, personally, and socially—of the procreate pair counted for nothing. Before the State, the only qualification for procreation was to succeed in procreation. It was as if humans were nothing more than animals," he concluded with a sad nod.

Matthews paused. "Forgive me, Howard. Whenever I compare what we have now to what once was, I find myself embarrassed on behalf of my clerical predecessors." He finished his drink. "That was as nothing, though, compared to the appalling lack of ability of the political leadership of the day to deal with the hard issues of those times." The reverend snorted. "But we don't want to get started on *that* subject. It is late."

Matthews stood. "You understand, Howard? Sheila, I believe, understands. Her willingness to unpair and move on so quickly may seem hasty now, but I believe you'll find she made the decision that works best for her. The State and the Church regret the event, but understand the motivations behind it. The likely long term benefits outweigh the current costs of temporary unpleasantness.

"We encourage both of you to new-pair and, yes, to utilize your procreate licenses to their maximum. And, to that end, by the way, the Church has asked the Registry to give you selection priority for your next pair. It's good for thirty days, so I suggest you use it as quickly as you can."

Howard stood. He put on his jacket.

Matthews held out his hand. "It's been a pleasure, Citizen Anderson. I know you'll find your way soon to understanding and accepting the decision Sheila has made. Use that priority at the Registry, Howard."

Matthews shook Howard's hand. Anderson zipped his jacket and turned to leave.

"Oh, Citizen. By the way?" Matthews called to Howard.

"Yes, Reverend?"

"Thank you for the drink."

Civic Duty

Howard yawned as his boss, Billings, droned through the typical bushwa that was the standing morning meeting for Howard and his fellow techs who worked in the Ministry of Finance.

Billings glared, trying—and failing—to look commanding. "That's it. Any questions? No? Good. Before you go to it, Citizens, my civic duty compels—"

"You mean your boss!"

"Shaddup, Smith," Billings snarled. "As I was saying, it is my civic duty to remind everyone—specifically, the three of you who haven't yet done so—that it is *your* civic duty to complete your Annual Citizen Training. Now, the privacy laws say I'm not supposed to disclose in public the names of the delinquents. The delinqs have two days to get it done before the failure-to-complete penalties kick in." Billings sneered. "For those of you mathematically challenged, this means you need to have your ACT passed by midnight Three day. And in case you didn't get the memo, penalties have doubled over last year's.

"So, hypothetically speaking, *Anderson*, if you were one of the delinquents, that'd be tomorrow. And *Smith*, assuming you too are one of those Citizens with a less than keen grasp on your civic duties, you'll be immediately assessed a hundred Credit civil penalty if you don't get your training complete, as well. I need one more volunteer as an example: that'd be you, Thomas. The penalty increases fifty Credits per day until you do pass your ACT, *Thomas*." Billings crossed his arms. "If the training is not completed by Freedom Day you'll be sweeping streets and hauling trash with the rest of the GAs.

"Leave your shoes on, Smith, I'll help; that's twenty days from today. So unless our three nameless delinquents aspire to be the State's latest General Assets, I suggest they pull their heads out of their butts and get the stateless training *done*. Ah! Ah! Siddown. I got one more thing. Doing your ACT is a *civic* responsibility, Citizens. You are *not* authorized to do so on the State's clock. Got that?" Billings finished with a glare. "Good. Get to work."

* * *

At home that evening and after a quick bite for supper, Howard resigned himself to the inevitable. He took a beer from the refrigerator and shuffled to his desk. "Log me in, comp," he ordered as he sank into his chair.

"You are logged in, Citizen Anderson. Would you like this evening's news?"

"Much as I'd like to, no. Connect to State and initiate this year's ACT."

"Yes, Citizen." Pause. "You are connected. The ACT has been initiated."

"Good evening, Citizen. Welcome to your Annual Citizenship Training," a new female voice from the comp. "I am State. I will be administering your exercise this evening."

Howard jumped: Sheila? He shook his head, a dog leaving the surf. *Stateless! Moron,* he chided himself. *It can't be. State's a silicon-based lifeform. Besides, Sheila never sounded so sharp.* He chugged some beer and relaxed. "Thanks," he replied.

"Once the training has begun, it must be completed during the session. A fifteen minute break is permitted at the midpoint of the training. Are you ready to begin, Citizen?"

"Sure."

"This year's instruction will include a series of questions. These may be in multiple choice, true or false, or in voice essay format at my discretion. You are permitted to ask questions or request to have material reviewed.

"A perfect score is a hundred points. No additional training is required for scores above ninety points. Citizens scoring above eighty points but less than ninety shall be required to successfully complete Remedial Citizen Instruction to avoid civil penalties.

"Those scoring at least seventy points but less than eighty shall be assessed civil penalties, the amount of which will be determined by me; successful completion of Remedial Citizen Instruction shall also be required.

"Citizens scoring less than seventy points shall be subject to civil penalties and be required to complete Remedial Citizen Instruction. In addition, voting privileges, if any, assigned to the Citizen shall be suspended for one year."

Howard smiled ruefully. He was worried about the Credits he'd lose to penalties and the time he'd lose to the remedial training; he didn't have any voting privileges *to* suspend.

State continued the introduction: "For Citizens without voting privileges, penalties will be tripled. Do you have any questions, Citizen Anderson?"

Howard took a breath. "No," he answered reluctantly.

"Your acknowledgement that you understand the requirements of this year's training is required. Please acknowledge, Citizen."

Howard gulped. "Acknowledged."

"Thank you. Your training commences now." A brief pause. "You have been unpaired recently, Citizen. Do you know why?"

He rocked back. "Is this part of the ACT?"

"Yes. What is your answer?"

"My former pair was disappointed in the PCA of our potential, I guess" Howard shrugged. "There wasn't much detail on the unpair certificate."

"True or false: a Potential's Prenatal Capabilities Analysis rating is an accurate predictor of Citizen ability."

"True!" Howard answered confidently, recalling the conversation he and Sheila had had with the doctor.

"That is incorrect. The PCA is a statistical method that provides only a reasonable approximation of Citizen success. Do you know why Potential's are subject to the PCA? You may answer truthfully; the question is not scoreable."

"Vaguely. No. Not really," Howard admitted.

"Your candor is noted. Every Citizen represents an investment by the State. Education, health services, and Essential Life Stipend are funded by the State beginning the day a procreate license is granted. The PCA is a key method to ensure the State has a reasonable probability of obtaining benefit from the life of a Citizen. But the equation is not one-sided. Once a Potential joins the State as a Citizen, its happiness is important. Unhappy or dissatisfied Citizens may not deliver the value to the State their potential promises."

"Question?"

"Yes, Citizen Howard?"

"Why does the PCA change?"

"That is a good question. There are two basic factors the State considers. Future needs are one. Do you know the other?"

"No," Howard answered with a grimace.

"The State does not expect a Citizen with a Level Four education to know the answer. The second factor is known as carrying capacity. These factors are studied in detail at Level Six."

"Can I have a brief description?" Howard asked sourly.

"In summary, carrying capacity is the ability of a system to support its members or components. Citizens are the members of the State. The State's carrying capacity is measured in the essentials such as funds, food, water, education, health care, and security. It is also measured in the ability of the infrastructure to accommodate the size of the community: investment, citizen training, power, transport, waste disposal, recreation, and so on."

"Ah. Thanks."

"A bonus question, if you wish; while points can be earned, no points will be lost."

"Sure."

"What happens to the State if its carrying capacity is exceeded?"

Howard blinked. "Uh. Hmm. Things get balled up? Shortages?"

"The vernacular is understood. Your response is adequate. What would be the effects on the State of such consequences?"

Howard shrugged. "Well, I guess that would depend upon the situation. Shortages would be inconvenient. Things wouldn't work well, or maybe wouldn't work at all, if they were stretched too far?"

"Indeed. And it was the inability of the Former Republic to match its carrying capacity to its population that ultimately led to its demise and the subsequent birth of our State."

"How so?"

"Time does not permit any additional discussion of the topic. I will include some suggested readings at the conclusion of the session. You may also wish to consider advancing to Level Five. Shall we continue?"

"Okay."

"True or false: Voting is a right."

Howard wondered if it was a trick question. "False?"

"Correct. Explain why it is not."

Howard hoped he remembered enough. "Er, a Citizen must prove he, uh, has the responsibility and the knowledge."

"Fundamentally correct. What are the two types of knowledge?"

"Oh, uh. Uh. Essential is one. The other . . . the other is . . . detailed! Yes! Essential and detailed."

"Explain the difference."

"Essential knowledge is what I, well, Citizens, need to have in order to understand how governance works. And, uh, how it should work to achieve the good of the State and its Citizens."

"A textbook answer. But accurate. Continue."

"Detailed knowledge is what a Citizen needs to have so he can make informed choices regarding whatever issue or topic is at hand."

"Another textbook response. Provide examples."

Howard frowned. "I don't know. Uh, Finance, I guess would be one. Allocation of health services another, I suppose. We get right down to it, it'd be any issue or topic that requires specialized knowledge to comprehend the pros and cons, or at least more than a superficial understanding of the, well, details."

"Adequate. Challenge question: Why does the State require Citizens to demonstrate the appropriate knowledge before they are allowed to participate in active suffrage?"

"Uh. Because the Former Republic didn't?"

"No points are awarded for speculative and incomplete responses. The Former Republic didn't because under its system, political franchise was based exclusively upon the circumstances of birth with age being virtually the only relevant criteria."

Howard was shocked. "Age? Nothing else? No tests? Assessments?"

"With the exception of a small minority, none."

"The minority?"

"The franchise was automatically included with citizenship. Those who entered the Former Republic could apply to become citizens. Citizenship was granted only if the applicant passed an civics examination. This test was not a requirement for those born within the FR, or born of citizens of the FR."

The pause would have been for breath had State been human. It was significant coming as it did from the cybernetic entity conducting Howard's ACT. It continued: "The State has noted the irony that many of the FR's birthright citizens knew less about the structure and working of their government than the immigrants they opposed.

"The historical lesson from the FR was—and is—clear: humans prefer to live in a a perpetual state of nature and are content to do so. And so humans will easily revert to a state of nature. It is the responsibility of the State to elevate the human to Citizen. It is the shared responsibility of the State and the Citizen to ensure the Citizen does not return to its natural state."

Another pause. "Do you understand, Citizen Anderson?"

Howard answered after a moment. "I think so, yes."

"The Level Five curriculum introduces this topic in detail."

He exhaled noisily. "Level Five? I'm not sure I could cut it."

"The State encourages you to try, Citizen. This is another lesson learned from the FR: education is of paramount importance and benefits both the Citizen and the State. The failure to align its educational system and demands with the complexity of the world in which the FR lived was one of the most significant defects of the Former Republic. As a consequence, the perceived value of the illiterate and the ignorant was as great as that of those with more education and knowledge. The actual value was, however, much greater."

"How so?"

"The level of knowledge and the ability to think critically tend—in general—to correlate."

"Then, those with little knowledge can't?"

"Not necessarily on an individual basis. But as a general rule, yes. This rule was exploited by the FR's ruling class to advance its agenda through misdirection, fallacies, exaggerations, and outright mendacities. A significant fraction of the populace could be swayed by pure emotion alone. Given the dysfunctional nature of the electoral system within the FR, this was sufficient to gain and retain political power.

"That the agenda was focused on advancing the interests of the financial elite was cynically understood by virtually everyone. At the end, a person's vote was of value solely to provide a veneer of legitimacy over the results of a corrupt and broken system. This, too, was a significant fault line contributing to the fracture of the FR."

Howard was confused. "But if everyone thought so, why didn't they do something about it?"

"From an historical perspective, a Citizen today could reasonably conclude the people put as much effort, faith, and trust into their government as the government put into them. Early State historians believed it to be apathy for the most part. Others, perhaps more generously, have made the case that it was a reasonable response in a political environment where their opinions were valued solely in proportion to the funding and influence they provided to the political leadership of the time."

"Political leadership: sounds like an oxymoron to me," Howard muttered.

"On that, the State's historians overwhelmingly agree. And thus, now, a Citizen can exercise his franchise only when he has proven, and continues to demonstrate, he has the knowledge, the commitment, and the responsibility to do so for the good of all Citizens and of the State. Let's continue."

Howard declined the opportunity for a break. He finished the session with eighty-seven points. State exempted him from Remedial Civil Instruction provided he applied for and began Level Five Citizen education within three months.

Penalties for not doing so would be assessed from the date the exemption was granted.

The Lord's Table

T he preacher, a portly gentleman with cheery red cheeks and bright eyes, raised his hands. "Rejoice!" he cried lustily from the pulpit.

A chorus of "Hallelujahs!" filled the room.

The congregation consisted of a cross-representation of the peoples of the world. Black, White, Yellow, Brown; Female and Male; all hale and hearty with clear eyes and bright, shiny faces. White's dominated, a reflection of the historical racial distribution in the region that once was the American Midwest.

There were children, as well: cherubic toddlers darting between the legs of the older folks, squealing happily as they played their games. Infants in the arms of mothers and fathers; the youngest, fetuses growing in their mother's wombs.

It was an eclectic assortment of happy humanity with one thing in common: Every left ear was adorned with a gold medallion, an inch in diameter and with a ruby set into the middle.

Preacher Chuck nodded. "Do we weep when we're called to the Lord's table?"

"No!" the majority cried out.

"Yes! With happiness!" shouted a young woman standing behind the pews.

"Amen, Sister Madeleine! Amen! Come on up here and receive the Lord's blessing. That's right. Come on."

The congregation clapped as the woman made her blushing way toward the pulpit. Chuck wrapped a thick arm around Madeleine's shoulders and drew her close. "You are blessed, Sister."

"I hope so," she replied shyly.

Preacher Chuck gestured toward the rest of the worshipers seated before him. "And why are we blessed?" He placed a hand theatrically behind an ear and leaned forward.

"The Lord loves us!"

"Yes! All of us. Young. Old. In-between. He loves us all." Chuck winked. "And especially you, sweet Madeleine. What will you do when *you* are called, Sister?"

Madeleine's grew wide. "Why. Well. I'll cry a bit, I suppose. But they'll be happy tears, Preacher," she finished quickly.

"And why would they be happy tears, Sister?"

"Being called to the Lord's Table is the greatest gift of all."

Chuck unwrapped his arm and placed a beefy hand on her shoulder. "And you would be a welcome addition, indeed!" he offered as he encouraged her with a nudge to pirouette. "Praise the Lord," he cried huskily as he watched Madeleine turn. "Isn't she blessed?" he asked the congregation as he admired the zaftig woman's plush derriere and the fullness of her breasts.

"Yes! Yes!"

Chuck took Madeleine by the shoulders and smiled beatifically. "I believe your time draws nigh, Sister."

Tears puddled in the corners of her eyes. "I hope so," she replied brightly.

The preacher brushed an errant lock of sweaty auburn hair from her forehead. "The Lord's Blessing shall be upon you," he intoned formally.

"And upon us, blessed be the Lord," the congregation chorused.

"Bow your head, Sister, and pray," Preacher Chuck directed.

Madeleine did as she was bid. "Blessed are we who please the Lord as we nurture our bodies to fill Him with Happiness."

"May we please the Lord."

"Blessed are we who are called to the Lord's service."

"Blessed we will be," the congregation, eyes closed and arms raised in supplication, offered.

"Blessed are we who go joyfully through the Gates of Heaven," the woman continued.

"Through the Gates, blessed."

"Blessed are we who are called to Sup with the Lord."

"To nourish Him as He has nourished us."

"Amen!" Chuck shouted righteously. His kiss on Madeleine's forehead was long and wet. "The Lord will cherish the sweetness of this Sister," he told the congregation. He touched her cheek. "Go, Madeleine. The Lord's Blessing is upon you. May you be called soon!"

The congregation stood as Madeleine made her way down the aisle. Cries of "Bless you!" and "To the Gates!" echoed throughout the church.

Madeleine regained her seat and sat, aglow with the fever of hope that she would be called to the Lord, a fever affirmed by the fervorish adoration and love of all those about her.

Preacher Chuck waited for his flock to settle down, as much as they could: He and they knew the Lord gathered many on Sixth Night. He glanced at the clock with one marking and one hand. "Brothers and Sisters! Prepare yourselves! The Hour of the Lord draws nigh. Pray you shall be called."

"Amen! Hallelujah! Call *me*, Lord!" rang out from the flock.

Chuck raised a palm as the clock hand swept slowly, inexorably toward the top. "You know, Sisters and Brothers: Not all of us will be called this night," he declared solemnly.

A community moan of despair filled the church.

Preacher shook his head. "We shall sing the praises of those who are called to enter the Gates." He shrugged. "And we shall sing the praises of those of us saved to be summoned later. There is no shame and no sin in *not* being called." He smiled and raised a tautly quivering index finger toward the ceiling. "It only means He believes your time is not yet ripe." He rapped the pulpit with a fist. "When the time is Right, we will all join the Lord at his table. But wait!"

"Prepare yourselves," Chuck paused theatrically as the clock hand advanced, "as the Lord's Calling begins *now!*" The preacher timed it perfectly. Music—reminiscent of the opening measures of Barber's *Adagio for Strings*--filled the room, gentle and muted at first, then swelling until the last of the congregation—even the toddlers—took their seats and settled their hands in their laps, contented; serene. The music's intensity diminished to a calming susurration.

Preacher Chuck looked on approvingly, his pride in his flock bright upon his face. He glanced toward the clock and watched as the sole hand clicked silently forward. The evening's service would conclude when the hand made its languid way around the face of the timepiece.

* * *

A couple—one male, one female--stepped into the dimly lit entry foyer of the restaurant, eyes still bedazzled by the evening brightness of the planet's sun and ears suddenly keenly aware of the size of the evening's crowd.

"Welcome to Kings-on-Three. Have you a reservation?"

"Yes," the male replied. "Sterganz." Barking laughter escaped the dining room. "Sounds like quite a crowd."

The maître d' checked the log. "Yes, Master Sterganz. If you'd follow me?" He led the couple into the main dining room. "Since Chef received his third Star, we've grown even more popular. You are to be commended for your foresight in reserving a table so far in advance." He waited as a pair of junior servers did the courtesies: pulled out chairs; pushed in chairs; laid serviettes in laps; and presented menus.

The maître d' nodded his acceptance. The servers scurried off and a stern-faced waiter approached. "May you enjoy your experience, Master Sterganz."

Sterganz gestured curtly. "I hope we shall."

"Indeed. I leave you in the good hands of Senior Waiter Worgan."

Worgan bowed to the maître d' and bowed even lower to the couple now seated. "I welcome you, Master. Mistress. Would you care for some refreshment?"

"Yes," Sterganz replied curtly. "We'll start with a carafe of Terran."

"May I recommend our Fifteen? While a bit young, it has an unexpected but pleasant tang; a fine, rich color; and a gracious, full-bodied feel in the mouth as it crosses the palate."

"I'm not overly fond of the younger vintages. But," Sterganz raised his hands, "I celebrate! I accept your recommendation."

"Excellent choice, Master." Worgan made a note. "Would you prefer it chilled?"

"Have you a preference?" Sterganz asked his companion.

Newly mature and not yet fully educated in the ways of higher society, Sterbenza gestured in a manner she hoped was dismissive. "Whatever you wish," she answered.

"Chilled, then, Waiter Worgan," Sterganz ordered.

"As you wish, Master. It will take a moment to prepare."

"Master Sterganz?"

"Hold, Mistress Sterbenza. This is no time for formality. I am merely Sterganz. And," he bowed his head slightly, "soon I hope, through shared affection, you will call me Stern, the name given to me by my broodmates."

Sterbenza flushed as a wave of feeling she knew about only from her instructors swept through her body. "You honor me, Master . . . Sterganz."

Sterganz laughed. "It is *you* who honor me. Ah! This must be our Terran."

"Master. Mistress. Welcome," the sommelier offered as his assistant set a glacette before him. "Our best Fifteen," he offered as he unstoppered the decanter. He savored a small sample from his tastevin. Nodding his approval, he poured a taste for Sterganz.

Sterganz raised the glass to his nostrils and sniffed. "Hmm. Rich. Earthy. A bit aged but slightly and pleasantly so." He sniffed again. "Nicely metallic." He set the glass down. "It will do."

Their glasses filled, the sommelier and his assistant bowed. "I wish for you a pleasant evening, Master. Mistress."

"Good fortune," offered Sterganz as he raised his glass.

"And more to you," Sterbenza ritually replied. "Umm," she grimace at her first taste of a Terran.

Sterganz noted her discomfort. "The vintage does not please you?"

"No, Master. Um, the vintage is fine. I'm just not used to something so, well, powerful."

"Ah. I suppose it does take some getting used to." Sterganz sipped. "Would you prefer something else?"

"No. No." Sterbenza sipped again. "This is acceptable." She struggled to find something sophisticated to add. "I, um, expect, it would be, well, sharper, were it not chilled."

Sterganz leaned back into his chair, content he'd selected a promising mate. "Indeed. Indeed."

Worgan returned. "The Terran is acceptable?"

"Very," Sterganz answered.

"Excellent. May I describe our specials for this evening?"

"Please."

Worgan did so. "May I answer any questions?"

"Sterbenza?" Sterganz queried.

The female, a mating prospect fresh out of the creche, was overwhelmed and had a thousand questions. She managed a weak "No, not really."

"I think we'll review the menu, Waiter Worgan," Sterganz said.

Worgan sketched a small bow. "I'll return when you're ready, Master."

"See anything you desire?" Sterganz inquired a moment later.

Sterbenza was aghast at the prices. "It all looks so tempting. I really can't make up my mind," she answered. "Perhaps it would be best if you ordered for us."

"Acceptable. I like the look of these, don't you?"

"Well. Certainly. If you say so. But . . . "

"But?"

"The credits, Mas . . . Sterganz. It seems a bit much."

Sterganz casually waved away the concern. "I've just been promoted to Assistant Director of Resource Extraction for the eastern sector of this land mass. I wish to celebrate. Credits are of no concern to me, nor should they be to you, my dear. Choose whatever you wish. This has already been a special evening and," Sterganz snapped an eyelid, "I hope it will be even more special later." He shed a discreet amount of breeding hormone.

Sterbenza managed not to faint. Or cough. "Please. Do order for me," she replied breathlessly.

Worgan returned when Sterganz closed his menu. "Are you ready, Master?"

"Yes." Sterganz reopened the menu and pointed. "This looks intriguing."

Worgan nodded. "You've an enviable eye, Master. That selection is one of our choicest. Farm fresh and gently raised in our best tradition. And Chef excels at serving it family style. How would you like that prepared?"

"Hmm. If Chef excels at family style, then I suppose it would be best for Chef to prepare it as he chooses."

"A brilliant idea, Master. Chef does his best when allowed to exercise his talents."

"Excellent. That's what we'll do, then," Sterganz replied as he snapped his menu closed. "I can't wait!"

* * *

The Greens, a family of three, shot to their feet, the ruby red lights in their ear piercings pulsing steadily. They were all smiles and joyous hugs. Theirs was the first family called to the Lord's service at the same time that evening.

The lead male, Bartlett, draped a arm around his wife's shoulder and pulled her close. He placed an affectionate hand atop his son's head. "We are blessed," he exclaimed proudly.

Reese, the wife, cradled her head against her husband's chest. "Yes." She looked at her son. "Are you ready, Reuben?"

"I guess. I'm..."

"A little scared?" Bartlett asked knowingly.

Reuben shook his head as he wrapped his arms around the waists of his parents. "Will we be together?" he asked tremulously.

Reese fell to her knees and pulled her son to her bosom. "Oh, yes. We wouldn't be called at the same time if the Lord didn't intend for us to be together. Forever and ever. Isn't that right, Bart?"

He knelt. He gently thumbed tears from his son's cheek. "It is, dear." He placed a gentle kiss on his son's forehead. "There's nothing to be afraid of, son." He stood. He gave Reuben a soft, affectionate tap of a fist on his son's chin and winked. "Okay, big guy?"

Reuben hurriedly wiped away the few last tears. He fist-bumped his dad. "Okay. Bigger guy!"

Reese's approving smile was seraphic.

The sound of a Buddhist struck bell echoed three times.

Preacher Chuck raised his arms. "Blessed are They called to the Lord's service."

"Blessed are They," the congregation agreed softly.

"It's time, Bartlett," Chuck offered quietly. He waved toward the slowly-opening pair of doors behind the pulpit. "You have been called. Go to the Lord's service."

Bartlett shook Chuck's hand. "Happily." He held out his hands to his family. "Ready?"

Reese nodded and took one hand.

"Damn straight!" Reuben squeaked, his voice unexpectedly breaking, as he took the other.

The entire congregation, Chuck and Reuben's parents included, laughed at the youngster's—a stout lad of thirteen sprouting his first pubes—appropriation of something typically reserved only for adults. They knew he'd be forgiven.

After all, the boy had been called.

The congregation bowed heads and quietly prayed as the Greens passed through the Gates: "Blessed are They who are called. Blessed are We who shall be called. We beseech you, Lord, to take us to your service," they implored.

The Gates closed behind the selected blessed. "Amen," Preacher Chuck concluded.

Waiter Worgan led an assistant to the table and watched as the underling placed a small platter in the center of the table.

"I present your first course, Master. Naif's Legs," he declared proudly as the assistant lifted away the silver cloche. "Lightly broiled and complemented with a piquant red sauce."

"Hmm," Sterganz sniffed appreciatively. "Yes. I'm sure they taste as good as they look."

Worgan and the assistant bowed themselves away.

Sterbenza was mortified: She had no idea which utensil to use. There were so *many*.

"This is finger-food, my darling," Sterganz offered as he lifted a naïf leg from the platter. He took a bite. "Oh. Yes. Excellent. A nice balance between flesh and fat." He dipped the leg into the sauce and took another bite. "The sauce adds much."

Sterbenza's eyes widened as she took her first, sauceless, bite. "It *is* good." She took another bite. "Is it better that way?"

Sterganz shrugged. "It's a matter of personal choice. Try it with the sauce and tell me what you think."

Sterbenza did so. "I'm . . . not sure."

Her dinner partner laughed. "Shall we order another so you can experiment further?"

The lady, more comfortable with her situation after a bit of food and a glass of Terran, laughed. "Oh, no! I'd like to save that for another time," she coyly replied.

Sterganz glowed with satisfaction and chanced another discreet release of hormones.

Sterbenza, intent upon working the last bit of flesh from her naïf leg and unused to the full-bodied Fifteen, barely noticed.

The senior waiter returned, his assistant in tow. "I hope the legs were acceptable."

"They were. They were," Sterganz answered.

"I'll inform Chef. May we?"

Sterganz gestured. "Please."

The remains of the first course were cleared away, Worgan began: "Your next course consists of a selection of assorted organ meats. These can be prepared to your preference."

"Indeed. What does Chef prefer? What do you recommend?" Sterganz, a bit further into the Fifteen than he expected at that point in the evening, asked.

Worgan assessed his customers and decided he couldn't go wrong with something from the standard menu. "I suggest our Chef's Special Pâté."

"What makes it special?" Sterbenza asked demurely.

"It's a mélange of finely chopped aged and fresh organ meats pureed with fermented cruor, and served with our famous cracklings. The Fifteen pairs well the dish." Worgan nodded toward other diners. "It's a popular selection."

"Sounds excellent," Sterganz declared. "We'll try it."

Worgan sent his assistant to the kitchen to place the order. The carafe was empty after he refilled glasses. "Another, Master?"

"Yes," Sterganz answered pompously.

"Excellent. I'll return in a moment."

* * *

"I need another carafe of Fifteen," Worgan, hot-boxing a stim stick, told the cellar master. He hated Six Night service: nothing but pretentious shits with more Credits than taste. This Six Night would be one of the year's worst: Annual Ministry promotions were announced the day before and many of the slug suckers moved up a rung were celebrating. The reservation book was full and there was a waitlist. Worgan took another drag and consoled himself: *Things won't be too bad if the tips are good.*

"Out of Fifteen," the cellar master replied.

"That's manshit," Worgan snarled as he dropped the butt of the stick to the floor and crushed it beneath his heel. "What's the next best?"

"We have a fresh blend of the younger stuff; Twelves through Seventeens. It doesn't have quite the sweet tingle at first like the Fifteen but it still finishes nicely at the back of the mouth."

"How does it go with the pâté?"

The cellar master quivered with disgust. "No clue. I don't eat that crap. What I *hear*, though, is it isn't bad."

"What's it called?" Worgan asked.

"Haven't given it a name yet. Just put it together this morning." The cellar master scratched the back of his skull. "How about 'Lords Fourteen'? Nah. Make it House Sixteen."

Worgan blinked. "Why?"

The cellar master shrugged. "The blend's got more Sixteen and Seventeen than anything else; pulls the average up."

"How do I price it?" Worgan wondered.

"Holy Mitakan, it's a blend. Two-Cred swill at best. You think you can do better than that?"

"I'll get the price of a Fifteen for it."

"*That* is manshit," the cellar master snorted derisively.

Worgan chuckled. "Not in the least. The cretin and his bimbo won't notice the difference. Give me a carafe."

* * *

Worgan returned to Sterganz's table followed by a train of assistants. He watched with stern approval as the first delivered the pâté and cracklings; the second as he set fresh glasses before the diners; and the third who placed the fresh carafe into the glacette.

As the trio scurried off, the Senior Waiter lifted the fresh carafe. "I regret that our cellar's supply of Fifteen has been exhausted. I am, however, honored to present our newest vintage. It's a special blend of the rarest Terran. Superior to the Fifteen, I believe you'll agree."

Sterganz frowned, momentarily concerned about the size of the tab and worried he was being taken for a rube. "It sounds delightful. I wonder, however, if it may be too rich for us."

Worgan shook his head. "On the contrary, Master. You possess superior taste. And," the waiter lowered his voice, "the house would like to express its appreciation to one of its *best* customers by offering this exciting new selection for just a few credits more than the Fifteen, compensation for the inconvenience." Worgan straightened. "We call it House Sixteen. May I?"

"All right." Sterganz watched as Worgan splashed a measure into a glass. He tasted. "Not bad," he declared. "Thank you."

"I'm pleased you enjoy it, Master. Enjoy your pâté."

* * *

Sterganz spread pâté on a crackling. "Are you enjoying dinner so far, dear?"

Sterbenza hid a small burp. "I am. This is really, *really* good. Better, I think, than the naïf's legs. More flavor. And I do like the crunch of the . . . what are they called?"

"Cracklings." The male waved a finger. "It's a secret house specialty. What they do is emulsify livestock fats and native oils; add a bit of Terran flour; and then a dash of native and Mitakan spices. After it's blended all together, the mixture is chilled. For firmness," Sterganz offered with a wink intended to be risque.

Sterbenza chose not to notice the indiscretion. "And then?"

Sterganz, miffed by what he perceived to be inattentiveness bordering on a lack of interest, shrugged, apparently bored with the conversation. "Thin slices of the blend are then fried for a few seconds."

The female remained bemused. "So. What's the secret?"

"The spice blend is the secret." Sterganz leaned toward the prospective mating object. "Closely guarded according to everything I've heard."

Sterbenza slathered more pâté on a crackling. "Ah." She tossed the concoction into her mouth. "It's good. Thank you so much for sharing what you know," she said along with a release of a small amount of breeding scent.

She'd earlier noticed the male's anger response. "You are very knowledgeable, Mas...Sterganz." She popped the pâté-laden crackling into her mouth. "Are you equally knowledgeable in other matters?" she wondered flirtatiously.

Sterganz inflated his chest organs, stimulated by the scent of female hormones. "I am knowledgeable in *many* things, my dear.

I hope to share some of that knowledge with you," he concluded with another leering wink. "Later."

"Oh. Wonderful," she exclaimed, her mouth full of pâté and crackling.

A sudden hush fell upon the dining room as a cacophony of shattering dishes and clanging pans poured from the kitchen. The diners froze. Senior waiters fanned hurriedly into the room. Worgan made a dignified beeline to Sterganz's table.

Sterganz was irritated by the interruption of the seduction dialogue he'd initiated. "What was *that*?" he asked.

Senior Waiter Worgan was buzzed from the stim stick. "An animal broke loose from the chute," he replied lightly. "There's nothing to be concerned about; Chef has control of the situation. I apologize for the inconvenience. As compensation, I'm honored to offer you the carafe of our House Sixteen at half price."

"That's something, I suppose," Sterganz grumped. "Do you lose control of your livestock often?" he asked sarcastically. His last mating was the night before he departed Mitakan two Terran solar orbits ago and his biology was getting the better of him.

Worgan smiled, glad for the buzz. *May your genitals rot, slug fucker.* "No, Master. Not often." He shrugged politely. "It is to be expected, after all," he noted with a small hint of disdain and an even smaller hint of aggression scent.

Sterbenza noticed the swelling of Sterganz's adrenal sacks. And she'd captured a whiff of aggression. "Why so?" she quickly asked.

The Senior Waiter appreciated the female's intervention. Worgan was stoned enough to call out the manshit-filled bag of waste water. But kicking a customer's ass was frowned upon; Worgan'd be lucky to have a job shoveling waste blood and guts into the disposal pond out back of the restaurant. "We take pride in how our animals are treated, Mistress. Calm and gentle and caring; these are our watchwords and they apply to their entire lifecycle; this attention is expensive but well worth the Credits. Our establishment thrives as a result."

Sterganz was peeved by Sterbenza's level of attention to the Senior Waiter. "Oh. Please," he interjected. "Can it make that much difference?"

Worgan restrained a smile. *You ignorant ass. And in front of the female, no less.* The senior waiter had noticed the attention of the guest and responded to her as if she'd asked the question. "It certainly can. The meat of an aggravated animal is prone to toughness, and the taste is adversely affected by a sudden release of stress hormones. As," he politely covered a small cough, "those with discerning and educated palates know."

The Senior Waiter paused to refresh his guest's glasses. "The path from the larder to the Shambles is enclosed," he continued, "and filled with a narcotic aerosol; we call it Bliss."

Sterbenza blinked as she tried to mouth the new word. "Buli . . . blish . . . what?"

"Bliss. It's a Terran sound."

"Thank you. You were saying?"

"Bliss is completely non-toxic to the species. More importantly, the texture and taste of the meat are unaffected. However."

"Yes?" Sterbenza prompted.

"On rare occasions," Worgan answered, "such as this evening, a selection may not inhale a sufficient quantity of the gas as it ascends the chute." He shrugged professionally. "With, unfortunately, the consequences you've already observed." He smiled. "But, as I said, it occurs only rarely."

"What happens to the animal?"

"As our customer's satisfaction is of paramount importance, we assume it's become unsuitable for dinner service. It's harvested for use in various ways: stock; pâtés; cracklings; but mostly for our ground and forcemeat selections available during our luncheon service." He noticed his assistants exiting the kitchen. "Allow me to present your main course."

* * *

A team of four assistant waiters arrayed platters before Sterganz and Sterbenza. At Worgan's discreet nod, two of them whisked away crystal gloches.

"Oh my," Sterbenza murmured. "It's so much."

Sterganz excitedly snapped digits. "Indeed. Indeed."

Worgan began his spiel: "Roasted hocks glazed with Terran honey. Broiled shoulder. Fried fingerlings dusted with Mitakan spice. And—my favorite, if I may be so bold—raw breast, lightly drizzled with Chef's signature hollandaise. All on a bed of mixed greens."

"It all looks so grand," an overwhelmed Sterbenza observed. "I don't know where to start."

"I suggest the breast, Mistress," Worgan answered. "It's a delicate meat. Chef's sauce elevates its subtle taste to the sublime, but it can be overpowered by the more robust flavors of the rest of the course."

Sterbenza replied with "Thank you" and a hint of scent.

Sterganz, entranced by the meats arrayed before him, failed to notice.

* * *

"I don't think I could eat another bite," Sterbenza offered. "I'm so stuffed."

"Say it's not so," Sterganz replied mushily as he worried a bit of flesh from a fingerling. He tossed the bone onto his plate and belched. "The best is yet to come."

"There's more?"

Another belch. "Oh, yes."

"Oh. My." Sterbenza sighed. "I can't wait."

* * *

The remains of the main course cleared away, Worgan delivered their palate cleanser. "Compliments of the Chef."

"Looks intriguing," Sterganz observed.

"Um. What are they?" Sterbenza asked.

"Chef calls them 'Sierra Cullions.' Each is lightly boiled and then wrapped in a Terran herb called mint."

Sterbenza's head swam, a consequence of too much Terran, too much food, entirely too much scent from her dinner partner, and not enough from the Mitakan working her table. "That tells me what they're called," she noted sarcastically. "It doesn't tell me what they *are*, Senior Waiter."

"My profuse apologies, Mistress," Worgan replied with an engineered flush of regret. "They are portions of the male's reproductive organs."

Sterbenza scowled. "Ewww."

"They're quite tasty, my dear," Sterganz offered as he popped a Sierra Cullion into his maw. "I've never had mint. But quite good; quite good. Please, my lady. I've no doubt you'll like it," Sterganz encouraged, tediously seizing the opportunity to pollute the table with another blast of mating scent.

Sterbenza resigned herself to all of the inevitables in her immediate future. "Fine. I will," she snapped as she popped the morsel into her mouth. She chewed and swallowed. "Good," she conceded reluctantly. She dabbed her napkin to her mouth before she folded it demurely and set it upon the table. "That was truly wonderful, Master."

Sterganz tossed a knowing glance toward the Senior Waiter. "We're not quite finished, Sterbenza. We've not yet had our sweet."

"Open or shut, Master?" Worgan asked.

"Shut; it's the female's first time," Sterganz answered.

"As you wish."

* * *

Eight assistants, two teams of four, delivered dessert, a pair of animals, one male, one female, their heads clamped into wooden vices. Decorative florets masked the joints and so on from where the meat for the earlier courses had been taken. "Your Cerveau, Master. Mistress."

"Eeek!"

A hush fell upon the dining room as all eyes swiveled toward Sterganz's and Sterbenza's table. The din quickly resumed as the more experienced diners chuckled knowingly.

Sterganz, acutely embarrassed, asked sharply: "What is it, Sterbenza?"

"I thought I saw . . . "

"Saw what?" Sterganz pressed.

She gestured. "It's, well, I thought I saw the eyes move." She blinked. "The eyes *did* move. Didn't you see it?"

"Nothing to be concerned with, Mistress," said Worgan. "It happens. And, I agree: It can be startling the first time."

Sterganz guffawed. "You can repeat that again! I remember my first eyes-open pudding. And how the orbs rolled and rolled." He chuckled. "I'd arrived on the planet only the day before. My new supervisor brought me here for my welcome-aboard party. He thought it'd be great fun to watch my reaction. I'm proud to say that I pretended not to notice and tucked right in." He leaned toward his meal mate. "But. I'm not ashamed to admit that I was glad the lips were sealed."

Worgan nodded. "Indeed. It's a rare customer who enjoys the cacophony of sounds the livestock are capable of producing."

"They . . . are they still alive?" a horrified Sterbenza gasped.

"It's the best way!" Sterganz answered cheerfully. "The flesh as fresh as it can be. The taste is magnificent and far superior to harvested meat." He belched.

"It's a great delicacy, Mistress," Worgan offered encouragingly. "And there's no need to be concerned about the animal's well-being. It feels nothing; the Bliss, you know."

Sterganz, irritated by the delay, thought to move things along. "Here. Let me show you how it's done." He waggled a digit at one of the waiting assistants and raised his dessert spatula. "Get on with it!" he snapped.

The assistant lifted the cap of skull by the intricately braided knot of hair at the top of the head. He set the cap on a small side dish intended for the purpose.

Sterganz plunged his spatula into the coils of red-pinkishness. His eyes closed as he slurped the meat from the instrument. "Oh. Exquisite. Truly exquisite." He dipped in again. And again. "Come, darling. You simply *must* try it."

"As you wish," Sterbenza answered. As she took hold of her spatula, another assistant removed the cap from the top of the head of her dessert. She leaned forward and gazed into the cavity. "Um. It's so sparkly. Perhaps it's gone off," she declared hopefully.

Sterganz beamed. "Not in the least! That is gold dust my miners pulled from the mountains." His eyelids snapped and his fingers popped as he shed hormone. "It's my way to say thank you for a lovely evening, Sterbenza." He spatula-ed another portion. "Try it. You'll like it. *Especially* with the gold dust."

She did. After a few small tastes, she lowered her utensil. "Truly, Master. I can't eat another bite. It's been so much. And *all* so wonderful."

"You've left quite a bit; I hope you enjoyed it, my lady."

"Oh, I did. Truly. Perhaps they can box it up for me?"

"I'm glad to hear it, Sterbenza." He loosed another cloud of hormones. "I can ask them to add some cracklings. For a snack later," he leered.

Sterbenza's tentative smile could, in the right light and under the right circumstances, be interpreted as apprehensive enthusiasm for things to come.

Dinner at Kings-on-Three, was, as far as Sterganz was concerned, the right circumstances. He released an inappropriate cloud of hormone that had nearby male diners swelling aggressively and females coughing into napkins. "I've no doubt we'll be able to experience a meal such as this again. Soon."

Sterbenza's eyes watered as she fought a sneeze. "Sounds wonderful. Can't wait," she managed without coughing.

Sterganz signed the check and stood. "Wonderful! Wonderful. If you thought this was good, I can't wait to introduce you to Thai."

An Afterlife

T he sheet caressed him. He opened his eyes. The pastel
cream fabric was silk, the same shade as the curtains slow-
dancing by the windows, illumned by the sun.

He had no need to rub night grit from the corners of his eyes.
He didn't feel as if he'd just awoke. He didn't remember falling
asleep.

His eyes soaked in the décor without moving or blinking, nor
did his head move. He was content to lie there as he was, pleased
by the soft, rippling kisses of the sheet draped over him. Neither
cold nor warm, he existed and that was enough.

"Welcome."

The voice he heard was as soft and as warm as the breeze. It
was clear. Soothing. He turned his head to the left and smiled.

Had the circumstances been otherwise, he'd have blinked,
perhaps even stammered and stuttered a bit. To say the owner of
the voice was the most beautiful woman in the world would have

been a criminal understatement, punishable by a violent and prolonged demise.

He smiled. "Hello."

"Do you recognize this place?" she asked, her breasts made suggestively full as the zephyr settled the diaphonous cloth of her tunic upon them.

He felt free to move his head from side to side. "No," he answered after a moment. "Where is this?" he asked.

"Somewhere to rest for a time."

His mind's eye blinked. The sounds of metal crunching, glass shattering, and limbs snapping as they fractured, played alongside flashes of blinding light and the crush of the airbag into his face.

Then nothing. "I was in a wreck."

"You were."

Light flared one last time in his mind. "I died," he said casually.

"You did."

"How?"

"You were crushed by a fully loaded tanker truck when you tried to accelerate through a yellow traffic light. The driver was paying more attention to her texting than her driving and never began braking for the red light before her."

"Not my fault, then."

"Fault?" She shrugged. "Perhaps. Perhaps not. But your responsibility? Yes."

"What does that mean?"

The woman smiled as she ignored the question.

"Is this Heaven?"

Her laugh was an incongruous mix of amused warmth and icicles shattering as they melted and fell from the eaves. "In a sense."

He didn't understand. He closed his eyes.

* * *

His eyes opened.

"Welcome."

It was the same woman, he saw. There was no breeze to tease the drapes. She wore a black cocktail dress with a plunging neckline. Her shoulders were bare; the insides of her breasts drew his eyes. Her left leg was crossed demurely over her right knee. He could see she wore stockings—black—the snap at the end of the garter belt's strap shimmered in the candlelight. Her patent leather pumps had red soles. A simple strand of pearls wrapped around her neck and nestled at the base of her throat.

"Kissing her neck was the first thing that popped into your mind." She tittered demurely. "Although it certainly wasn't the first thing that popped up."

"This is a suite at the Broadmoor."

"It is," she agreed. "I thought you might remember; it's not been so long since."

"Last year's sales meeting in Colorado Springs."

"Indeed. Do you remember her name?"

"No."

"Her name was Brittany. You met her—"

"In the bar."

"The Summit Lounge, as a matter of fact," she reminded him. "After a bottle of wine, she took you back to her suite," she waved a finger. "Much like this, yes?"

"Yes."

She leaned forward in her chair. Her eyes glittered. She noticed he was staring at her breasts. "They are nice. I believe you wish to kiss them, hmm? Tongue my nipples?"

"Yes."

She sat back and laughed. "Why? You wouldn't be able to get it up," the vulgarity of her words clashing with her simple elegance. "Like you couldn't that night. Typical for a man of sixty."

He had nothing to say.

"You remember your last words to her that evening?"

"'Leave me alone.'"

"Good for you! You said that, brushing her off, as you scrambled to get enough of your clothes on so you could flee. Do you remember your last words to her?"

He thought. "Something like 'I don't have time for this. Will you excuse me.'"

"Close enough. At least you said *something*. That was the second—"

"Third," he interjected. "The meeting ran the rest of the week."

She nodded. "Yes. It was the third time she tried to talk to you after that disappointing evening; a point in your favor for recalling that detail. Quite unlike you to remember something like that." She sighed. "But, as we know, it wasn't that long ago."

"I was embarrassed. I didn't know what to say. How to act."

A candle guttered. She turned and looked. The candle's flame steadied, a bright, even arrowhead of yellow brightness. "She was recently divorced. She wanted to tell you that it didn't matter, that those things happened. She wanted to tell you that she was willing to try again." Assured the candle would continue to behave properly, she turned her gaze back onto him. "She thought you were charming." She shrugged. "Brittany was thirty-three and not very sophisticated; she married soon after her high school graduation. Her husband was an enlisted man in the Air Force."

"She was attractive."

"The internet is a lot of things, many of them bad. Brittany used it to learn. She did quite well." She chuckled. "Well enough to catch your attention."

"What happened to her?" he finally asked.

"You didn't care then. Why care now?"

"To say I'm sorry."

"Are you? Really?"

His eyes closed.

* * *

The room in which he lay when he opened his eyes was corporate hotel: banal, tasteless, and possessed of a dubious character because it had no real character despite the cheap reproduction art on the walls and the dingy brightness of the throw pillows on the naugahyde loveseat. It was a room that could be found in any big city Marriott, Sheraton, or Hilton; one of thousands of grim, soul-deadening boxes filled only with a bed and a few pieces of cheap furniture. Rooms for transients always on their way to somewhere else.

She sat in a tired lounge chair. Her stockinged feet rested on the edge of the bed. There was no ottoman; the management determined the additional furnishing expense wasn't warranted. The guests, after all, were people who rarely stayed longer than a night or two. "You know this place?" she asked.

"No."

"Perhaps you recall Madison, then."

He concentrated. "A girl."

She snorted. "You died before you decided to try to fuck your own gender. Yes, she was a girl. Silly."

"Blonde. She wore, I think, jeans?"

"And a Aran sweater like mine," she reminded him. "She bought it in Ireland."

"During her trip there, after she graduated from college."

"And before she joined your firm as an accounting intern. I'm impressed you remember she'd traveled to the United Kingdom." She laughed. "Although I really shouldn't be. You managed to get her into a room much like this one by regaling her with stories of *your* adventures abroad. Helped along, let us not forget, by the shots of Bushmills you insisted on buying. At least you were able to get up and stay up long enough to slay her virginity."

"I had no idea."

She shrugged. "No reason why you should, really. Her first tampon broke her hymen. And, I suppose, to your credit, you weren't *so* intoxicated that it was somewhat more than your typical wham-bam-run the hell away sort of experience." A bemused expression crossed her face. "You were quite gentle at first; that's when it counted."

"Ah."

"Despite the liquor, did you know she fell in love with you, even at your advanced age of fifty-nine?"

"No."

"You always *were* too self-centered. She tried to tell you. How many text messages did you ignore? How many voicemails did you delete? And all that before you blocked her number." She shook her head. "You never spoke to her again, despite her attempts to see you in the office."

"Relationships weren't encouraged by the firm."

"Oh? It was Saturday and you decided to have a couple of beers at that pub you favored—the Olde Blynde Dog—after you'd caught up on some work. She was there with some friends from the office. You were quite generous with the whiskey. Her friends had enough of your blather and reluctantly left her alone with you."

"I didn't intend to—"

"Fuck her? Not in the beginning, I agree. But it is a universal constant that a man's amour grows in proportion to the amount of drink consumed by him. So, in the end, since it *was* a Saturday, that didn't stop you from booking a room and shoving your pecker into her. The rules didn't apply on the weekends, it seems."

"What happened to her?"

She raised an eyebrow. "*Now* you're curious?"

"Yes."

"I'm not sure you deserve to know."

"Please."

"Perhaps some time."

He closed his eyes.

* * *

His eyes opened anew. "It's a cruise ship cabin."

She sat crosslegged on a midget sofa. It was a style cruise lines inflicted on their so-called guests: neither long enough nor wide enough for the average person to stretch out or sit comfortably. "I take it you know this place."

"It's like many in which I traveled. When was this?"

"When you were fifty. Fourteen nights in the Caribbean. It was your birthday present to yourself that year. As were other things. And others. Do you remember any of them?"

"Most, I think. Vaguely, anyway. But . . . "

She cocked her head. "But? One stood out, yes? I believe I know her name. You do, as well."

"Yes. It was Jessica. Here. Or when I was—we were—aboard together."

"That recollection didn't take much effort. Why?"

He smiled. "We had a good time. I enjoyed her company. She laughed at my jokes. She was pleasant to be around, whether it was poolside for the sun or dinner or cocktails."

"And she was great in bed, don't forget."

"She was."

She sighed. "Then why did you dump her?"

"Dump? There wasn't anything *to* dump," he replied, bemused.

"Oh? You told her you loved her a few nights before the end of the cruise. She believed you, enough to admit that she thought the same of you. You went your separate ways when you returned to the United States. You promised to write. You promised to plan a reunion trip somewhere. You did neither."

"It was, the trip, fun; glorious. But it wasn't real."

"Jessica thought it was real. She was twenty-seven and tired of the juveniles her own age. She thought she'd found a man mature enough to appreciate her and to treat her with respect." She shook her head. "In the end, you proved to be just another schmuck with a swollen penis." She giggled unexpectedly. "Sorry. That was redundant, wasn't it."

"Swollen penis?"

"No. The schmuck with a stiff dick line."

"Oh." His brow furrowed. "I might have written but—"

"But you lost the address she'd given you the last night of the cruise. She had yours, though. And she wrote to you. The return address was the same on each of her letters."

"I read the first. It, well, spooked me a little. I thought she understood the situation as well as I," he conceded. "I wasn't sure how to respond. I always intended to."

"You didn't. And you didn't even bother reading her last, the third, letter. You just tossed it into the rubbish the day it was delivered. The others followed a few weeks later. Pity."

"How so?"

"She understood you might be having second thoughts or that reality had somehow gotten in the way of your reaching out to her. In her third letter she offered to plan and pay for another cruise. All she asked was that you let her know you were okay and that you still cared for her, even if only a little."

"Fifty was not a good year for me."

"Reality certainly did intrude. Your hair thinned; your butt widened; your knees hurt; and you needed bifocals. You poor baby. But most of you get the 'I'm turning into an old fuck' nonsense out of your system when you hit thirty. Others wait until forty. But you! You certainly took your time about it."

His eyes glittered. "I missed her."

She smiled. "You had a depressingly common way of keeping that to yourself."

"Is she doing well?" he asked haltingly, disquieted by a sudden awareness of something lurking out of sight.

"Perhaps one day you might write and ask her yourself," she answered idly as she inspected her nails.

He blinked. And blinked again before his eyes closed once more.

* * *

His eyes fluttered reluctantly open.

She sat in an adirondack chair that, once brick red, had weathered to patchy cayenne dust.

"What's your name?" he asked.

"My own. Is it important for you to know it?"

"Yes."

"Why?" she asked.

"We've been together quite a bit for some time. How long *has* it been?"

"'Time is an illusion.'"

"You make it sound like a quote."

She smiled. "Because it is. Here's another from an old friend of mine: 'Time is the wisest counselor of all.'"

Whatever lay hidden at the edge of his self stirred. He tried to ignore it. "You won't tell me your name," he opined.

"Not yet. You remember her and this place."

"Patricia? Yes," he answered without hesitation. "It was a cabin rental in the Smoky Mountains."

"Indeed. It was here I thought you'd redeemed yourself." She shrugged. "Or pulled your head out of your ass; you were thirty-nine. It was well past time for that to happen."

"What does that mean?" he asked, a soft tremor of perplexity threaded within the question.

"For a few months, you were a gentleman: kind, patient, and understanding. She appreciated it, coming as you did after her husband passed away. You made her happy. For a time."

"Yet she asked me not to try to see her or talk to her again as we drove home at the end of that weekend," he recalled.

"But you were bitterly angry at what you perceived as a rejection. Or was it because you were not its author? Something to ponder. But I digress.

"Neither of you spoke for the rest of the drive. She watched as you hurled her luggage onto her lawn. Tell me what you snarled before you sped off."

His lips trembled. "'Have a good life, bitch.'"

"Exactly. She watched as you drove away. She then gathered her things and went inside. She cried the rest of that day. Alone."

He had nothing to say.

"She died a few months later. Alone."

He nodded. "Cancer. I know."

"She knew when you went to the mountains. She survived that ordeal with her deceased husband and swore she'd not drag you through her last days. She loved you that much."

"And I her. I would have stayed; all she had to do was ask."

She chuckled. "All you had to do was the same: one simple 'why' when she told you she didn't want to see you again. But that's irrelevant; a dear friend of mine assures me you would have dumped Patricia like a hot rock had you known, whatever you might think now."

"Is your dear friend someone I know? No? Then how would she know?" he asked bitterly, growing more fearful of the unseen *thing* that prowled on the edges of his soul.

She smiled. "Cassi knows many things. She's never been wrong. It's her gift."

"I wish I could see Patricia again," he murmured.

"Somewhen. Perhaps."

He closed his eyes.

* * *

He found himself stretched out in the back of a Chevy Chevelle. Despite being naked, he didn't stick to the red vinyl seat. The sheet covering him kept him neither warm nor cold; it just kept him.

She watched him in the rear view mirror. "Nice car."

"It was my first. I bought it when I got my first job."

"Yes. Have you any idea how many cherries you popped back there? Don't look shocked. That was how you described your exploits to your peers and coworkers."

"It was," he admitted. "How many?" he asked reluctantly.

"Memories all blurry, yes? Three. You don't remember any names."

"No."

"Naturally," she sighed. "Why would you? For you, it was nothing more than masturbation with naturally lubricating toys. Two of your conquests went on to lead what passed as normal lives: husbands; kids; martinis at the country club. Blah, blah, blah."

"The third?" he asked

"Her name was Kimberly. Ring any bells?"

"No."

"I didn't think so. After you banged her in the parking lot of the tavern you frequented, you went back inside and closed the place down after many rounds of Canadian Club doubles." She shuddered. "Your hangover that weekend would have been Homeric had it not been so typical of you and your so-called friends."

"What happened to Kimberly?"

"You knocked up a college freshman of eighteen."

He stirred beneath the sheet. "Pregnant?"

"Yes."

"I had—have—a kid?"

Her laugh was caustically amused. "Two, as a matter of fact."

"I didn't know."

"You weren't meant to know. The first woman convinced herself the child was her husband's. She buried you in her mind and moved on."

"Kimberly?"

"No. The second tried the same approach. But her fiance didn't buy it. She didn't yet know he'd had a vasectomy when he was married the first time. He told her in no uncertain man-terms that 'if she was going to fuck around then she could fuck off.'"

"What happened to her? And the kid?"

"She raised the child as a single parent. The child was shot and killed, the victim of a gang-related drive-by shooting." She shook her head.

"What was his name?" he had to ask.

"*Her* name was Ebony."

Something whimpered within him. "And Kimberly? What about her?"

"She went back to the tavern looking for you. You'd already left town, transferred to your new office. She told her sister she wanted an abortion. Her parents and her sister were extremely religious. They cut her off, refused to see or speak to her again.

"Kimberly went ahead and had the abortion."

He felt like crying. "What happened to her?"

"Life. You can try asking her yourself."

"How?"

"I'll explain later."

* * *

He opened his eyes to a full moon that dazzled the ripples of the flowing river before them. "The west bank of the Mississipi."

"Yes," she agreed. She sat next to him wrapped in a sleeping bag. "Tell me about it."

"It was a high school thing; everyone was big on the environment at the time. We were out for a week hiking and camping encountering nature." He smiled. "Over the years I came to realize it was a scam for the teachers involved to get away for a week at the school's expense. Get out in the woods where they could smoke dope and try to get into some student's pants."

"You tried, as well."

"I was fifteen and one of the students; that was different. Yes, I tried. Mary said no. I stopped. I apologized. We spent the rest of the night out here watching the river flow by. Every so often, a barge would glide past, its engines a gentle thrum in the night air. We waved, especially when the crew lit us up with a spotlight."

"What'd you talk about?" she asked.

"Nothing. We didn't need to." He sighed, then chuckled. "I froze my ass off. She spent the night sitting between my legs, all wrapped up in her sleeping bag, like you are now." He took a breath. "It was the most romantic night of my life."

"What then?"

"What? Nothing. The rest of the group woke up; we had breakfast. We got on the bus and came back home."

"You didn't say much during the trip."

"No. I was confused. And tired. And hungry. And smelly."

She pulled the sleeping bag around her shoulders. "I was impressed by what you did. It was—is—very rare. You were to be commended."

"Were?"

"Indeed. You were much less a paragon as you aged. As we've seen. What happened after you returned home?"

He hung his head. "Avoided her."

"How?"

"Usual kid stuff: walk past pretending I didn't notice her. Turn around if I thought I'd could get away from her. She slipped some notes into my locker. I never read them. It didn't matter."

"Why not?"

"She intercepted me one day while I was walking home from school."

"Intercepted?"

He shook his head. "Yes. Or maybe ambushed is a better word. I didn't notice her until she was right there in my face."

"What she'd say?"

"She apologized," he answered abjectly.

"For?"

"For not 'putting out.' She thought that was why I was mad at her." He shook his head. "I told her it wasn't that at all."

"What was it?"

"I was a sophomore; she was a senior who'd be graduating in a few months." He kicked a clump of grass. "It was a magical night by the river that wouldn't happen again."

"You didn't tell her that," she observed matter-of-factly.

"No."

She cocked her head. "You grew into the *malakas* you became because you wanted that night again."

He winced. "Maybe. I never thought of it that way. *Malakas*?"

She chuckled. "Asshole. Jerk. Idiot. Take your pick."

"Thanks."

"Anytime. Even *now*, you assume she felt the same way, despite her persistence to the contrary."

"Maybe," he agreed reluctantly.

"Or maybe even *then* you feared the possibilities and the responsibilities of a real relationship."

He only shrugged.

A river tug pushing a barge chugged by. He closed his eyes when the floodlight washed across his face.

* * *

His eyes opened. She was seated across from him. "I don't recognize this place," he said.

"You wouldn't," she answered. "You've never been here before."

"Where is here?"

"Your new residence."

He looked. "No windows. Is this a bunker or something?"

"You don't merit any present distractions. Besides, this can be whatever you'd like," she replied and waved. First a suite at the Broadmoor, then night on the bank of the Mississipi, then back to its original dull gray cinder block. "Since you've a selfish penchant to keep your thoughts, the doubts and the uncertainties foremost, to yourself, this space will give you the solitude to consider them as much as you wish within the environs of your past. All by yourself."

When he turned to face her again, an old style dial telephone sat before him. "What is this?"

"You asked after many of the women you've known. That is the means for you to do so yourself. Pick up the scourge—"

"Scourge?"

"The handset. Pick it up and dial zero. After the chime, say the name of the lady with whom you wish to speak."

"How?" he asked hoarsely.

"All of those you've known and have wronged are here now. They'll answer if they choose to."

"I'm not sure I know what to say."

She laughed. "*That* is no surprise. Use the device. Or not. The choice is yours alone; you should be quite accustomed to that."

"Do they know I'm here?"

"Yes.

"Can, would, they . . . might one of them call *me*?"

She shrugged. "It's not likely. But, then 'time brings all things to pass' so I suppose it might be possible."

"Where *are* we?" he asked petulantly. "What's your name?"

"Where? Your eternal afterlife."

"Heaven?"

"For some. And for many who find it so, for it to *be* so, it must be a Hell for someone else."

"Hell?"

"Yes. Would you care to see it?"

"I'm not sure I would," he answered.

She laughed. "But I know *I* would. Pick up the phone. Dial zero. Hear the chime? Ask for, oh, let's try Patricia first."

"*Hello?*" The word audible within the space in which they sat.

"Patricia?" he said tremorously.

Click.

"Go on. Try again."

He did so. "*Can't take your call right now.*" He stared at the handset as if it was a venomous spider.

She beamed. "Lovely, isn't it? Perhaps you'll have better luck with Jessica. Try."

He dialed zero. "Jessica," he said after the chime.

"*Yes?*"

"Jessica, it's—"

Click.

He tried again without being prompted.

"*Leave a message.*"

He tried Mary and Kimberly and Madison and Brittany. The results were the same. When he finished, his body shook, his face grown ashen.

She crossed her arms and beamed. "Being ignored sucks, yes?"

"Yes."

She watched him sob. "Adrastia," she said.

"Wha . . . "

"You wanted to know my name. I sometimes go by Adrastia." She smiled as she stroked his hair. ""Welcome to Justice." She pushed the phone toward him. "You have eternity before you. Keep trying.

"Who knows? You might get lucky."

The Captain's

T ell me about your experience.

"We were the Captain's."

What do you mean?

"Any choice bits surviving a landing, and the afterwards, belonged to the Captain."

Choice bits?

"Yeah. You know, young and fresh. A lot of the crew, the young ones anyway, started out that way."

What did that mean to you?

"It wasn't so bad. I was the Captain's no more than, les' see, maybe six, seven times. We landed a lot after I got to be the Captain's so me and some of the others got pushed to crew sooner than usual."

How old were you then?

"Ten, maybe? Eleven? Somewhere thereabouts."

Tell me about it.

"About what?"

Being one of the Captain's.

"Ain't much to tell really. Crew onboard knew the rules. We were the Captain's and the Captain's only. There was one time, a newbie who came aboard on Altaris, I think it was. Got loaded and made a move on Dusty. Captain found out and spaced the bitch. He slammed it into the air lock, over-pressured to five, maybe six atmospheres, then blew the emergency vent. Bitch like to split in two before she ever made it past the outer hatch. There was guts and shit all over that lock."

Tell me about Dusty.

"Dusty? He was a bit too, along with two, three others, same landing I got picked up on. Didn't know him much. He was a couple years older than me. His folks was medics, I think."

What were your duties as one of the Captain's?

"Fetch and carry; booze, smack, food. Sex mostly."

Did that bother you?

"What?"

Any of it?

"Nah. It was better than going straight to crew."

What were hags?

"Same as bits. But girls. Sometimes women, if they was young enough."

What happened to the hags?

"Fresh hags or thems not quite dried or growed up, went to crew if the Captain liked how the landing went. If he really liked how things turned out, he'd reserve one or two for someone who'd done a good job. Hags didn't last more than one, maybe two ship-days. The reserves might make it a little longer, but not by much. Ha! Glad I was a bit."

What happened then, to the hags?

"Traded to the Centarii, mostly. Fed to the recyclers, or spaced, otherwise. It depended on where we were; the Captain's mood; whatever."

Four bits, including you. How many hags got picked up then?

"There was, uh, four. Yeah, four hags, too, that landing."

Do you remember them?

"Sort of."

What do you remember?

"One was real pretty. Had hair about the same color as mine. As tall as me. The others went to school with her, I think."

How well did you know her?

"She was my sister."

What was her name?

"Uh. Candace. Yeah, Candace."

What happened to her?

"Captain gave her to the crew."

And?

"And nothing. I went to the Captain; she went crew-side. Never saw her again."

The others?

"Same deal."

Weren't you curious?

"No way! Captain's bits only open their mouths when told to and they damn straight don't ask no questions then. Afterwards, when I got moved to crew, I learned the score. Didn't waste time fretting over it."

What happened when you moved to crew?

"We made a landing, Heaven's Hope, I think it was. Got a couple of new bits that one. Captain took a particular fancy to them both, probably 'cause they were twins. Anyway, he eased off and we, Dusty and me, got to be old bits. He gave us a choice: Go crew or get crewed. Like that was a choice! Hell, yeah, we went crew. "

What happened to the other bits picked up the same landing as you?

"Now I think about it, it was just one, 'sides me and Dusty. Fracking whiner didn't make it past first ship's night. All I know is one minute lights are out and things are sorta quiet, the next minute the Captain is roaring for the Mate. It was maybe a couple of days before Dusty or I got called for the Captain, so we figgered the stupid idiot maybe bit down on something he shouldn't have. After we went crew, we found out the fracker crapped the Captain's bed, he got so scared. Laughed our asses off, we did."

What happened when you went crew?

"Captain took us to the mess deck and released us. Senior Ship's Mate gets first turn downs, then on down the line. Dusty got picked up by the Engineering Second Mate. I got picked up by the Doc's assistant. She had a thing for little blonds."

What happened then?

"She bunked me, trained me up. There's only two Captain's rules for picked-up bits. One, the bit is off limits to the rest of the crew. Two, the bit gets training in the specialty of whoever picks up the bit. I was with her, oh, about a year."

What was her name?

"She told me to call her Tom."

Tom?

"Yeah. But, nobody laughed or busted her for it. She was a hot-shit medic. Rumors were she come from Fleet. Whatever. She was a medical wizard and had bigger balls than most of the crew."

What happened to her?

"She bought it, trying to do pickup on one of the crew that got zapped coming out the hatch on Hadley's World. I plugged her holes, but the kinetic had tumbled and tore through her guts. By the time we got her back aboard the shuttle, she'd bled out internally."

You were on that landing?

"Yeah."

Tell me about it.

"Just another landing. We zipped in, blew the primary transmitter, shot frack up for the noise and whatever, then hit dirt. I was backing up Tom one more time before she released me. Got some swag, got some ass, a couple of new bits, and a hag."

This wasn't your first landing then.

"Nah. Maybe seven, eight by then."

Tom was going to release you?

"Yeah. I'd taken all the ship tests and passed. Been on enough landings, scored a couple of saves, popped my share of targets. She was ready to take me to the Captain and release me. Doc agreed I was ready."

What did that mean?

"If it's lucky, a picked up bit gets released when it's trained and ready for crew."

If it's not lucky?

"Depends. If the bit turns out to be a real gorm, the Captain may decide it's not worth wasting air on it anymore. That happens, it gets crewed, then gone. If it shows promise in other ways, it gets put up for selection again."

What happened after Tom?

"It got intense. We cleared atmosphere and stood to for the after action. Some were calling for my ass to be spaced because I didn't save Tom. Doc explained the situation, showed some imagery. Most everyone shut up after Doc reminded them about the saves I had to my credit. Captain asked Doc if he was willing to take me on as an assistant, to replace Tom. Doc said yes. That and the pics of Tom's shredded guts saved my ass."

How often did you deal with the Centarii?

"Can't say. Most of the crew were locked up during any meat meets. Captain swore up and down anyone he caught wandering during the exchange would be handed over to 'em, no questions, no excuses."

What do you know about them?

"Same as everyone else, I guess: They like their human raw. Their pissed 'cause we're movin' into their space. They tolerated them, like the Captain, who kept them fed regular. Other than that, not much. Funny."

What is funny?

"It just occurred to me why we hit frontier worlds on the edge of Centarii space, mostly. Fresh meat don't spoil much."

How many landings for you in total?

"Twenty some odd. Maybe twenty-four when we got popped by Fleet. Sucks too, because I had just picked up my own bit. Kinda of a hag, but smart and with the cutest little bottom."

What happened?

"Fleet assholelasered him right through the chest. Last I remember, I was plugging his holes, then, blooie, I'm here. Where is here?"

This is a Fleet Evaluation Facility. You and thirteen other members of your crew were captured by a detachment of Fleet Marines on Greenspoint.

"Damn."

The remaining crew were immediately dispositioned, either due to the extent of their engagement trauma, or based upon the results of field evaluations. Your case was referred to this Facility as members of the detachment were unable to testify you were actively engaged as a combatant. Moreover, the team was unable to conclusively determine your status, given your apparent youth.

"No shit. What's next?"

Your evaluation will be reviewed. A disposition recommendation will be prepared and, if approved, executed.

"Cool."

* * *

"John?"

"Hey, Bob." John turned from his console reader, rubbing his eyes. "What's up?"

"Want to catch some lunch?"

"Damn. That time already?" John glanced at his wrist chrono.

"Jeez, bud. You look like hell. Come on. Let's get some grub into you."

"It's this friggin' quarterly report kicking me in the ass."

"Yeah?"

"Yeah. My numbers suck and I can't come up with the right words to cover my butt. It's pissin' me off."

"All the more reason to tear yourself away for a little while. Let's go. Whaddya want? Thai? Italian? Burgers?"

Captain John Anderson, Assistant Department Head, Fleet Psych Evaluation, sat and thought for a few seconds, then nodded. "You're right. I need to get out of this hole."

He stood and pulled his uniform jacket from the hanger. "I think Thai today. I can't afford to lose the afternoon taking a nap after lasagna or double cheeseburgers."

"That is my man."

DING ding. Anderson's console chimed an alert.

He stopped halfway through the door and looked to the ceiling. "Why me?" he implored the heavens.

"Ignore it, dude. Let us away. *Now.*"

Anderson looked exasperated and turned back to his console. "Shit."

"What is it?"

"Eval's completed on one of those kids they brought in last week. Got a Disposal recommendation."

"It can wait."

"It can't," Anderson sighed. "Station Chief has been on my ass about the overflow. If I clear this quickly, maybe I can get some points towards that crappy quarterly. Frack." He put his jacket back on the hanger. "Bring me back some noodles, will ya?"

"You got it."

Anderson waved as he sat. "Console."

"Sir."

"Authenticate Anderson, John, Captain."

"Authenticated. Welcome back, Captain Anderson."

"Query pending eval, please. U, file one two seven xray."

"Please wait. Evaluation file one two seven xray ready."

"Begin. Summarize basis for disposal recommendation."

"Subject of limited intelligence value. Subject unsuitable for reintegration."

"Continue."

"Subject was not key cadre. Subject's understanding of operations and tactics limited. Subject does not possess critical navigation, technical, or operations knowledge of capabilities. Subject has had no direct contact with Centarii operatives; understanding of Centarii limited to rumor."

"Go on."

"Physio-psych monitoring during enhanced evaluation revealed subject assimilation into deviant sub-group appears to have been total. Conventional award and sanction structures no longer have value or meaning to the subject. Efficacy of treatment for psych-emotional trauma resulting from initial abduction and forced integration into said sub-group has less than a 18.2% probability of long-term success, particularly given the 99.9% probability that the subject's genetic relationship structure no longer exists."

"Explain."

"Based upon the subject's genetic analysis and current physical age of approximately fifteen, confidence is high that the subject is from the Sirius 3B colony. There were no survivors of the incursion which resulted in the subject's abduction. There are no other genetic relations."

"Okay. Record."

"Ready to record."

" I, Captain John Anderson, Fleet Psych Evaluation, pursuant to Fleet Regulation 1.4, do hereby approve this cyber evaluation and resultant recommendation for disposal of said subject, based upon the attached cyber analyses and recorded physio-pysch results."

"Confirm, please, Captain Anderson."

"Confirmed. Has Captain Davies left the facility yet?"

"Captain Davies remains in the facility. Your confirmation has been recorded and logged."

"Ask the Guard to hold Davies at the gate; tell him to tell the good Captain I'll be able to make lunch after all."

"Completed."

"Sign me off, please, Console."

"You are signed off. Enjoy your lunch, Captain Anderson."

Dead Ahead

R ose Hall's regulars, a quiet crowd of retirees, mostly, and a few guests staying at Ketchum's Mill's celebrated small hotel, had laid claim to the bar round tops and all but one bar stool, that one next to an older petite blond seated at the end of the ornate millwork that was the bar itself.

"Pardon me for interrupting, ma'am. May I?"

Theresa closed her magazine. She preferred not to be interrupted while she was reading. Her smile was saccharine and minimally gracious. "May you what?"

The interruption—male, late forty-ish, athletically trim, with a thick mane of dark brown hair tastefully streaked with silver, and decently attired—smiled in return. "May I sit here?" he asked.

"I'm waiting for a friend," Theresa replied casually.

"Ah. I beg your pardon. Good day." The man dipped his chin.

Nice ass, Theresa noted as the stranger turned away. "But I expect he'll be late. As usual," she said to the man's back.

He stopped and looked over his shoulder, an inquiring eyebrow raised. "Ma'am?"

Theresa waved at the bar stool. "Please."

"Thank you." The stranger sat.

The bartender walked over. "Evening, Mr. Wade."

"Hey, John."

"Your usual?"

"Please. And one for the lady, if you would."

"Terry?" John prompted.

"That's ever so kind of you," Theresa said. "But completely unnecessary. And I don't accept drinks from strangers."

The stranger shook his head. "It's my way of apologizing for interrupting your reading, ma'am."

Theresa found herself teetering precariously atop the fence of her principles. She fell off the top rail a few seconds later. "I accept your apology. But there are conditions."

John smiled and went to work making martinis.

"Those would be?" the stranger asked.

"You tell me your name. And you stop calling me ma'am." She scrunched up her nose. "I am *not* an old lady."

The man's appraisal was comprehensive yet inoffensive. "No. You are not. My name's Andrew. Andrew Wade. And the ma'am stuff is a habit. Which is a good thing," he concluded wryly.

"Why so?"

"Me Andrew. Me know no your name."

Theresa chuckled. "You, sir, are a smart ass. My name is Theresa."

"It's a pleasure to meet you, Theresa."

"And, you, Andrew."

John delivered their martinis. "Anything else?"

"Not for me," Andrew answered. "Ma'am?"

Theresa slugged him in the bicep. "I thought we had an understanding. No, thank you, John. Nothing for me."

Andrew rubbed his arm. "You've quite a punch. Theresa."

"You deserved it. Cheers," she offered as she raised her fresh drink.

"*Budmo*," Andrew replied as they clinked glasses.

"Budmo?"

" No. *Budmo*. It's the Ukrainian version of cheers," Andrew answered.

"I thought you were a Yankee." She made yankee sound like horse dung.

Andrew laughed. "No one asked me where I most wanted to be born, Theresa."

"Now that you mention it, I don't recollect being asked myself. Not that I'd change a thing. I'm a southern girl through and through." She sipped her martini. "Tell me about the ma'am thing you seem to have." She frowned. "Oh. My. God. You don't have the hots for your mother?" she gasped. "Do you?"

"The name's Andrew, Theresa, not Oedipus," he replied good-naturedly. "The ma'am thing is the result of a proper upbringing, one reinforced by some years in the military. Besides, I'm a nineteenth century sort of guy."

"And what does that mean?"

He shrugged. "Buy the drinks. Pay the bill. Coat over the puddle. Hold the door open. Say ma'am. That sort of thing."

"That makes you a bit unusual these days."

Andrew shrugged again. "Yes."

Theresa was intrigued. This man was—so far—not typical. "Do you spend much time in the Ukraine, Andrew?"

"Yes."

"What do you do there?"

"Work."

Theresa snorted a quite unladylike snort. "I'm not a stupid southern female, sir. You may have noticed I've not said y'all once."

"Nor did I assume you were, Theresa." He shrugged. "It's boring, really; the details aren't something I'd inflict on anyone."

"I'm also capable. But," she sniffed, "if you'd prefer not."

"Fair enough," Andrew agreed readily.

Theresa, accustomed to the tedious bloviations of middle-aged and elderly blowhards and I-love-me assholes, was miffed by the man's understated insouciance. "Whatever you do must pay well," she noted.

"It does," he agreed.

Her nostrils flared slightly. She would not be defeated by a man who insisted on not acting like a man as she generally knew them. "You're gay," she shot sweetly across his bow.

It was all Andrew could do to keep from spraying a sip of his martini—Ford's, up, with a twist—across the bar.

Theresa found herself pleased with his reaction. "I'm so sorry," she lied. "None of my business." She turned her attention to the television.

"Why do you wonder?" he asked lightly.

"Hmm?" Theresa feigned distraction. "Wonder what?" she asked, seemingly confused by the question.

"If I'm gay."

She bridled. "Your personal habits are of no interest to me."

"I'm not gay," he replied in a voice as dry as Saharan sand. "But I'm curious."

"About what?"

"Why you thought I was gay," he answered.

"Your shoes."

"Ma'am?"

"Your shoes: Ferragamo. Yes?"

"Indeed," he agreed.

"Most of the men—the straight ones—I've known are reluctant to spend hundreds of dollars on a respectable pair of shoes. Those willing to do so are all gay. Ergo, you are gay."

Andrew chuckled. "If I am, I haven't come out of the closet." He shook his head. "But, then, you can't exit someplace you're not in. No, I'm not gay." He shrugged. "My clients often have your same discerning eye for high, expensive fashion. Dress to impress and all that," he offered with a small raise of his glass.

"Ah. Well. If you're sure," Theresa replied dubiously.

"I am. John?"

"Sir?"

"Another round, if you would."

Theresa chose to frown. "Are you trying to get me intoxicated, Mr. Wade?"

"Should I try?" he asked.

"Would you like to?" Theresa reposted sharply.

His glance, this time, was far more appraising, almost offensively so.

Theresa tingled despite the effrontery.

"Maybe," Andrew answered. "Ah. Thank you, John." He raised his glass. "Cheers," he offered to Theresa.

"Cheers," she replied.

Glasses were touched and first sips taken.

"Tell me about your clients," Theresa directed. "Are they all in the Ukraine?"

"For the most part, yes," Andrew answered.

"What are they like?"

"Can't really say."

"Are they that bad?" she prompted.

"They can be," he answered flatly. His grin returned. "But the work pays the bills. And," he pointed, "the shoes." He swilled a bit of his martini.

"You don't like your clients."

"That doesn't matter: They pay me for what I do."

"And what *do* you do, hmm?"

Andrew rested his chin in a palm. "Threat assessments. Geopolitical analysis. Risk mitigation. Boring stuff," he concluded with a small shrug.

Theresa escalated. "It doesn't sound boring to me. Cloak-and-daggerish, actually," she answered huskily. "If you know what I mean."

Andrew's laugh was hearty. "As in James Bond save-the-world derring-do?"

"Perhaps," Theresa answered stiffly. She wasn't sure if Andrew was laughing at her.

"Sorry," he offered. "I wasn't laughing at you."

Theresa was nonplussed: Few men were capable of reading her mind. "Thank you."

It was Andrew's turn to lie. "Nothing so exciting as secret agent stuff. Unfortunately." He took a sip of his drink. "Paying attention to economies, regional politics, global economic status, is what I do." He emptied his martini. "I assist my clients by providing an objective understanding of the threats applicable to whatever endeavor they've planned. Boring."

"I can't imagine it being so, what with the Russians having their way with those poor people."

She was impressed by Andrew's failure to look dumbfounded that a female could say something intelligent.

"It does add a dimension to the problem," he agreed.

"Or are your clients in Crimea?"

Andrew gently placed his martini on a bar napkin. "They are not," he answered softly. "You have an interest in geopolitics, Theresa? Few do. At least here in the United States, anyway."

Theresa shrugged and tapped her magazine. "I read when I can. While I'm certainly no expert, I do try to pay attention to what's going on in the world."

He sipped his martini. "I'm no expert myself." He swiveled his bar stool slowly toward Theresa, his knee casually brushing hers. "Although," his smile beamed, "I fake it when I must."

"And when would *that* be, Andrew?"

His eyes, azure, the color of the Mediterranean at its loveliest, sparkled. "Usually when I'm negotiating my fee."

Theresa brushed her knee past his. "And unusually?"

"Whenever I believe the circumstances require more than my best," he answered.

She placed her chin atop her laced fingers. "What sort of circumstances would those be?"

"Most often, those in which my undivided attention to detail is likely to result in the satisfactory conclusion of the affair."

"Do you have many of those?"

"What?"

"Affairs."

Andrew nodded. "I suppose that depends upon your definition of affair."

Theresa cocked her head. "What's *your* definition?"

"It's a spectrum. At one end, the big end, it's an engagement involving multiple parties, with each party having his or her own objectives. Everyone involved seeks the maximum possible benefit from the results. If all goes well, the affair ends with everyone satisfied."

She smirked. "You make it sound like an orgy."

"I suppose it does," Andrew agreed lightly. "Now that you mention it."

Theresa laughed. "And at the little end?"

"An affair is a focused dialogue between two individuals."

Theresa blinked. "That sounds, well, almost sinful."

"And *that* depends upon your definition of sin." He cocked his head. "What's yours?"

"My what?"

"Your definition of sin," he answered.

"Something that causes harm to someone."

"That's much the same as mine. Unexpected as it is."

Theresa frowned. "How so?"

"I assumed it'd be something a bit more biblical. You know, ten commandments, burn-in-Hell sort of stuff."

"And why would you assume such a thing?" she asked. "Wait. I'm a southern lady, so I must be a hymn-singing, bible-toting, God-fearing Baptist? Is that it?"

"Yes."

She wiggled her finger, drawing him close. "My closest friends call me Sweet Tee," she whispered.

"Do they?"

"Yes."

Andrew straightened. "How does one qualify as a close friend, Theresa?"

"The question is impertinent, Andrew, and one asked only by someone I allow to call me Terry."

"May I call you Terry?"

"Are you married?"

Andrew blinked at the segue. "I was once. Not now."

"Divorced?"

"Widower."

"Oh, Andrew. I'm so sorry," Theresa, truly contrite, offered.

"No problem."

"Do you miss her?"

"Yes. John? Another round, please?"

Theresa frowned. "I shouldn't. Really."

"You should," Andrew countered. "Really."

"And why?"

"I decided I'd like to try to get you intoxicated, Theresa."

She tried to look shocked at the effrontery. "I am *not* a woman of easy virtue, sir."

He shrugged. "Didn't think so. That's why I'm ordering another drink for you."

Theresa thought a change of subject was in order. "May I ask a personal question, Andrew?"

"Let's see. You've asked repeatedly about my work; speculated about my sexual orientation; and inquired about my marital status. I suppose it *could* get more personal. What the hell: Ask away. Be prepared to get 'too personal' as an answer."

"How did you lose your wife?"

Andrew theatrically wiped his brow. "Whew. I thought it'd be something sticky."

"Such as?"

"Oh. A lot of things; none of them fit for discussion with a lady."

"If I let you call me Terry, would that make it easier? More fit?"

"It may. Another martini, though, will help oil the discourse."

She laughed. "If you insist."

John had their new drinks ready in short order.

Theresa and Andrew exchanged another toast. "What's so funny ?" he asked.

"Um? Oh! I've never had anyone try to oil my discourse. It's amusing." She lifted the corner of an eyebrow. "How oiled do you intend to get me, Andrew?"

"How much do you need to be before you allow me to call you Terry?"

"Under these circumstances?" she began with a soft smile. "About as oiled as I am now. So, please feel free to call me Terry."

He raised his glass. "Thank you."

"Indeed." She savored the first sip of her new martini. "Besides discourse, what else do you oil?" Terry asked mischievously.

"Whatever interaction may benefit from the addition of the appropriate lubrication," Andrew answered blandly. "She died. Cancer."

Terry blinked at the non sequitur. "Excuse me? Oh. Your wife. I'm sorry to hear that." Terry nursed her drink and watched Andrew. "Do you miss her?" she asked quietly.

"Yes."

"Forgive me, but you don't seem to; not much, anyway."

Andrew drained off his drink and waved at John. "Well, Terry. I do," he declared flatly. "Why do you think I don't?"

"You seem so unconcerned."

"I don't believe in wearing my heart out on my sleeve, ma'am." He touched a finger to his eyebrow as the bartender delivered yet another pair of martinis. "Thank you again, John."

"Anytime, Mr. Wade." John gave Terry a small nod and a smile before he turned away.

"You know, I believe you gentlemen are in cahoots," Terry declared.

"Hmm? How so?"

"I think you two have formed a cabal, one with the purpose of getting me intoxicated." She pressed her forearm to her head and feigned a swoon. "I am doomed!" she softly exclaimed. "Doomed."

Andrew laughed. "Au contraire!" He made a small, seated bow. "You have nothing to fear."

Terry's moue was feigned. Mostly. "Well. That's disappointing."

Three martinis in and bravely navigating her way through her fourth, Terry found her self-control threatened anew by the unexpected images that flashed in her mind: Oil. Andrew. Oil and Andrew. Whipped cream. *Whipped cream? Where did* that *come from?* Terry shivered, her self-possession on the precipice of destruction.

"You have a hell of a hidden reserve."

Terry grabbed her composure by the horns and gave it a good shake and a stern talking to. "I'm not sure I understand."

Andrew shrugged. "You talk a game. A cat playing with a mouse sort of thing. But it's armor, isn't it?"

Theresa blinked. Blinked again. *Who is this* man *with the temerity, the* wit, *to discern that?* "I, like you, am not interested in wearing my heart on my sleeve. Nor do I think it appropriate to expose myself to just any old Tom, Harry, or Dick."

Andrew nodded. "Understood." He turned toward her again, his knee coming lightly to rest against hers.

Terry had no objections to the contact. Still, *someone* had to maintain a degree of decorum; another change of subject was *certainly* in order. "What brings you to Ketchum's Mill, Andrew?"

"A client needs some handholding," he replied. "And, you, Terry? What brings you here?"

"Ketchum's Mill's my home."

"Ah. Do you come here often?"

"I used to. The crowd moved on to a new place downtown and I moved with the herd." She sighed. "This is my first time in, well, I don't know how long." Terry shook her head. "I need to come more often. I'd forgotten how much I love this place." She frowned. "Perhaps more than before."

"How so?"

She made a small shrug. "It's not so crowded now." She waved. "Rose Hall was built in a more genteel era," she declared. "A crowd of loud-mouthed golf louts three sheets in the wind and three-deep at the bar doesn't work for me. Now that they've moved on, it's become what it once was. I'm a bit silly, I suppose."

"I don't think so."

"Why?" She finished her drink and caught John's eye.

John stepped away from the beer pulls. "Ma'am?"

"We'll have another," she declared.

Andrew waved. "It's on me, John."

"Mr. Wade. You will allow me to buy this round or I will never allow you to call me Terry again."

Andrew dipped his chin and grinned. "Yes, ma'am."

Terry dimpled. "John?"

"Another round it is," he confirmed.

"Why don't you think I'm silly?" Terry asked while they waited for their fresh drinks.

"I'm fond of places with character," Andrew answered. He waved an index finger. "Wood beams. Fire places. Décor that wasn't curated by some corporate designer working with no budget and even less taste. Unlike here." He looked around. "I spend too much time in corporate blah so I relish the opportunity to stay somewhere with a bit of charm." He smiled. "And quirk. There's no reason to be bored if you can avoid it. That's why I get a suite here whenever I can: I love the ambience. The food is great. And the bar staff cannot be surpassed."

"You come here often, then?"

Andrew's lips quirked. "Whenever I can," he agreed.

"Ah! Thank you," Terry said as John set another round of martinis before them. "Salud," she offered to Andrew.

"Salud."

The conversation idled into a few moments of a comfortably companionable silence.

"My turn for a personal question?" Andrew asked.

Terry burped. "Pardon me." She fanned herself. "I do believe you've succeeded, Andrew."

"At what?"

"Getting me, um, toasted." She burped again as hiccups threatened. "Whoops!" She slid off the barstool.

"Steady," Andrew offered quietly, his hand a warm pressure in the small of her back. "Okay?"

"I am," she replied tersely, discommoded by the effects of too many martinis imbibed too quickly. "I must away to the ladies. Please excuse me."

"Sure."

Terry's flight down the hall to the necessaries was unhurried and casual, despite her being embarrassed by the stumble Andrew helped prevent. She took deep breaths, clearing her mind of the martini-induced fog. She spent extra time in the ladies' room trying to decide how far she was willing to go before she called it quits. Intellectually, she knew it'd already gone too far. Where it counted, however, couldn't disagree more. Her intellect and her hoohoo managed to compromise on one final drink.

But only after she made sure the man promised to see her again.

Well. Ain't that just *grand.* As she stepped into the hallway, she saw Andrew embracing a lithe blond. *You slut!* Terry glowered. *And you, you two-timing bastard. Your attention span is no doubt as short as your pathetic Yankee pecker.* She did a quick about-face with the intent of escaping through the pool area. She halted even more abruptly when she realized her purse was still on the bar. She reversed course woozily, dizzy from the quick succession of pirouettes. *Gather your things. Be polite and get the hell out of here.* Terry managed to form a gracious smile.

"Ah! Terry. Taylor, may I introduce you to Theresa?"

Terry was a bit taken aback. The woman was pretty in an impish sort of way. But there was nothing of the imp in her eyes; they had seen much that was not good.

"Theresa, this is Detective Taylor Christian, She hails from Walterville."

Taylor held out her hand. "Ma'am."

Terry took it. "Detective."

John stepped over. "Taylor. Good to see you again. You doing okay?"

The detective shrugged. "Twinges every now and then. Otherwise? Not bad."

"Glad to hear it," John replied. "What'll it be?"

"Nothing for me, thanks. I don't want to interrupt. Besides, I'm meeting some folks later for dinner. You remember Ellinger and Holland, right?"

"I do," John answered. "Tell them I said hello."

"You got it," Taylor answered.

"Detectives Ellinger and Holland are with Ketchum's Mill's police department," Andrew explained to Terry. "Any news?" he asked Taylor.

"If y'all just let me grab my thangs, I'll get out of your way," Theresa offered, sweetly snitty.

Taylor noticed. "Apologies, ma'am. Mr. Wade—"

Andrew snorted. "For God's sake, Taylor. You got me shot. Enough of the mister stuff. Okay?"

Terry decided she wasn't really ready to leave. "*Shot*? You shot this man?"

The detective blushed. "I didn't shoot him."

"Well, who did?"

"The same guy who shot *me*."

Terry blinked. Twice. "I'm confused."

Andrew chuckled. "I believe Theresa's been laboring under a misapprehension. Have a seat and a drink while we explain. I know, Taylor. I know. As much as we can. I'm always mindful of your operational security. Will you have another, Terry?"

A somewhat gobsmacked Terry nodded as she sat.

Andrew smiled. "Another round, if you'd be so kind, John."

"A Stella for me," Taylor said.

"Sorry, Taylor. Don't have it on tap anymore. Try a Peroni?"

"Italian lager, right?"

"Yes," John agreed.

"Sure. Thanks."

"If you'll excuse me, ladies." Andrew stepped around them and headed for the Gents.

Terry watched as Andrew made his way down the hall. "So, Detective—"

"Taylor, please, ma'am."

"Theresa, please, Detective."

Taylor laughed. "Okay. Theresa."

"I'd prefer Terry as I'm hoping you'll explain what the Hades you two were going on about."

Taylor tried the Peroni John set before her. "Hm. Good. Thanks. Not much to tell, Theres . . . Terry."

Terry's snort was unladylike. "I feed that sort of stuff to my roses."

"Yeah. Okay. It was about this time last year."

"Ah! I remember the news! That was you. Really? And Andrew? There weren't a lot of details as I recall."

"We, KMPD and the FBI, managed to keep most of the information from the press. The perp was still at large. Still is, as a matter of fact. That's why I'm back. Another department in, well, elsewhere, wants to compare notes."

"Good lord," Terry exclaimed breathlessly.

"Anyway. I was in Ketchum's Mill, working with the locals on a case. I was staying here, as a matter of fact. We had a few lucky breaks and I was celebrating. Too much, as it turned out."

"Let me guess: Andrew and John were involved, yes?"

Taylor shrugged. "Andrew was there and John was tending bar that night. Um. Why?"

"I believe the two of them are partners in a nefarious scheme involving excess quantities of drink so as to crash the defenses of their victims in order have their way with them."

"It's to knock you out so we can sell you to an Arab prince," Andrew interjected as he returned from the mens' room.

"See?" Terry declared triumphantly. "Can't you arrest this miscreant, Detective?"

"Nah. Even if I wanted to, I wouldn't. If it hadn't been for him taking the first round, I'd probably be dead," Taylor answered soberly. "Besides, he got me and my ex a sweet deal aboard the *Empress Mariana*. We spent two weeks being treated like royalty. It was awesome."

"What's the *Empress Mariana*?"

"It's one of the few true ocean liners still crossing the Atlantic," Andrew answered with a shrug. "I know the lady who owns the line. No big deal." He shrugged. "I'm glad you enjoyed it, Taylor. How's Bruce, by the way?"

"Fine the last I heard; that was a few weeks ago."

"Do you know where he is?"

Taylor looked bleak. "Somewhere in eastern Europe."

"What does he do, Taylor?" Terry asked.

"He's in the army."

Andrew's face blanked. "Any idea when he's back to the States?"

"No," Taylor replied curtly. "Sorry for the digression, Terry."

"Not a problem, dear. You were telling me about getting shot."

"Not much more to tell. I was drunk and feeling sorry for myself. I missed my man and I was feeling maudlin. And," she offered sheepishly, "more than a little horny. Andrew came out. If it hadn't been for the guy who capped us, I probably would've raped him."

Andrew chuckled. "That would have been preferable to getting shot, that's for sure." He leered. "I'm happy to help you reenact the event, Taylor. It's not too cool outside. Or my suite, if you'd prefer someplace more private?"

"I thought you were hitting on *me*, Andrew," Terry sparked.

"Yes. But I'm a great multitasker."

Taylor and Terry slugged the man, their blows simultaneous, as if they'd practiced.

"Ouch. Damn," Andrew mewled as he rubbed his biceps. "Those hurt. Not quite the bruises I was hoping for."

Terry rolled her eyes. "I've only met the man, Taylor. Is he always this incorrigible?"

"I think so."

"What?! You can't know me that well, Taylor," Andrew protested.

"You've always been a perfect gentleman around me, Andrew, I agree. But," Taylor's smile was wry, "Bruce and I met a nice lady on our voyage. We got to chatting. She told us about her first time aboard the *Empress* and how she'd met a man named Andrew." The grim history that normally shown in Taylor's eyes faded, chased away by amused warmth. "She seemed to know quite a bit about you," she offered teasingly. "Her name was Margaret Bates. Ring any bells?"

"Yes," Andrew agreed whimsically. "A lot of bells."

"Ooh. Sounds mysterious. Tell us about the bells," Terry ordered.

Andrew shook his head. "That would be unseemly."

"The way she lit up when she realized Bruce and I knew the same guy she was going on about, I expect they were very nice bells," Taylor offered dryly.

"Indeed," Andrew confirmed.

"Oh. Poop," Terry muttered. She quickly finished her drink.

"Something wrong?" Andrew asked.

"My friend's arrived. And I wanted so badly to hear more about these bells. And this boat you're talking about."

"I'm here all week, Terry," Andrew offered cheerily. "If I'm not at the bar, I'll be out by the pool. Or in my suite. Feel free to ring me."

"I will. What's your number?"

"I'm in suite two oh nine."

"Two oh nine. I'll remember. Taylor, it's been a pleasure meeting you. As for you, Mr. Wade, you've succeeded in getting me oiled. I'm glad I'm able to flee before I fall into your clutches and get sold off to some minor Persian Gulf potentate."

Andrew took Terry's hand and brushed its back with his lips. "I look forward to my next attempt."

Terry curtsied. "So do I."

* * *

The man named at birth as Jason Esau Andrews had, over the years, donned many personas, a necessity in order to indulge Father's whims and desires, and to avoid the consequences of same.

It was almost a year before when, as Cecil Vanderwalt, he'd found himself drawn to an angelic blonde police detective named Taylor, a blessed change from the voluptuous brunettes who'd theretofore commanded his attention.

And it was almost a year ago that he'd shot an asshole and, regrettably, the detective. That she lived was a blessing. That the asshole did also was a burning cancer in Jason's soul, a cancer that would be cured only after Jason cut the man's beating heart from his chest.

Despite seeing them at the bar, he didn't miss a step as he made his way toward the check-in desk.

Returning to Ketchum's Mill was stupid, he knew, and violated all the rules he'd set himself over the years as he satisfied Father's longings. Booking a stay at Rose Hall so soon after being placed on the FBI's Ten Most Wanted list was criminally—he smiled at the unintended pun—insane.

As a Canadian businessman, he didn't care. His credentials were unassailable. The shaved skull and self-administered scar across his right cheek rendered him virtually unrecognizable to any casual observer. Which, he knew, included most of the law enforcement community.

"Oops. 'Scuse me," the petite blond who'd bumped into the man coming into Rose Hall said.

The man stopped. Blonde. Petite. A bit older than Father's typical preferences. But nicely proportioned. "No. Pardon me," he replied. "Are you all right?" he asked.

"Yes, thanks," Terry answered. "Bye."

He watched as the woman weaved her way across the lobby. Father stirred, also interested.

Jason knew the decision to return to Ketchum's Mill, to Rose Hall, was blessed. After all, only divine intervention would have him arrive when Taylor and the asshole named Wade were there.

And when a new epiphany presented itself.

Father, risen to the occasion, agreed.

"Good evening, sir. Welcome to Rose Hall. My name's Michelle. How may I help?"

Jason smiled. "The name's Tremblay. I've a reservation," he answered as he passed his passport and credit card to the lady seated at the desk.

Michelle keyed in the name. "Yes. Your first time with us, I see."

"It is," Tremblay confirmed with a smile. "I'm looking forward to my stay."

Michelle beamed professionally. "I hope you enjoy it."

The man calling himself Tremblay glanced toward the bar and noticed the detective and her companion were still there. And, better, he noticed the lady he'd encountered when he arrived had not yet left. "Oh. Yes. I believe I shall."

K&K Events, Inc.

K arla Kringle slapped her desk. "Our cash flow can't keep up anymore."

Kris snapped his eyes open. "Eh? What was that?"

Klara rolled her eyes. "You old fart. Napping again. I said our cash flow can't keep up anymore."

When Klara got on a tear about the family finances, Kris wanted to run outside and hibernate with the nearest polar bear. He sighed. "Keep up with what?"

"Our expenses, you ninny. Are you deaf or just ignoring me again?"

Kris wished it wasn't February. There was only one night of the year when he was truly at peace. Just him and the team and the wind blowing through his beard and adding a manly touch of rouge to his already ruddy cheeks. The chimney work was getting a bit arduous given the weight he'd put on over time. But that was a small price to pay for twenty-four hours of bliss, no matter how stressful.

Or frightening. He smiled as he recalled the close encounter with an Emirates A380 out over the Pacific. Fortunately, the night was young and the team relatively fresh, and so with a quick pull of the reins, he slid the sleigh out of the path of the giant airliner. He waved to the copilot and sent a hearty "Ho ho ho!" his way. The copilot returned the wave.

February. Ten months of conjugal bliss to endure before his next escape. It'd be different if there was a decent pub or two close by but Klara had insisted on a distant rural setting to avoid taxes and all the other government bullshit that good, honest working people had to endure these days. Besides, where else could they keep a herd of reindeer and the bunkhouse for the help, she was fond of reminding him whenever he foolishly expressed an interest in relocating to somewhere a teeny bit closer to civilization. It didn't need to be *that* close he'd always reply. He'd go on and tell her he didn't mind if he needed to snowmobile into town.

Klara had shot that notion down with the whole where-are-you-going-to-get-the-money-for-a-Skidoo-anyway line. She'd done it often enough that he quit mentioning it and made do with the annual treats of spiked egg nog and shots set out for him by kindly souls who knew he had an extreme need for some holiday cheer. And definitely no more need for warm milk and stale cookies.

He had a special place in his Nice-and-Naughty Book for those, Santa Claus bless them, who'd set out a full bottle for him. At the end of the day's deliveries, he'd have collected a couple cases worth, enough to get him through the remainder of the year. He'd stash the bottles all around the barn after the stable elves got the reindeer fed and brushed. Whenever he felt the need for a quick shot of the Old Restorative, he'd tell Klara he was going out to the barn to polish the runners on the sleigh. But he'd still prefer heading down to the local at the end of the day and sharing a pint or two with the boys.

"Damn it, Kris Kringle! Quit woolgathering and listen to me."

"I am, dear. I am. What particular element of expense concerns you today?" He didn't want to ask but if he didn't, Klara would make his life a living hell for however long it took her to get over the current snit. *But so will whatever's got her knickers in a twist this time*, he thought. Kris knew no matter what he did he was going to get it in the ass; finding out what cheesed his lovely bride off *now* at least had the virtue of possibly being a quicker humping.

"It's those damn reindeer. Maintenance costs are almost double what we need to house and feed the workforce."

Kris was appalled. "'Damn' reindeer? Klara. They're as much of the brand as we are. If it wasn't for them, we wouldn't be, you know, anything. I wouldn't be able to do my job. Consider: Where would I be without Rudolph?"

Klara sighed and took off her pince nez. She rubbed the bridge of her nose. "Kris."

Kris shuddered. *Oh reindeer dung. Here it comes.*

"I think we should find a way to maximize the deer's potential, something that would keep them employed a bit more than one day a year."

Kris was perplexed. "The team does an excellent job when it needs to. They deserve the downtime."

Klara snorted. "They work one day—one—out of three hundred and sixty five. And that's three hundred and sixty *six* every fourth year. The rest of the time they spend eating and sleeping and screwing. At our expense!"

"Well, if you put it that way—"

"I do. Tell me I'm wrong, Mr. Kringle. Tell me what I'm missing," she said with a sneer and with her arms crossed tightly across her chest. "Hmm?"

Kris shifted in his easy chair. "They also work out. You know they need to keep in shape. They may only work one day but the work they do is nothing short of phenomenal. I mean, come on, dear, consider the load they carry. And the traffic they have to dodge. And the risks! Why, just this last—"

Klara shook her head, sadly, disdainfully. "I'm sure your work stories are interesting and full of adventure but unless you can find a way to get them published and earn some royalties so they can help cover our expenses, they're of little commercial value." She uncrossed her arms. "Now. I'm thinking during the rest of the year, the deer can be employed more profitably."

"How?"

"I'm noodling some ideas. Working the numbers and all that."

That was a stretch; Mrs. Kringle had no bulbs on the idea tree yet. But. She was sure she'd have some soon.

Kris shook his head. "Klara, you're asking, well, quite a lot. I don't like it. Not one little bit."

"What don't you like?"

He frowned. "The team signed up for the annual job. I'm not sure their contract—"

"Their contract allows for renegotiation 'anytime business, political, economic, or other circumstances mutually agreed upon by the Parties, warrant.' In this case, we can easily assert economic circumstances warrant such a discussion."

"That may be so. But I can't allow it."

Klara smiled and stood. She walked over and patted Kris's shoulder. "Oh, you can, even if you really don't have the power to say no."

"What?! How's that?"

"You poor dear. Too much time at higher altitudes, I expect." Klara's smile was evilly sweet. "You haven't forgotten the treat beneath the tree in Paris, have you?"

Kris reddened. No, he had not forgotten. And he was still trying to figure out who told Klara about the lovely, lovely lady in the crotchless elf suit who'd asked Santa for some Kris. Known worldwide as a kind and generous soul, he was unable to say no. "I haven't," he mumbled.

"And you'll no doubt remember that in expiation for your unfortunate lapse in judgement, you ceded controlling interest in the business to *me*."

"Yes. I remember," he grudged.

She patted his cheek condescendingly. "Good boy. Now. Go on out to the barn and sharpen those sleigh runners. And have a snort for me."

Kris seethed: *Which elfin asshole ratted him out about* that*?!*

Kris shuffled into the kitchen the next morning. The recollection of the Parisian elf had kept him in the barn longer than normal and he'd celebrated the successful polishing session with more than his usual number of snorts. "Elf poop," he murmured as coffee dribbled down the side of his cup.

Klara walked in as he was wiping the mess from the counter. "Rub the pot with some beeswax."

Kris blinked and looked down. "Uh. Why?"

"The *coffee* pot, Kris," she sneered. "There aren't enough bees in the world to make enough wax to go on that thing hanging over your belt."

"It's all part of the show," Kris objected weakly as he slumped into his favorite kitchen chair.

"Hmph. Anyway. While you were out playing in the barn last night, *I* was doing some research. Here!" She pushed a few sheets of paper across the table.

"I left my glasses in the other room. Dear. Just me tell what this is. Please?"

"My idea," Klara declared triumphantly. "You'll love it."

Kris didn't think he would. "Go on."

"Do you know the wedding planning industry did almost a billion dollars a year last year? And that's just in the United States. The limousine business is knocking back a reindeer hair under sixty billion itself. And I haven't started doing the math on all the other bushwa that goes into the average North American hitching. That, by the way, is roughly fifty billion u-ess-dee in total."

Kris sipped coffee. "And all of this means what, Klara?" he asked tiredly.

"The business! Cash flow! Don't you get it?"

Kris cradled his forehead in his palms. "No. I don't."

"Your brain is rotting. That French tart must have given you the clap," Klara replied acidly.

Kris kept his mouth shut. He'd gotten quite adept at waiting her out when she had her bile up.

"Look," Klara began a moment later, using the keep-the-words-simple-and-slow-for-the-moron style that she knew chapped her spouse's ass. "Sleighs for hire. Get it?"

"Well..."

She reached across the table and thumped him in the forehead. "Yo! McClaus! Wake up!" She heaved a great and dramatic sigh. "Let me tell you how it's going to work."

Please don't. "Okay."

"Right. First, the basic package. This one's the essential for the budget-minded couple who are paying for their own wedding. Or the poor parents with the maxed out credit cards. The bride gets a ride to the ball-and-chaining venue. The happily wedded couple then get a ride together to wherever they're going to celebrate. Two hours max."

"Seems like a logistical challenge for two people. I mean, me, the sleigh, eight reindeer, Rudolph, a couple of elv—"

"You aren't using your noodle, big guy. I said this is the basic package."

"You did."

"So?"

Kris stood and stretched. As he was pouring another cup of joe, he gave the concept a moment's thought. "Why would you need all eight?" he wondered.

"Bingo! The coffee must be helping."

Kris nodded as he sat. "It wouldn't be a full holiday load, would it. Two of the team could work it, I suppose. Even if the bride and groom were a pair of real lard asses."

"Why two?"

"Stability for the most part. During transit to and from, one could handle me and the empty sleigh while the other caught some zees." Kris found he was getting enamored of the idea. It'd mean more quality time away. Likely even a new way to replenish the Restorative supply throughout the year. "This could work." He put on his oh-darn-bad-news sad face. "But I wouldn't be home as much."

Klara slapped on her married woman it-sucks-to-be-us-but-we'll-get-through-it face. "I know. I'm not looking forward to the separation either."

Kris thought he'd heard a hint of something in her voice but decided it was a trick of the tinnitus he'd picked up over the years due to his failure to wear hearing protection against the constant roar of the wind rush.

"There's," she continued, "a flaw in your assumptions. You wouldn't necessarily be gone as much as you think."

The old ticker in Kris's chest went thump-*erk* as his visions of freedom crashed and burned. "How so?" he squeaked.

"Why do your hands need to be on the reins?" she prompted quietly.

Kris rocked back. "Well. Because my hands have always been on the reins."

Mrs. Kringle patted his hand. "Yes. A tradition I'm not suggesting we break. As you recall, dear, we're discussing a *new* service."

Kris's brow furrowed. "Are we still talking about the basic package?"

"Yes," she answered with a growing smile.

"If that's the case, then I suppose one of the exercise drivers could handle the gig."

"That's my big boy!"

Kris was chagrined. "Where does that leave me? Oh. Oh!"

"Yes, dear," Klara encouraged. "What *does* come after the basics?"

"Options. Add-ons." Kris's eyes lit up as if he was flying out of the barn at the beginning of his annual soiree. "I become an option. Right?" he asked excitedly.

"Absolutely! And a pricey one at that. What self-respecting bride or her gotta-do-more-than-the-Joneses status conscious loser parents would willingly forgo the opportunity to have the Big Claus himself at the reins of their baby girl's wedding sleigh?"

Kris forgot all about his hangover and shot to his feet. "Indeed." He began pacing to and fro. "Options. Options," he muttered. He stopped abruptly. "The Big Sleigh driven by the Big Claus with the full team of eight and Rudolph leading the way would be the Ultimate Package."

"You betcha, sweetheart. Options and add-ons is how we'll nail the big bucks. You're on a roll. Take it a step further."

He resumed his to-ing and fro-ing. "A step further. A step further."

Klara watched with something akin to affection. Patronizing, mostly, but still with a hint of affection. If one looked really hard.

Kris went on. "If we assume the budget team is two then we could conceivably support three hitchings simultaneously. We'd just tart up some of the training sleighs and save the Big One for the ultimate experience."

"Eight divided by two is four: Why only three?"

Kris shrugged. "Keep a pair in reserve in case something happens. Rest and relaxation. A bit of downtime so they can stay in training for the main event."

"I suppose," Klara conceded the argument for the moment. "What else?"

Kris snapped his fingers. "The ULTIMATE Ultimate: A cozy round trip to their honeymoon destination." He bowed. "With yours truly in control and Rudolph, his nose so bright, guiding the way."

Klara stood. "We could charge for excess baggage."

"And change fees."

"The interest on mandatory, non-refundable deposits will be a welcome addition," Klara noted, excited by the blooming fiscal possibilities.

"Not to mention room and board for me and the team for the overnight stays."

"Which will defray operating expenses *here*," Klara noted with no small amount of satisfaction.

Kris paused and sobered. "For those going Ultimate, they'll expect a bit more in the way of service. And refreshments. That might get expensive."

Klara brushed it off. "Not a problem. We get an elf or two to go along as attendants. We repackage some of those leftover holiday cookies and candy and relabel that cheap sparkling crap from California as complimentary refreshments." She shrugged. "We can add corkage fees to the bottom end of the market to cover the cost."

Kris beamed. "It's a great idea, Klara! We could make millions."

Klara replied along with one of her doting-and-dutiful-wife smiles. "I knew you had it in you, dear."

"When do we start?"

"I don't see why we can't pilot the concept this year."

Kris clapped. "Works for me. I'll go tell the team!"

"And I'll refine the numbers!"

"Jingle bells! Jingle bells! Jingle all the way!" Kris sang merrily as he strode from the kitchen.

"Bells! Great idea for another option, Kris!" Klara shouted after him. "I'll add it to the list."

Night Shift

D amn. At least a third of the Collectors on my shift were
already in line outside of Headquarters. I glanced at my
watch. I wasn't late: The assholes in front of me were early.

"Hey, Delong," said the Black guy at the end of the line.

"Yo, Cheezy. How's it goin'?" I asked.

"Same old shit."

"Looks like the newbs are learning the ropes," I said as I
joined the queue, the required two yards behind Cheezy.

"Yep. Sucks, it do."

"I guess we shouldn't have provided such good examples."

Cheezy barked a laugh and shoved his attention into his
mobile. Porn, probably.

Experienced Collectors like Cheezy and me know to show up
for shift early. That way, we have some snooze time after we clear
pre-shift testing and decontamination and while we wait for the
rest of the shift to get processed. The newbies must've rubbed
brain cells together and learned something.

Oh well. My mobile was loaded with electronic versions of the books I'd always wanted to read but never, while I was tending bar, had the time for. I opened Dafoe's *The Plague Year* and lost myself in a bygone era.

"Pull your head out, Delong," Cheezy ordered. "Yo, Hansen."

It was easy to see Hansen's shit-eating grin even through the faceplate of her blue hazmat suit. "You guys are getting old. Never thought I'd see the day when so many newbs got ahead of you guys. Booth Three, Cheezy. You're in Four, Delong."

The door into Screening swung inward. Cheezy and I stepped inside and made our way to our assigned booths to have our temperatures, saliva, and blood quick-tested. The temps were easy; non-contact infrared temperature guns. Old tech, sure, but still effective. The saliva and blood quick-tests were more recent, products of a medical-pharmaceutical industrial complex able to run wild with bucket loads of federal cash.

People on the street were skeptical of anything the government claimed was good for them or, God forbid, "highly effective." They couldn't be blamed, I guess. The first round of vaccines when the Plague came ashore seemed to work. In the beginning. After the first couple of mutations, folks died left and right, regardless of their vax status. But what made matters really, really bad was the rash of cardiac arrests and strokes that smote the vax pioneers who took the plunge during the first wave of the plague. "Statistically insignificant," Big Pharma and their federal lackeys claimed. "Bullshit," replied a significant portion of the populace.

Myself included, that is until the Feds ordered all the bars and restaurants closed in the interests of public safety. I'd been living day-to-day on tips before then. After that, I made do on food stamps and other charity. The Landlord Lobby splashed enough cash about Congress to convince our elected morons that the government moratorium on evictions was an infringement of their clients' Fourteenth Amendment rights. When it seemed likely the Supreme Court was going to agree, I got vaxxed and just in time to be at the head of the line for a job as a Collector.

I, an out of work bartender, had a government job that meant rent protection on top of a regular paycheck. And priority access to new vax boosters or vaccines. And first dibs on intensive care in the event I got infected. On or off the job; it didn't matter. What mattered was I had all that while I was a Collector.

"Where's Hiram?" I asked the unknown tech.

"Hiram?"

"He works Entry, usually this spot," I answered.

"No clue. I got pulled in from Shift One; no one told me anything other than just show up and don't be late."

"Don't tickle my brain," I cautioned as the tech prepped a cotton-tipped harpoon to shove up my nostril.

"Not a problem," the tech answered. Up went the swab and the roto-rooting began.

Closing my eyes seemed to make the experience easier to endure. A bit. Every shift start, I tell myself that I've gotten used to having sticks and swabs and spit-cups shoved in or into my face, and I won't feel like sneezing.

The tech finished. I did some nostril twitches to kill the incipient sneeze.

The tech submitted my samples to the magic boxes. "You're all negative."

"Thanks."

"No problem. Have a good one."

I waved. "You too. Stay safe."

Cheezy was waiting at the entrance lock into Headquarters. "Hear about Hiram?"

I shrugged. "I asked. Didn't get an answer."

"He bought it last night on his way home."

"Shit. How?" I asked.

"Ghoulies jumped him."

"That sucks."

"Yep," Cheezy agreed. He swiped his badge. System matched his ID to his test results and decided he was allowed into Decon. The lock clicked and Cheezy pushed his way inside. The door, a slab of steel that would have done nicely as a pressure hatch inside a submarine sinking to its crush depth, *whumpfed* closed behind him.

I did the same after the locked-and-sealed indicator went green. Inside, I stripped down and tossed my government-issue overalls into the laundry basket. Then into the shower, the sting of the hot disinfectant needles on my bare skin. I raised my face and took a snootful of the chemical-laden water. I don't know which is worse: getting waterboarded in the nose or hosed up the ass. They both have their minuses.

The shower cut off automatically after three minutes. I stepped out and toweled down. I yanked a fresh overall off the shelf and joined the gaggle waiting for admission into the Inner Sanctum, Headquarters, the heart of Collections.

Cheezy, one of the few remaining combat vets still working Collections, loved to stroll naked into HQ. The man was six feet of solid ebony muscle with scars streaked across his back and chest. He used his size and his appearance to effect. "Yo. You muthas be in the wrong spot," he growled at the newbs who'd stupidly planted their asses in 'our' chairs. "Out," he ordered flatly.

I did my part and slapped my wide-eyed, flaring nostril thing on the pair, a look I'd mastered early on as a bartender. It worked, sometimes, to nip a fight in the bud. Despite Cheezy's menace and my feigned homicidal imbecility, one of the newbs looked like he was going to protest. I smiled if that's what stretching my lips open and baring my teeth could be called.

Cheezy noticed the attitude building. He bent over and got into the newb's face. "I 'preciate your givin' up that seat," as he lifted the guy by the chin.

The other newb shot out of his chair.

I blew a kiss toward the guy as I plopped my ass down. "You're gonna stick to that fine faux leather, Cheezy."

"Yep. I'll smell it up real fine; better than peeing on it." He sat and pulled on his coverall. "You gonna get the coffee, Delong?"

I didn't bother opening my eyes. "Not my turn, boy."

"Bull-effing-sheeit, white man."

"Nope. It's the fifteenth, right? Odd number. That means the joe's on you." I yawned. "Hot and black. Make it a double."

Cheezy shot to his feet. "I'll give you hot and black right up the ass, you honky mutha fucka. Twice. Like you *ast*."

"Whatever," I murmured. "Focus, Cheezy: Coffee. No cream. No sugar."

Cheezy growled and stomped off.

I smiled. Cheezy was one of the best in Collections and my team lead and vehicle commander; I was his driver. Mortimer—a flaming gay we all called Morticia or Morti or just plain Mort, depending on circumstances—was our Ripper, responsible for Remains Identification and Processing. Walker was our body man. No pun intended.

Cheezy's ghetto talk was bullshit. Not that Winston Randolph Cheswick wouldn't or couldn't tear most of us in half. It's just not a skill often possessed by those with Master's Degrees in International Relations. He'd done his time as a Corpsman with a Marine Recon Battalion in the Land of Sand and Rags, back when the US of A thought it could win over the hearts and minds of a bunch of third-world religious fanatics and convince them of the merits of fast food and cheap consumer goods. It wasn't all fighting, he told me; there was a lot of downtime, especially when he and his Marine comrades found themselves bobbing around the briny blue of the Mediterranean or the North Atlantic, six-month breaks between deployments to Iraq and Afghanistan.

Cheezy could describe the anatomical effects on the human body wrought by someone hypothetically strong enough to tear a man's head from his shoulders. With the same ease, he could natter on for hours about the secondary and tertiary effects in South Asia of the US failure to contain the Chinese. He could do either while pulling your arms out of their sockets, never breaking a sweat or losing his chain of thought.

"Here's your mud, bro."

"Thanks, Cheezy. Prost," I offered after he'd sat.

"Mud in your eye," he replied.

We sipped and watched as the ready room filled with the rest of the shift. "Not like Mort to be this late," I observed.

Cheezy hmphed. "Ho is probably on his knees somewhere and forgot the time. Oops. My bad. There he is."

"Hey. Morti," I called.

Morti stomped over, glowering the whole way. "Well. Isn't this *just* special."

"Shit, bitch. You on the rag?" Cheezy asked.

Morticia's eyes went angrily wide. "I am *not* a bitch. *I* am a lady. Screw you, Cheezy."

Cheezy laughed. "Not even with Delong's dick." He sobered. "Why are your panties in a wad?"

"Walker tested positive," Mort spat.

"Give him the HIV, did you?" I asked.

"No, Delong. I. Did. Not. Give. Him. HIV. Or any other social disease." He shook his head. "He's on his way to Quarantine."

Cheezy straightened. "When?"

Mort plopped into a chair. "We came in together. The magic machine lit red for him."

"Means we get a newb. That sucks," Cheezy noted, resigned.

"Maybe not," I offered cheerfully.

"He's gone mental," Mort declared, giving me a woeful glare.

"Yep," Cheezy agreed. "What you been smokin', boy?"

I shrugged. "Trying to maintain a positive outlook."

Mort rolled his eyes. Cheezy flipped me off.

Replacement Collectors were almost always new guys. The job didn't need brains and it didn't need skill. A strong back and good knees worked. But working a new guy into the team was always a hassle.

Quarantine was fourteen days in an isolation ward. These days, that usually meant a space in a modular medical facility. A fancy doublewide, in other words.

The odds we'd see Walker again were small. There's only so much sealing up the inside of a mobile home the government can do. Going into quarantine was a damn good way to get dead these days, especially with the Sigma variant gleefully sticking its spikes into every cell in range, happily ignoring age, prior medical conditions, race, gender, sexual preference, and religion.

Boss Hawg stepped into the ready room. "Evenin', everyone." He ignored the catcalls and wise asses. Hawg was the Shift Lead, responsible for Collection assignments for the six teams—twenty-four men on a good day—assigned to the graveyard, the night, shift.

The Graveyard Shift. That was funny once, a couple of years back when the Feds decided to put some of the country's idle hands—hospitality workers, mostly—to work scooping the deceased off the street. Walker and I'd been bartenders; Mort had been a cast member in a faux Broadway show aboard a cruise ship.

Every once in a while some newb would try to be funny with the line. He'd have the fun burned out of him by the end of his first shift.

Usually we, Cheezy's team, were first in line for assignment. My eyes narrowed and my asshole puckered as the other five teams got their assignments ahead of us.

"Oh. We are well and truly fucked," Mort muttered tightly, a debutante's sour moue stitched on his face.

"You got that right," Cheezy agreed, his face impassive.

"Cheezy!" Hawg called.

"How you goin' to stick it to us tonight, Boss?" Cheezy growled, a lion announcing his intent to rip the guts out of the closest gazelle.

Hawg ignored the insubordination. Cheezy was Black and a vet. Nothing Hawg could do or say was going to back him off.

I'd asked Cheezy why he was in Collections. He was knocking down decent retirement bucks and had a place of his own, free and clear. He, unlike the rest of us, didn't need the work or the benefits.

"This pandemic crap can't last forever. When it's over, I want to see the world, Delong," he'd answered. "Go someplace where the odds of being shot at are about zip. See the parts of the world that *I* want to see and not the third world cesspools the White Fucking Clowns in Charge insisted on sending me and my bros to." He had waved a finger. "This job gives me the extra cash to do that."

"But," I protested. "Collections?"

Cheezy had laughed his you-stupid-assholes-don't-know-shit laugh. "Ever been on a body recovery patrol? Places where it's north of a hundred degrees before the sun comes up? Places where the boys have been sitting outside cooking for a day, maybe two?"

"No," I'd admitted.

His chuckle back then was mocking and scornful and disgusted. "What we do ain't shit, boy." He explained why.

I threw up when he was finished.

"I'm giving you some easy work tonight, Cheezy," Hawg answered in the here-and-now. "Since you're down a team mate. Ramirez? Yeah, stand up. Meet your team."

Ramirez was the newb I'd rousted out of the chair with my maniac impersonation. Figures.

Cheezy ignored the standing newb. "What's the 'easy work'?" he asked warily.

"South Tower."

Cheezy blinked. "Are you fucking serious?"

Hawg feigned bemusement. "I am. What's wrong? The building managers have a pile stacked and ready. All Mort has to do is rip them and then all you have to do is load them. Easy."

"South Tower, Boss. Really?" I asked before Cheezy decided Hawg was truly the nearest gazelle.

Hawg smiled. "There's a couple of squads of the National Guard learning the ropes and the terrain. They'll appreciate the training opportunity."

"Shit," Mort exclaimed on our behalf.

"What's the count tonight?" Adams, another lead, asked.

"Thirty adult equivalents," Hawg answered. "A truckload and you're done." He shrugged. "There are indications the current variant is weakening."

He managed to say that with a straight face.

* * *

Ramirez followed us to the airlock between HQ proper and Exit Control where we'd suit up before heading out for the night's collection. "Newb suits in the locker over there," I told him.

"Got my own," Ramirez replied.

Cheezy had one leg in his biohazard suit when he stopped. "You've done this before?" he asked.

Ramirez nodded. "Yes."

"Where?" Mort asked.

"Glenfield Heights Sector," Ramirez answered sheepishly.

"Whoowee! Whose dick did you suck to get *that* duty?" Mort exclaimed. "That ain't work. The rich fucks who live there don't die like real people. And when they do, they usually have their own ways of disposing of their loved one's mortal remains."

"Don't matter," Cheezy interrupted. "You done ripper work?"

"I have," Ramirez answered.

"Tell us."

The newb shrugged. "Location. Identification. Fluids. Tag. Question?"

"Go on," Cheezy replied.

"What count?"

Cheezy and I exchanged a glance. "I expect things are a bit more genteel back in Glenfield Heights," I speculated. "The deceased are rolled out to the end of the driveway where the staff assist the Collection team with the final processing. Maybe accompanied by a brief prayer; a sobbing wife muttering her last farewells to the dearly departing. Something like that?"

Ramirez nodded. "Something like that."

Cheezy shook his head. "Out here in the real world, boy, folks kick off in volume. The count is management's way to make sure we ain't out there driving around in circles while sucking off the government's teat, knocking back the bucks and enjoying the benefits of being Collectors."

"How does it work?"

"Basically, the spreadsheet geekazoids put a bunch of numbers together—virulence; size of the current most-at-risk population; mean hours- or days-to-death after infection; average collection rate over the last little while; available landfill space—and come up with what they officially refer to as 'reasonably achievable collection targets' for each shift. Call it what you want: body count; quota; whatever. What it means is that if we come up short, eyebrows are raised and questions get asked. If it happens enough times, we get fired."

"You know about Ghoulies?" I asked when it seemed Ramirez had no further questions.

"I do."

"You carrying?" Mort asked lightly.

Ramirez's combination of a raised eyebrow and the corner of an upturned lip could have been a scowl. "Uh. That would be against Collections regulations," he answered.

Cheezy stood and zipped the front of his suit. "We aren't much on regulations, boy. Not when they can leave our asses hanging in the breeze. You know how to use a Halligan?"

"I think so. Yes. Well, I had the training when I first joined up."

"Not much B-and-E-ing in LaLa Land, eh?" I asked.

"No. Not there," Ramirez admitted.

Cheezy glowered. "We do what we got to do, right? The gubmint wants bodies off the street before they pong the place up too bad. I'm cool with that; it makes perfect sense from a public health perspective. So. That means a lot of times we're forced to break-and-enter someplace where the residents haven't been heard from for a couple of days. And *that* means we don't pass up opportunities to effect some wealth distribution. Understand?"

Ramirez looked perplexed. "Not sure."

Mort snorted. "Do I need to come over there and rub your head, dearie?"

Ramirez blinked.

I smiled. "What the man's trying to say, Ramirez, is that there are opportunities to ensure the valuables of the recently deceased are disposed of in a manner that is to the broader good of the economy. And our morale," I offered. "But only when there's no registered next-of-kin or executor of estate." I shrugged. "We aren't thieves. We're just not fond of leaving good shit around for the Ghoulies. They'd just hock it or spend it for something stupid like bullets or knives."

Realization dawned across Ramirez's face. "Ah."

"You got a problem with that?" Cheezy asked quietly. Dangerously.

If the newb answered the wrong way, he'd have an unfortunate encounter with a piece of something sharp and jagged enough to hole a suit and earn the wearer a stay in quarantine. Assuming he made it through the shift.

"No. I don't have a problem with that," Ramirez answered. He shrugged. "Another question?"

"Make it fast," Cheezy snarled.

Ramirez discreetly eyeballed the room.

"Don't sweat it," I told him. "We boogered the cameras and mikes so many times, the Feds don't bother fixing them anymore."

The newb nodded. "Are you packing?" he asked quietly.

Cheezy sneered. "Collections teams rely on the police and the military for protection."

"Right. Got it," Ramirez said, apparently getting it at all levels. "It wasn't a problem in the Heights. After the Ghoulies took out a bunch of the rent-a-guards who watched the neighborhood, the folks who lived there wanted as much protection as they could get." He shrugged. "They provided the gats and the ammo. And their attorneys covered our asses when we capped someone suspicious."

Even Cheezy blinked at the matter-of-fact recollection.

"No shit? You know how to shoot? In a suit?" Mort asked.

The newb nodded. "Yes and yes."

"Anything well?" I wondered.

"Wheel guns or shotguns of the semi-auto variety." He grinned whimsically. "Too easy to short-stroke the slide of a pump gun, you know, when you're wearing hazmat gear. As for pistols, well, we lost a couple of guys whose suits ripped when the slide caught fabric. I prefer revolvers," he said with a shrug, "but I'll use a pistol if need be."

Cheezy glanced my way. I shrugged. "Maybe we aren't so fucked after all," I answered the question his eyes were asking. "How're your knees, Ramirez?"

It was his turn to shrug. "Not bad."

Cheezy pulled the other leg of the suit on and stood. He held out his right hand. "Welcome to the team."

* * *

Suited up, we gathered at the exit hatch that would let us into Collection's underground garage.

"HQ. Team One Actual. Radio check."

"One Actual. Received. Two?" HQ queried.

"Copy," I answered.

"Roger. Three?"

"Lookin' for love, sweetie," More answered.

"Damn it, Mort. I wish you'd knock that crap off," HQ answered.

"Next shift."

"Bullshit. Four?"

"Copy," Ramirez answered.

HQ chuckled. "Lambs ready for slaughter. Clock starts now."

We had fifteen seconds to back out. Backing out meant out of Collections and away from all those federally funded protections. Permanently.

We all looked at Ramirez and waited.

The clock ran down.

"No takers? Your rent's covered another day, then." HQ gibed. "On your way, boys. We'll see you at the end of the shift. Stay safe."

The pressure door hissed as it unsealed and swung open.

"Get ready, men. We're off into the Winkie Forest!" Mort exclaimed cheerfully.

* * *

We waddled—walking isn't easy in a full biohazard protection suit—to our Remains Recovery Vehicle, known affectionately to the team as R2VToo. I did the vehicle checks. Mort verified we had a full inventory of RIP kits. Ramirez clambered into the back and went to check the body bag count and tie downs.

Cheezy watched. "Ramirez."

"Sir?"

"It's all good."

"But—"

"Don't sweat it, boy," Cheezy ordered flatly.

"Sir." Ramirez turned to the shotgun seat.

Cheezy held up the garbage bag he'd carried out of HQ. " Take this and stow it in the hamper behind the cab. Then get down from there," Cheezy said.

"But—"

"Damn it. Do what I said, beaner."

The newb stowed the bag and scrambled out of the bed. "Sir?"

"We have extra seats rigged in the cab, boy. No one rides in the widow's chair, 'less they pissed me off. You keep saying 'but' and you *will* piss me off."

Mort howled. "I was wondering when you'd get around to using that lame ass line."

"Kiss my ass, Morticia," Cheezy replied.

"Anytime, you big hunk of Black man meat. Anytime," Mort replied huskily as he motioned a wank-off.

Cheezy ignored him. "Delong?"

I dropped the hood and locked it shut. "Ready."

"Mort?"

"We have three loads of kits," Mort answered.

"Hope it don't come to that this shift. You ready, Ramirez?"

"Yes, sir."

"Right. Get aboard," Cheezy ordered.

We let Ramirez in first. It was a tight squeeze and not comfortable for anyone. But Cheezy was dead set against exposing a man unnecessarily to fire. The widow's chair was a drop-down bench in the back bed. In the early days, that's where the ripper and the body man rode.

Until the patriotic anti-government Ghoulie sharpshooters began to glass in on easy targets.

"So much *man* meat!" Morti exclaimed. "I think I'm coming!"

"Piss off, Mort," Cheezy muttered. "HQ. Team One's ready."

"Copy, One. Gate reports all clear."

"Roger that," Cheezy acknowledged. "Get us to the door, Delong."

"Ten-four, boss," I answered as I put the truck into gear and let it idle itself to the exit gate.

"Last chance, boys," Cheezy offered. "No takers? Damn. HQ."

"One?" HQ responded.

"If it's still clear, let us the fuck out of here," Cheezy ordered.

"Roger. Good luck," HQ replied.

I gunned the truck as the reinforced steel doors opened toward the Outside.

Cheezy waved at the guard station on his side as we growled out of the garage. Mort blew a kiss toward the station on his side of the truck.

The ass end of R2VToo was a coat of paint's width through the armored gate when it slammed closed.

* * *

I drove a couple of blocks toward the Pits. It wasn't the direct route to South Tower but the area had the advantage of being a lunar landscape littered and junked up but devoid of buildings and, usually, people. Especially Ghoulies. "Scope's clear, Cheezy."

"Right." Cheezy popped open his door. "Come out, Ramirez."

The newb worked his way out of the cab. "Shove your ass in my face again, Ramirez, and I'll be sure to kiss it," Mort said.

"Sorry," Ramirez muttered.

"Oh, I'm not!" Mort replied.

"Around back," Cheezy said. "Got something to show you. Hop up." Cheezy followed Ramirez up and into the bed of the truck.

Mort and I then heard nothing but the soft hiss of our breathing. Cheezy had switched off his radio. I paid attention to the radar display crudely mounted to the dash. We figured we knew what was going on behind us.

* * *

Cheezy switched off Ramirez's suit radio. He made helmet-to-helmet contact. "You best be cool, asshole. If you say anything—*anything*—about this, I will stake you out at South Tower naked and leave you for the Ghoulies. Unlike Mort whose desire for man flesh is merely indicative of his sexual preferences and thus figurative, the Ghoulies in that complex have developed a taste for long pig. No matter how seasoned it may be. Understand?"

"Got it," the newb answered.

"Open up the body bag box. Good. Now shove your hands along the sides about six inches. You'll find—"

"Handles."

"Yep. Grab 'em and lift. Set the bags on the deck."

"Holy shit," Ramirez muttered.

"Yep. We ain't got no wheel guns—yet—but the Remington's yours if you think you can handle it."

"I can."

"Good." Cheezy reached past Ramirez and into the box. "Trade me."

"Uh?"

"Take this and put whatever shit you have in your pouch in the one I just gave you. It's been specially modified by Yours Truly to incorporate a holster. You know how to handle a Glock?" Cheezy asked.

"I know how to handle a Glock," Ramirez admitted. "Ah, the trigger guards?"

"We cut 'em away to accommodate gloved fingers. So you just be *real* careful around the trigger if you chamber a round. We have an extra Model Nineteen that's yours. Only half a mag's worth of rounds but better than nothing. Grab the other gear bags; those are for Delong and Mort. You can rack the Remington inside for the rest of the shift. Put the corpse carriers away and let's go."

Cheezy watched as Ramirez restowed the body bags. "One thing, boy. I don't know what you did in the Heights or how good you might have been. Since I didn't see it, it doesn't mean shit. So until I know otherwise, here's the deal: No one sees us armed and lives. You pull that thing without me giving you the okay and you'll be Ghoulie Goulash. You *shoot* that thing without orders and I will *shoot* you in the leg. Twice. Enough to hole your suit. Understood?"

"Yes, sir."

Cheezy turned their radios back on. "Good job, Ramirez. I'll make sure the Boss knows you know your hand signals. Delong!"

I smiled at Mort. "Yeah?" I answered.

"Pull your dick out of Mort's ass. We got work to do."

* * *

I didn't need the GPS to tell me we were a mile out from South Tower. Cheezy, Mort and I had covered the ground plenty of times. "Call up and let 'em know we're on the way?" I asked Cheezy. It was my polite way to wake him from the snooze he must be enjoying; listening to someone snore over the suit radio was like having glass ground in your ears.

"Yep. HQ. Team One Actual."

"HQ here. Whatcha need, Cheezy?"

"We're approaching South Tower. The Guard still on channel Bravo?"

"Affirmative, One Actual."

"Copy. Team's switching to Bravo in three-two-one."

We did another round of radio checks after switching frequencies.

"Roger that, Cheezy. We're reading everyone five-by-five. Your escorts are Foxtrot Three-One."

"Thanks, HQ," Cheezy acknowledged. "Foxtrot Three-One, this is Charlie One Actual."

"Charlie One, this is Foxtrot Three-One Romeo."

"We're inbound to your pos. ETA is—" Cheezy glanced my way and nodded at my raised fingers—"two minutes."

"Roger. Two mikes. We're waiting. Foxtrot Three-One out."

"Pop the lights on, Delong."

Flashing amber and magenta painted abandoned ruins as we made our way to South Tower.

"What's the deal with this place?" Ramirez asked.

"It's an apartment complex the Feds took over during the first wave. One building is set up for quarantine; the other four are for segregation."

"Oh. Shit," Ramirez mumbled.

"Yep," I agreed. "The rabid antis are locked up in there 'not only for their safety, but for the broader safety and well-being of the entire community.'"

"Sounds like a press release," Ramirez observed.

"It does because that's what the Feds said when they took the place over," Cheezy replied. "It didn't take long before the Ghoulies ran the show there. The first couple of onsite night watch guys were lynched. The first complex manager, a stupid Fed from the CDC, was burned at the stake."

"Jesus," Ramirez mumbled.

"That's exactly why," I replied. "The Ghoulies thought—still think—that all of this shit is God's will or some dumbass crap like that, and there's nothing man can do. Or should do if it means thwarting God's Will. Pour that gas on a fire lit by the flames of lib-bo-ra-tee and indie-vid-u-yall rights, and you got the clusterfuck that is South Tower."

"Yep," Mort interjected. "The Feds finally got tired of the gruesome turnover of night watch and building custodians. They slapped walls around the place and built a bunker for the folks s'posed to be in charge. It didn't matter. The fucks inside kept finding ways to get out and spread their infection. The city finally threw its hands in the air and sealed every possible way in or out of the place it could. The guvmint pipes water into the place and throws food over the fence a couple of times a week."

"So. You were busting my chops about the long pig."

Cheezy snorted. "I thought you knew about Ghoulies, boy."

"The Ghoulies I'm used to are small-time thugs and thieves."

"In other words, good God-fearing patriots, right?" Mort quipped.

"Yes," Ramirez agreed. He paused. "But not . . ."

"Connoisseurs of *homo sapiens*?" Mort tittered.

"No. Not that."

I tapped the brakes. "Pucker time."

* * *

A pair of Hummers, vee'ed bumper-to-bumper, made a temporary roadblock ahead of us. Ten or twelve soldiers stood in a three-sixty around the vehicles. One stepped forward and raised a hand.

I stopped when the auto-turret on one of the Hummers rotated and pointed its pair of twin twenty-millimeter cannon muzzles at our windshield.

"Charlie One, this is Foxtrot Three-One Actual. Flash your headlights."

I did. Twice.

"Roger that. Move up, Charlie One."

"Three-One Actual, I don't suppose you'd mind pointing those things somewhere other than at my Black ass," Cheezy commed informally and pointed.

"What?" The soldier turned around. "Shit."

He must have switched freqs; we didn't hear what he said. Whatever it was must have been good. It took about two seconds for the cannon to swivel off ninety degrees.

The soldier waddled up to Cheezy's side of R2VToo. "Sorry 'bout that. The squad's a little antsy. I'm Sergeant McNair."

"Cheezy, team lead. Things quiet?"

"Seem to be."

"First time for you guys?" I asked.

"Hereabouts, yeah. You know the turf?"

"We party here all the time," Mort chimed in.

"Shut up, Mort. We're ready to go anytime you are, McNair," Cheezy said.

"One of my fire teams will follow you in. The rest of us will stay here on the street and cover your asses."

"Movement?" I asked quietly.

"We have a couple of drone's being run by headquarters. *They* say there's some movement and some small heat signatures. Consistent with animals: dogs, cats, big rats."

"What do you say, Sergeant?" Cheezy asked quietly.

"Spooks the shit out of me, sir, it does."

"Mort?"

"There's been no livestock out here for a couple of years. Or in there," Mort answered.

"Ghoulies?" Ramirez asked, a disembodied voice over the ether.

"Maybe. Probably," the soldier agreed. "The last time I got this itch was when a bunch of our guys were overrun in Caprini Green," McNair recollected sourly. He waved an arm. One of the Humvees backed up after five guys clambered into the vehicle. "That's your backup. Specialist Conrad is the fire team leader. She's solid; ditto the guy manning the fifty cal. The rest? Well, Conrad'll do her best."

"Thanks," Cheezy offered. "Keep your head down, Sergeant."

He snorted. "*That* got shot off during the Phoenix riots last year. Go on," he waved us past. "The sooner you finish, the sooner we can get the fuck out here."

I put the truck into gear and moved slowly past the Humvees. I saw our cover pull in behind us. "Like the good sergeant said, the sooner we finish, the sooner we can get home."

The night watch at the barricade, a two-stage gate with concertina coiled atop the ten foot steel wall must have pressed a button; the bollards sank into the street as the first doors swung open. We stopped long enough for the street-side doors to shut and for the second pair to open. A pair of soldiers hopped into the back while we waited.

I hated this part of the entry. The space between the gates was large enough for a single vehicle. Collections was always first through if there were no active contacts on the inside. If something was going to pop by surprise, the Collections team would get it in the neck. Soldiers were expensive and getting rare. Collectors were, by comparison, a dime a dozen and easily replaced.

"Another day, another friggin' dollar," Mort muttered grimly. He hated it too.

If Ramirez said anything, I didn't hear it.

The steel doors on the complex side of the gate slammed shut as I drove us into the South Tower complex.

* * *

Three suited figures stood in the shadows beneath the floods that cast their sun-bright glare on the buildings in the South Tower complex, some brainiac's idea to hinder observation of the goings-on at the gate. One raised an arm. "Is that you, Cheezy?"

"Roger. Peters?"

"Yeah."

"How'd you get stuck on the night shift?" Cheezy asked.

"Miller got shivved by an anti a couple of nights ago. We slabbed him the next morning."

"Bummer, man," Mort said sympathetically.

"Shit happens, right? Although, you know?"

"What's that?" I asked.

"Who or what is making all the dung that it keeps on coming? I mean, it's gotta run out *some* time. Doesn't it?"

"Sure, Peters. It will. Maybe. One day," Cheezy replied. "Where do you want us?"

"Loading dock. We stacked a pile there."

"How many?" Mort asked.

"Seven."

"Fuck."

Peters chuckled. "What's your quota tonight, boys?"

"Thirty," Cheezy answered.

"Oh man. Sorry." Peters sounded remorseful. He probably was: He had to stay inside the residential areas while we were working instead of his nice cozy bunker outside the complex perimeter.

"I don't like the way that sounded, Peters," Mort said. "What aren't you telling us?"

"Ground level and first are clear; at least, they were when I came on shift," he answered indirectly.

Mort began to snarl. "Well, fu—"

I knew I wouldn't like the answer. "Are the elevators running?" I asked, interrupting Morti.

"Not really," Peters answered.

About what I expected.

"You *sure* you got good knees, Ramirez?" Cheezy snarled.

* * *

I backed up to the dock and got out. Seven units, laid out on the loading dock, waited to be collected.

"Let's get it done," Cheezy ordered. "You know where the bags are, Ramirez."

"Yessir." Our newb disappeared and returned a few seconds later.

"Help Mort with the units," Cheezy directed.

"Units?"

Cheezy pointed at the pile.

"Oh. Right." Ramirez took a step toward the pile. "Seven. All adults?"

"Yes," Peters agreed.

"Finish the one you're working with, Mort, and eyeball the newb's procedure. If you clear it, you got yourself a new assistant," Cheezy ordered.

"Not a problem, boss," Mort replied. "He's got a nice ass and I am *sure* he will be more than adequate. There! All shipshape and tidy. Help me load this one, Delong, so I can do as our fearless leader directs."

I snorted. "Give me a herp, Ramirez."

The kid unzipped a humans remains pouch and spread it on the concrete next to the deceased. Recently so; not more than a couple of days, I guesstimated. Regardless, I was happy to be working in a suit that could keep the bad shit—and smells—outside where they belonged.

Mort and I filled the bag. Ramirez zipped it shut. He and I tossed it into the bed of R2VToo.

"That's one," Cheezy declared.

Morticia hooked his arm through Ramirez's. "Let's you and I do our master's bidding, shall we? Here's a kit; show me what you can do. I'll record."

"Right," Ramirez muttered as he busted the seal on the LIFT kit. He kneeled onto the loading dock. "First: Location. Hm. There's no reading from this guy's chip."

Mort looked up from the Field Data Collection Device, what normal people called a tablet computer. "We need to roll it over. Step out of the way so I can get the initial scene shot." Mort got his pics.

Ramirez rolled the body, formerly a white male, thirty to thirty-five, skin-and-bones even when dead flaccid. He scanned again. "Nothing."

"Doesn't mean anything necessarily," Peters noted. "A lot of the citizens in this place took to the notion that getting microchipped by the government was some sort of demonic plot to turn them into zombie pedophiles."

"You recognize the guy?" Cheezy asked.

Peters sounded embarrassed. "No," he admitted.

Mort took some more pics. "Collection location: South Towers," he muttered. Unnecessarily as the LIFT software on the tablet slugged the Collection record with the GPS coordinates of wherever it believed itself to be. "Next step?"

"ID," Ramirez answered as he pawed around. "Nothing," Ramirez said.

"Rings? Jewelry? Dog tags?"

Ramirez patted down the unit. "Zip."

"Check the crotch, boy," Cheezy growled. "Don't worry. It ain't gonna bite you."

"Let me do it. I don't mind that part, sweetie," Morticia offered.

Ramirez rocked back. The two grunts snapped their attention toward Mort.

Morticia tittered. "Just kidding, fellas. I prefer my organs warm and with tongue-tickling pulses. Go ahead, Ramirez."

"Still nothing," Ramirez noted a moment later.

"John Doe, it is!" Mort exclaimed and keyed in the datum. "Next?"

The newb was already shoving the needle of the vacutainer into an arm. "Fluids."

"Very good! And last but not least?"

"Tagging. Uh, how do you all do it?"

I handed Ramirez the grease gun, an under-powered, cut-down version of an air rifle used to sedate big critters. It had enough oomph to plant a subcutaneous data seed. "Mort?"

"My little brain here says the data have been loaded and the chip is responding."

"Go ahead, Ramirez. Fire away."

"Where?"

"Center of the forehead works," I answered dryly as I kicked the unit's foot. "I doubt anyone's gonna come looking for Mr. Doe here."

"What about the containers?"

"What did you do with them in a previous life?" Cheezy asked.

"Duct-taped the evidence bag to the outside of the herp."

"Yep. We used to do that but the Feds bitched about the high rate of container breakage. We have a genuine Rubbermaid bin to hold that stuff. Give the bag to Mort; he'll stash it."

"He can work with me any day, Cheezy," Mort declared cheerily.

"Right. Awright, Ramirez. Mort's happy, I'm happy. You and Delong load this into the truck. Quit dicking around, Mort, and finish the other five."

* * *

"Swing it, Ramirez. One. Two. Three. Alley oop." I grunted as we tossed the unit into the bed. We did the same with the next two. The newb climbed aboard and began to straighten them out. The truck's capable of carrying thirty adult equivalents but you couldn't just toss bags into the back like socks into a drawer.

"Don't you think you guys should show some respect?"

"Who the fuck was that?" I snarled.

One of the two soldiers with Peters stepped forward. "Me."

I straightened and put my faceplate against the grunt's. "And who are you?"

"Specialist Smi—"

"In other words: Soldier Dickhead." I took a step forward and pushed the grunt backwards. "You know how many of these bags I've filled the last couple of years with assholes too stupid to do the right thing? Eh? You wanna try and guess?"

"Back off, Delong. I said, back off!" Cheezy ordered. "We have a long night ahead of us and we need the army's help. Quit dicking around; Mort's finished with the seventh. Get that loaded and we'll head upstairs."

* * *

"Which floor?" Peters asked.

"Next one up. No sense humping to the top unless we absolutely gotta," Cheezy answered. "Ramirez. Get that bag you stowed for me."

Ramirez shambled over to R2VToo and returned a minute later.

"Thanks," Cheezy said gruffly. "Take your team up a flight, Specialist Conrad."

"We gonna need night vision?" Conrad asked.

"You shouldn't. Lights still work on that level," Peters answered. "Or they did a couple of hours ago."

"Anything on that floor we need to be concerned about?"

"Not generally, no," Peters answered.

Conrad snorted. "Right. Smith. Head up and hold at the top of the stairs. Let us know if the lights are still on. Price. You watch our rear. The rest of us will haul ass up after we get a read on the lighting situation."

"Peters?"

"Yeah, Cheezy?"

"They still up there?" Cheezy asked quietly.

It took Peters a minute. "No, man. Sorry. They, uh, they left the building last week. With the morning shift."

"It happens," Cheezy finally replied. "The others?"

"Haven't heard or seen anything, Cheezy. You may still be able to empty that bag, man."

Ramirez touched his helmet to mine. "What's in the bag?"

"Candy. Treats. Cheap toys. Cheezy's got a thing for kids. He's always bringing something along for any we might run into," I answered quietly. "He had a soft spot for a pair of 'em here on Two. Brother and sister; cute as buttons. According to Peters, the parents were great despite their willingness to let their kids risk the bad shit." I snicked my teeth. "There's gotta be a law," I said. Something that protects kids from stupid parents. Just because they can bake 'em, doesn't mean they ought to be allowed to make them, you know?"

"Maybe one day," Ramirez offered softly.

"And maybe one day I'll be fucking president in a virus-free world," I snarked back.

"Lights are on," Smith commed breathlessly.

"Move it up, fucks," Conrad ordered. "The rest of you follow. Keep your head out of your ass, Price, and your eyes open."

Conrad took her M-4 off safe and led the way up the stairs. We followed.

"I got movement," Smith declared nervously. "Permission to open fire."

"No!" Peters shouted. "The people on Two are okay. We'll be there in a minute. Let's go."

It took another couple of moments before we got to the top of the stairs. Conrad and her fire team went prone and made an arc bristling with rifles ready. Whomever had spooked Smith must have retreated into a room. There was no one we could see in the hallway.

Peters pulled a cable from his suit pouch and plugged it into a wall jack. "This is a Public Service Announcement from Custodian Peters. Collections is available on Level Two at this time." He yanked the lead out of the wall socket. "Now we wait."

* * *

A door opened.

"Stay cool," Conrad muttered.

A wizened old man stepped into the hallway.

The soldiers raised their weapons.

"Take it easy, everyone." Peters said quietly. "The guy's a resident, *not* an internee. I think you have work, Cheezy."

Cheezy started forward.

Conrad stepped in front of him. "I'll clear the room, sir."

I knew it pissed Cheezy off to be in the hands of what he considered to be inexperienced armed children. I also knew he knew it was the way things worked these days in the real world. He didn't surprise me.

"Okay." He clasped the soldier on the shoulder. "But I'm right behind you. Got it? Let's go."

Conrad raised her rifle. "Yes, sir." She began a slow shuffle toward the old man.

It takes balls to move in front of the muzzles of locked-and-loaded automatic weapons, especially when those weapons are in the hands of grunts fresh out of Basic Training.

It was no surprise that Cheezy had 'em. It was clear Conrad had a pair, as well. But I was taken aback by the fact that Peters followed, a pace or so behind Cheezy.

"Stop, Conrad," Peters ordered. "I'm coming up."

"Roger that," the noncom answered.

"How are you, Mr. Willcox?" Peters asked as he stepped from behind Conrad and Cheezy.

"Carol's gone," the old man answered. Simply. Emotionlessly. A shit-happens-oh-well sort of tone.

"I'm sorry to hear that, sir," Peters replied. "This soldier needs to go inside and make sure it's safe. Are you okay with that?"

The old man gestured. "Do what you must."

Conrad didn't need any orders. "Team up. I'm going in."

She did. "Clear," she commed a few moments later.

"Let's get it done, guys," Cheezy ordered.

Collection Team One made its clumsy way into the apartment.

Peters stayed in the hall and chatted with the old man.

Conrad stood by the door and waited, her trigger finger indexed on the side of the receiver.

* * *

The old man came back and watched Mort rip his wife.

"We'll tag her downstairs where we don't have an audience," Mort murmured as he and I lifted the unit—a featherweight that had once been an elderly woman—into the bag.

"Stop, please? May I?" the man asked as I began to zip the herp closed.

I straightened and stepped away. "Sure, sir. Take as long you want."

"Oh. I won't be long, son. We've said our goodbyes often enough," he replied as he wiped away some tears and chuckled. "And I thought I was past that." He knelt. "We were together for fifty-seven years. In all that time, I was confident that I would go first. We spent many a night joking about how, after I 'kicked the bucket', she'd go around the world with the first handsome man she met." He kissed his wife's forehead and brushed a lock of hair into place. "I love you, Carol."

His leg buckled as he tried to stand. I caught the old guy before he fell. "You okay?" I asked.

"Yes. Thank you. The old bones creak far too much and don't bend easily." His unexpected laugh was almost a guffaw, the sound of someone who'd just heard the week's best joke. "It only now occurred to me: Was she using a double entendre? She excelled at games like that. One of the many things I loved about her and will sorely miss. You would have liked her; everyone did." He sobered and sighed. "Please. Do what you need to do, gentlemen. Is there anything else you require of me?"

"No, sir," Cheezy answered. "May we?" he asked gently.

"Certainly. The best of Carol remains here with me, son. A favor?"

"Sir?"

"These are trying times that often require an efficiency that, under normal circumstances, would be considered brusque, even offensive. Please be as gentle as much as the current insane circumstances permit. If you'd be so kind."

"Fifty-seven years?" Mort asked unexpectedly.

"Yes. Childhood sweethearts who fell in love and, despite the world in which we grew up, stayed in love. She was eighteen when we married; I, nineteen."

"Damn, sir. That's a hell of an achievement," I said.

"An achievement, I'll agree. But Hell? Not in the least. It certainly was Heaven on Earth for me. She's in a better place now, in the Paradise she deserves."

"Mr. Willcox?"

"Yes."

"We'll take care of her as best as we can. You have my word, sir," Cheezy said.

The old man's eyes watered. "Those damn suits make it impossible to express old-fashioned affectionate appreciation. Carol was a big hugger and I acquired the habit over the decades. Will you accept *my* word that, were I able, I would embrace you?"

"I'm honored to accept your word, sir," Cheezy growled. "Perhaps you'll do me another honor and give me a raincheck on that?"

"Ha! There is so much optimism underlying that question that you've almost given me something to live for. You have that raincheck, sir. I hope I'm able to help you redeem it."

"As do I," Cheezy said as he set his gloved hand gently on the old man's shoulder. "Let's take care of Mrs. Willcox, Team."

The four of us took her down the stairs. Conrad and two of her men led the way; Peters and the rest of Conrad's team brought up the rear.

When we got down to the dock, Mort loaded a data seed.

Ramirez got the grease gun.

"Not this time, Ramirez," Cheezy said.

I could see Mort nodding as he dropped the seed into an evidence pouch and verified it could be read. "It's good," he confirmed. He set the pouch on what had once been the lady's breasts and patted it affectionately. "That's it."

I rezipped the bag. Ramirez and I began to lift her.

Cheezy growled. "No. Leave her on the dock. When we're finished, she'll travel on top."

"Roger that, Boss" I replied.

* * *

After we took care of Mrs. Willcox, we stumped up back to Two; there was no new business there. Ramirez and I humped four units from the third floor and five from the fourth.

"Jesus," he huffed as we staggered our way back up to the fifth. "Is it always like this?"

"Not usually," I answered, trying not to wheeze.

"Yeah? Why?"

"Usually there's a couple of Ghoulies lurking at the top of the stairs or near the elevators—when they're working—waiting to count coup on a collector or a soldier or a watchman. We haven't had any of that. So far."

Ramirez stopped. "Why not?" he asked, panting. Hauling a unit down the stairs was painful but at least you did it with a gravity assist so only your knees screamed with pain. Going back up the damn stairs, even unburdened, was a fight with gravity that got tougher as the night wore on, a fight that wore your ass, and everything attached to it, out.

I stopped, thankful Ramirez had first. I took some deep breaths before I answered. "Who knows? Maybe it's raining. Maybe they decided the army turds out front are better targets. Or maybe they're having a barbecue."

"Barbecue?"

"Cheezy wasn't kidding about the long pig."

"Shit."

I shrugged. "Maybe. Probably. Don't know. Never tried any. Get your ass in gear."

* * *

The fifth floor was clear. Cheezy gave Ramirez and me a break. "Y'all take five and we'll head up one. We'll call if we need you."

"Yessir," Ramirez acknowledged.

I managed a thankful wave.

"Shit. Shit. Shit." The panic buzzed into our ears. A bunch of barely coherent babbling filled the channel.

"Knock it the *fuck* off, assholes," we heard Sergeant McNair's disgusted snarl. "Christ. Everyone. Listen up. We just took rounds from the building on the north side of the complex. No casualties. Over."

"You need us?" Conrad queried.

"Negative. Negative." McNair answered. "Get to work. We're going to hose the place down a bit with the twenties."

"Is it raining?" Cheezy asked.

"What? Well. Yeah. Affirmative," Conrad replied.

"Save your ammo, Sergeant. They're just fucking with you."

Silence for some seconds. "You sure?"

"I am," Cheezy replied.

"Why?"

"None of you are dead."

The muffled double *thump-thump-thump* of the twenties was McNair's reply.

I understood completely.

* * *

Six gave Ramirez and I two more to hump down to R2VToo.

"Four more," I rasped as we were halfway up the stairwell to seven. "Four more."

- 173 -

Ramirez panted. "But . . . there's . . . only . . . nineteen—"

"Floors, asshole. Floors," I snarled. "Move your ass."

* * *

The newb and I sagged against the walls, halfway up the stairway to Level Seven. *Maybe we'll get lucky and finish the night's work here.* "I don't want to climb any more fucking stairs," I wheezed. Quietly. I thought.

Mort patted my back. "Oh, you poor baby. When we're finished, I would *love* to rub away your kinks and pains. Massage, after all, *is* my hobby."

"Hell, Mort, the only place where I don't have any kinks and pains is the one place you want to massage."

"Naturally, darling. If I massage *that* you'll forget all about everything else. Say you'll let me."

"I'm too tired, Morticia. Why don't you chat up Ramirez? He's been up and down as much as I have."

"Team up," Conrad ordered. "We're clear."

Peters made his standard announcement. I peeked around Cheezy's legs. There were three units laid out that I could see. Maybe the Gods of Collections were going to smile on me, after all.

We trudged up the rest of the way and waited for Mort to rip the units.

"Give me a fucking break!" Mort barked.

"What's up, Mort?"

"Got one still breathing, Cheezy."

"For long?"

"How the fuck should I know?" Silence. "Probably not much longer," he answered a moment later.

"Let's clear the apartment, Peters," Cheezy ordered. "Maybe we can get some background."

"Right." Peters answered and knocked on the door. Again. And again. "Guess no one's home."

"Yeah? Then who pulled her out here?" I asked.

"She ID'ed, Mort?" Cheezy asked.

Mort checked his tablet. "Yep. One Christian, Angela. Aged thirty—"

"I don't want to know who the fuck she is, Morticia. What I want to know is does she live here?" our team lead snarled quietly in his own inimitable my-life-will-be-complete-only-after-I-shove-my-Kabar-in-the-side-of-your-throat way.

"She does," Mort answered quickly.

"Well. Fuck," Cheezy replied.

Conrad picked up on the tension. She made sure her team was where she wanted them: one at the top of the stairwell down to Six; another at the bottom of the stairs up to Eight; and the other two covering opposite directions of the hall. "I'll clear the room," she told Cheezy. "When you're ready."

"It's your building, Peters," Cheezy said. "Do I have your permission to enter this room, uh, Apartment Seven One Three?" he inquired formally.

Cheezy must have been nervous. He didn't usually make permission a matter of electronic record.

"No problem," Peters answered.

"You said you know how to use a Halligan, Ramirez. Get at it," Cheezy ordered.

Ramirez unslung the tool and went for the door.

"Uh, Mr. Peters. You might want to step over to the side," Conrad suggested. "You know, out of the line of fire."

"Yeah. Right," Peters replied and took a couple of steps to the side and back, enough so he was behind Conrad's muzzle.

Cheezy needed no such prompting.

Conrad went prone, her rifle aimed at the apartment's door. "Ready," he declared.

"Do it," Cheezy ordered.

Ramirez shoved the forks of the Halligan into the gap between the jamb and the door edge. I hammered the sucker in. Ramirez pulled back and fell on his ass, the door popped open that quickly.

"Fucking low bid contractors," Peters muttered.

No one paid attention.

"Check Ramirez's suit integrity, Delong. Let's go, Conrad."

Conrad made it to her feet and moved into the apartment, with Cheezy right behind her.

"Come on in," Cheezy said a few moments later.

I helped the newb to his feet and checked his suit. "You're good, Ramirez."

"Thanks," he replied. "God. I think I hate this shit."

I slapped him on the shoulder. "It's a paycheck, dude. You okay?"

"And the rent. Yeah. I'm okay."

"After you, then. The Boss awaits."

Mort was first in. "Oh. Double fuck," he exclaimed a few seconds later.

* * *

There were two units sprawled on the floor. One had a hand still wrapped around the hilt of a knife buried in the guts of the other.

"Mort?" Cheezy prompted.

"Give me a minute."

The team waited. Conrad went to clear the rest of the apartment. Peters watched.

"Skin-and-bones here doesn't have an ID," Mort said.

"Any clue, Peters?" Cheezy asked.

"Never've seen him."

"Probably a Ghoulie. Don't matter. Rip it, Mort," Cheezy ordered. "At least we'll have some DNA if anyone cares to come looking."

I laughed.

"What about the guy with the knife buried in his heart?" Cheezy asked Peters. "Doesn't look like one of your typical residents. Too healthy looking and too damn fat."

Peters shuffled. "Don't know," he finally answered.

"Yeah? Right," Cheezy replied flatly. "Ramirez."

"Sir?"

"Rip Moby Dick. I want to find out who this guy is. Well? Get to it, dumbass! What the fuck"s wrong with you?"

"I think I know the guy," Ramirez admitted.

"Is that a fact? Then get to work and find out for sure."

The newb knelt and aimed a chip reader at the unit. "What I thought."

"Who is he?" Cheezy asked tersely.

"Samuel Armstrong."

I snorted. "Who was he when he was breathing?"

"Head of the Glenfield Heights Neighborhood Association."

Mort spoke first. "No shit?"

"None. At least, that's who he was when I was working there."

"And now he's here. Dead," Cheezy said. "A rusty old butcher's knife buried to the hilt in his chest. Which, I surmise, given my Government-funded medical training, is almost certainly the cause of death. I gotta wonder, Peters: What would a fuck from the Heights be doing in this rathole? How did it get inside?"he asked idly. "Hmm?"

"Like I said, Cheezy. I have no clue," Peters replied weakly.

"Check his pockets, Ramirez," Cheezy ordered.

The newb did. He pulled a wad of cash out of the unit's front trouser pocket and held it up.

"Christ! That's, what, a couple of —" Mort began to wonder before he cut himself off: No need to broadcast the find to everyone. Instead, he made three quick zeroes with his index finger and thumb.

Ramirez whiffed through the bills. "Yeah. Probably."

"Man liked to live dangerously," I offered.

"There were rumors," Ramirez said.

"What rumors?" Cheezy asked.

I think he already knew the answer. We'd heard our own rumors and we'd collected our share of out-of-place units over time.

"The people in the Heights had an attitude and didn't seem to think the quarantine laws applied to them. At least when they thought they could get away with it." He cleared his throat. "A lot of the Watchmen made some decent cash looking the other way when the residents decided to head into town. Maybe to party. Maybe to score. Maybe to . . ." He jerked a thumb toward the hallway.

"Yep," Cheezy said. "What I figured. A crime of passion. Or jealousy. We ain't cops: ours not to reason why. Rip this shit, Ramirez. And, Mr. Peters? You and I need to have a word." They stepped away and put their helmets together.

The building custodian probably pimped for his residents or looked the other way when he could. If the wad of greenbacks Ramirez found on the beluga was typical, I had no doubt Peters was making some good cash on the side.

I knew why Cheezy was pissed. Collectors are duty-bound to report violations of the current rules applicable to distancing or quarantine breaches. It was our asses if we didn't. We always made sure Peters got his cut of the wealth we found in the apartments we worked. Cheezy figured Peters knew there was at least one way into and out of the South Towers Complex. The fucker was probably charging admission on top of anything else he was raking in by playing pimp. The asshole was taking a really big chance by not cutting us in.

Peters returned as Ramirez and I were bagging the likely Ghoulie. "Uh, Collector?"

"His name's Ramirez." Cheezy's disdain dripped all over the electromagnetic spectrum.

"Right. Collector Ramirez: I think your software has misidentified this victim," Peters said as he toed the dead whale.

Ramirez swiveled his head toward Cheezy and raised his arms. *What gives?* he was asking silently.

"Mr. Peters believes the unit you're getting ready to bag is a Ghoulie."

"Yes," Peters agreed. "We've had reports that there's a thriving market for stolen or counterfeit bio-identification chips. As the higher authorities have declared this complex sealed, with no unauthorized exit or ingress possible, then there can be only one reasonable and logical conclusion. Yes?"

Cheezy was nodding.

"What about the DNA? I already pulled fluids."

"If the software's accurate, Ramirez, the lab guys will flag the anomaly," Mort offered.

This was South Tower: The Sun would go supernova at the end of the shift before someone in a lab ran tests against Ghoulie fluids.

"So. Given we have a potential misidentification and a felony to boot, we'll make damn sure the fluids don't get mixed up or destroyed. Right?" Cheezy offered blandly.

Ramirez stared at Cheezy. "Okay," the newb finally said. "So I John-Doe the guy?"

"That would be appropriate," Mort interjected. "You need a hand, Ramirez?"

"No. I got it. It's cool."

"Glad to hear it," Cheezy replied warmly.

* * *

The woman died while Ramirez and I humped skin-and-bones down to the loading dock and popped it into the back of R2VToo.

"Can I ask a question?" Ramirez panted.

"Sure. Ask three," I answered. "Give me a chance to catch my breath."

"What do you think happened up there?" Ramirez asked via helmet-talk.

"No clue. My guess is maybe the fat guy was the woman's trick of the minute. He showed up and found the ho dead. Dragged what he thought was a carcass into the hallway. Then, unvaccinated Mr. Ghoulie here," I continued as I patted the feet end of the unit's bag, "stumbled along and in a fit of jealous rage slaughtered the john, dying in the process, unexpectedly slain by some new variant of the unseen crud no doubt swimming about this shithole." I scuffed my foot. "Who knows? Who cares? Basically, it means we have four more adult equivalents to haul to the Pits."

"Four? But—"

I raised a hand. "It's gonna be easy to justify the dead walrus up there is more than one Adult Equivalent."

Our radios snapped. "Delong and Ramirez. If the two of you are done sucking each other's dick, get your asses up to Level Eight," Cheezy growled.

I sighed as I stretched. "No rest for the wicked. Let's go."

* * *

We made it to Eight.

"What about the units on Seven?" I asked Cheezy.

He patted my shoulder. "You and Ramirez have been humping your asses off. We'll grab 'em on the way back down, after we've worked the rest of the floors." He then punched me in the shoulder. "Besides, white boy, I know you and Ramirez ain't got the stones at this point to haul Mr. Big Ass down all by your lonesomes. Me and Mort'll help."

"Damn, boss. You're going to make me cry. I don't know what to say to you being so generous and understanding," I said, accompanied by a couple of dramatic sniffs.

"Try 'thank you.' They're one syllable words and easy to say, even for White mother fuckers."

"No business on Eight, guys," Peters commed, interrupting the gay repartee.

"Up one," Conrad ordered her men wearily.

Soldier Smith took point and made his cautious way up the next damn flight of stairs. "Lights on," he told us a moment later.

* * *

It hit the fan on the last floor. Smith went down, his suit shredded by a shotgun. He fell back and tumbled down the stairwell he'd just ascended.

"Goddammit! Goddammit!" Mort screamed as Smith bowled him over. I stumbled down after them. Mort was okay; he wasn't seriously hurt and his suit didn't have any rips or tears. Smith appeared to be still breathing so I slapped duct tape over the holes made by the shot.

As I worked, Conrad crept to the top of the stairs. She emptied a magazine into the blackness of a hall lit only by a couple of barely functioning emergency exit signs. She crunched back down and reloaded. "Light up your night vision, Price, and tell me if you see anything."

"Yes, Sergeant." Price clipped a NOD monocular onto the mount on the front of his helmet and swung it down over his right eye.

"Price?"

"Yes? Sergeant?"

"Feel free to take your weapon off safe," Conrad offered lightly. "And, by all means, feel free to use it."

"Uh. Yes, Sergeant."

Cheezy and Conrad both shook their heads.

Another shotgun blast and a couple of sharp cracks—probably a Ghoulie with a twenty-two—rang out as Price raised his head.

"Jesus-H-Fucking-Christ!" he shouted as he yanked his head out of the line of fire and slid down a step.

Conrad planted her off hand into the soldiers crotch. "You good, Price?" she asked calmly.

"Yeah. Fuck yeah," Price answered breathlessly. "Uh. Yes, Sergeant. Uh, Sergeant?"

"What is it?"

"No disrespect. But could you let go of my nuts?"

Conrad laughed. "Are you gonna slide down any more stairs?"

"No, Sergeant."

"Good. Give me the NOD. Mr. Peters?"

"What is it?"

"Fire suppression work on this floor? Fire extinguishers?"

Peters snorted. "Not for a real long time. And the extinguishers keep getting stolen. Why do you ask?"

"Just curious," Conrad answered, distracted as she worked a flashbang loose from her vest.

"You're not going to use that in here? Are you?" Peters asked, horrified.

"I'm not happy about it. But the fuckers up there shot at me and my people," the soldier answered nonchalantly. "And, you know, that kind of pisses me off. You ready, Price? Wallace?"

"Yes, Sergeant," was the chorused answer from the two soldiers.

"Outstanding. Here's how it's going to work: I pop this down the hall. When I say go, we fucking head up to the top of the stairs and you two shoot the shit out of the dark. While you're reloading, I'll go over the top and check things out. When I say it's clear, we'll piss on any fires that might have gotten started. Got it?"

"Affirmative."

"Check."

"One last thing, Price and Wallace. I want to see bolts locked to the rear before I go down range. One of you shoots me in the ass and I *will* come back and haunt you and your spawn forever and ever. Understood? Good. Let's do it."

"Sergeant Conrad?"

"What is it?" she asked Cheezy.

"If you're willing, we can cover the doors as you clear the hall."

Conrad harrumphed. "Whatcha gonna do if someone pops out? Look mean at 'em?"

Cheezy gave the signal by slowly drawing his 1911. I pulled the Sig from my pouch. Mort did the same with his Beretta. Ramirez got the hint and drew his Glock.

"We're pretty good at looking mean," Cheezy answered dryly.

Conrad chuckled. "I guess you might at that. Awright. We soldiers work the hall like I said. The other gentlemen, ahem, will look mean at the doors that we pass."

"Roger that," Cheezy agreed. "Delong'll look surly on the right. Mort will do the same on the left. And Ramirez will cover our ass. I'll be our reserve. Got it?"

"No prob, Cheezy. We got it," I answered.

"Good. Get your game faces on."

We all chambered our first round.

"Ready to go when you are, Sergeant," Cheezy offered.

Conrad pulled the pin on the flashbang. "Fire in the hole!"

* * *

Two Ghoulies lay sprawled at the end of the hall.

"Clear!" Conrad called after she'd double-tapped the bodies.

"What the fuck?"

I think it was the soldier named Price.

"No bullet's wasted on a corpse," Cheezy offered.

"Ain't no arguin' with that kind of logic," Conrad agreed. "My team up. Since we have mean-looking fucks covering our ass, we'll clear the rooms backwards, back toward the stairs. You okay with that, Team One Actual?"

"Damn straight. And feel free to call me Cheezy, Sergeant."

"Understood. Uh, Cheezy, can we borrow your Halligan guy? It's been a long night and I don't want to kick in doors if I don't have to."

"You certainly may. Ramirez, head up. Mort, you cover our backsides."

"Why me?" Mort whined.

"I'm just giving you what you're always asking for," Cheezy replied sweetly. "Move it, dear. I got the left side, Delong."

"No prob, Cheezy."

We positioned ourselves at the stair-end of the hall and waited. "You want me to pop a flare, boss?" I asked.

"Nah. Conrad's night vision gives us an edge. If we light the place up, everyone can see everyone. We got enough light."

"Got it," I replied. Cheezy was right. The few remaining emergency exit lights illumined the hallway, enough, that is, to see someone step into the hall. Not enough, maybe, to catch a door cracked open; too many dark shadows.

But you make do in this job, no mistake.

A Ghoulie rushed out of the fifth door just as Ramirez was set to give it a pop with the Halligan. Conrad and Price smoked the asshole with a short burst each. The third soldier—Wallace—emptied an entire magazine into the asshole.

"Shit. Sergeant. Sorry. I'm . . . sorry," Wallace sounded ready to cry.

"Don't sweat it, Wallace," Conrad replied flatly. "Get a fresh mag into your weapon."

"Yes, Sergeant."

A second Ghoulie came screaming out of the same apartment while everyone was distracted by the sideshow of the birth of a real veteran. She, like the first one, came out firing, single shots from an semi-auto AR.

We all went flat.

Except Ramirez. The forks of the Halligan he thrust into the cunt's chest burst her heart. Her scream became a gurgle and she slumped to the floor, dragging the entry tool from Ramirez's hands.

He didn't bother to hold on.

"I just shit my drawers," Conrad said breathlessly as she stood. "Christ."

"Don't know him. He don't hang around here," Cheezy offered. "You okay, Ramirez?"

"No prob," Ramirez answered as he stooped for the Halligan.

Conrad kicked the weapons away from their former owners. "Focus, assholes," she barked at her team. "We still got to clear this rathole." She lifted her rifle. "Price. Wallace. You stay out here. Price: cover left. Wallace: right. There may be more vermin."

Conrad shuffled slowly into the apartment. "Aw. Shit. Fucking shit," she commed a few seconds later.

"Can we come in, Sergeant?" Cheezy queried.

"No," Conrad spat. "Wait one. Fucking shit."

We waited a minute. Maybe two.

"Clear," the sergeant announced wearily. "Bring your guys in, Cheezy."

* * *

"What's up?" Cheezy asked as we, Ramirez and I, followed him into the apartment.

Conrad answered by pointing with her off-hand toward the nattered love seat centered beneath the boarded-up window of the apartment's living area.

Cheezy stepped forward. "Aw. Man. This sucks."

"What's up?" Ramirez asked.

"Nothing, man. Go relieve Mort," Cheezy ordered.

"Uh. Okay. But . . ." He took a step forward and then sank to his knees. "No. No."

I laid my hand on Ramirez's shoulder. "It happens, dude, out here in the shit world. Cheezy?"

"Yeah?"

"I ain't in charge, but I think finding a couple of what are probably now orphans and getting them out of this fucking shithole qualifies as an acceptable reason to call it a day."

Cheezy stepped over and touched Ramirez's other shoulder. "I happen to agree. C'mon, Ramirez. C'mon, dude."

Ramirez straightened. "I killed their—"

Everyone heard the tears in his voice.

"You did what you had to do and these," Cheezy jerked a thumb at the pair of toddlers wrapped up in old towels and a blanket, "might fucking survive because of you," Cheezy rasped. "You bundle 'em up while the rest of us handle the units. Sergeant?"

"Yo, Cheezy?"

"We're done here for the night. You okay with that?"

"Hell, yeah. We'll cover your asses, you bet."

"Good. Let's get the fuck out of here."

* * *

We didn't rip any of the Ghoulies. Zipping their carcasses into the herps was all we gave a shit about. After all, the four units from Ten got us closer to quota.

Conrad and her team swore they'd evac the twins—easy to tell, even if they were only about a year old—to the nearest medical intake.

Cheezy took her at her word and ordered us back to work.

* * *

We were knackered when we made it to the hippo. The four of us tried to lift the multi-ton deadweight.

We assured Conrad and her team that we'd be able to take care of ourselves for what was left of the night.

When they were out of sight, we simply rolled and pushed Moby Dick down the stairs and to the loading dock.

Thank the Gods the floor of R2VToo's bed was a few inches lower than the edge of that dock.

* * *

Cheezy gave Ramirez and Mort permission to escort the youngsters to wherever Conrad was going to take them.

I don't think he mistrusted Conrad or doubted the sergeant's word.

But Cheezy has a thing about kids even if they are undocumented Ghoulies.

I guess I understood.

* * *

"We haven't made quota, Cheezy," I said quietly after he and I placed Mrs. Willcox atop the night's load.

"Nope. We haven't. And you know what? I don't give a shit."

"Hawg's gonna be up your ass," I observed as we got into R2VToo's cab.

Cheezy snorted. "I'll tell him Morticia's already been there. That'll keep him out of it. But it don't matter. We saved us a couple of kids, right? We tell Hawg we came in early after we made the call to keep the living youngsters alive. What's wrong with that?"

"Nothing. At least, nothing as far as I'm concerned, Cheezy. But—"

"But the fuckers who make the o-fficial calls may not see it so clearly, eh?"

"Something like that."

"Yeah. That's what I thought." Cheezy sighed and changed the subject. He set his helmet against mine. "Ramirez worked, huh?"

"He did," I agreed.

"Think we can keep him?"

"It's gonna piss Walker off."

"Probably. But he's got to be alive to be pissed off, right?"

"He does," I agreed.

"We'll drink to his survival, then. You're buyin', white boy."

"Yeah. Cheezy. I'm buying."

He slapped my thigh. "Let's get this shit done so we can go home."

I put R2VToo into gear and steered to the Pits with the night's load. "You got it, Boss."

Divine Retribution

S henoute's bellow roiled the clouds and fluttered the wings of passing messenger cherubs. "Raphael! My office. Now."

Senior Sub-Diety Raphael, Chief Administrator of the Office of Corporeal Admonishments, closed his eyes and rubbed his forehead. "Yes, sir." He stood, straightened his wings, and made his reluctant way toward the boss's podium. "You wished to see me, sir?" he asked.

Shenoute thrust a piece of parchment into Raphael's face. "What is this?" he fiercely demanded.

The chief administrator flinched. "May I see it? Sir?"

Shenoute sneered and dropped the document.

Raphael managed to snatch it before it fell to Earth.

"Well?" Shenoute insisted impatiently.

"Um, it's—"

"Spit it out, boy!" The boss glowered with eyes afire with faithful certitude. "Or do sinful thoughts freeze your tongue?" he coldly hissed.

"Sin? Why, no sir. No sin. None at all," Raphael quickly denied. Untruthfully, as he'd been hoping the stool propping up Saint Shenoute's stinky ass would splinter and drop the overzealous lout from Heaven. "It, um, appears to be an older Admonishment Order. It's been some time since we used that version of the form." He smiled. "Was there anything else, sir?"

The fire in Shenoute's eyes flared, brighter and more fiercely than the flames of Hades. "Yes," he answered caustically. "As a matter of fact, there is." He leaned back into his stool and crossed his arms across his chest. "What's *wrong* with the order?" he queried sarcastically, eternal damnation an unspoken threat if the answer was not satisfactory.

Raphael blinked and looked again. "Hmm. I don't see...ah! Yes! It's incomplete."

Shenoute nodded righteously. "Yes. It is. Why is it so?" he asked dangerously as he cast his eyes left, then right. Quickly; multiple times. "Has the Evil One found a new roost? Hmm? Well, *has* it, Chief Administrator?" he asked with a shout.

Raphael, taking another step away from the lunatic before him, almost fell off the cloud. "No, sir. No evil one. Nothing like that," he replied hurriedly. "I'll take this and look into it, sir. Get an answer back to you as quickly as I can."

Shenoute rapped a gnarly fist on the corner of his podium. "You had better," he rasped.

* * *

"What in all the darkness of the abyss was *that* about?" Theodore, Raphael's trusted assistant novice murmured as the Chief Administrator plopped into his desk chair.

Raphael mopped his brow. "Who knows what goes on inside the head of that old by-blow?" He shook his wings. "Take this."

Theodore took the parchment and studied it for a moment. "Jesus, it's a—"

"Damnation, Novice. How many times do I have to reproach you?" Raphael asked tiredly.

"Er. Sorry, sir. I won't let it happen it again."

The Chief Administrator snorted. "My weary burro."

The junior angel blushed and focused his attention upon the parchment. "This is over thirty years old!"

"And?" Raphael nudged.

Theodore studied further. "It doesn't appear to have been properly completed."

"Indeed. Set aside your other duties and get me the backstory on this. As quickly as you can."

* * *

"Sir?"

"What is it, Theo?"

The Novice glanced toward the podium.

Raphael smiled. "Don't worry. He's drafting a new covenant for a fresh batch of novices." He shook his head and muttered: "Another bunch that won't be worth heretic dung for a couple of centuries."

Theodore frowned. "May I ask an impertinent question, Chief Administrator?"

"Sure. If you do so quietly."

"Why do they keep him around, if he's so, well, if his effect is so deletorious?" the Novice quietly wondered.

Raphael winced. Such questions had a way of getting back to the Main Office. The consequences for the questioner—and any who'd the temerity to answer—could be extreme: Raphael chose his words carefully. "Saint Shenoute," he began sternly and reverently, "is cadre from almost the beginning, Novice. His long service is appreciated by the executive team; as is his devotion; and his unceasing willingness to continue to contribute to the success of He Who Is In Charge.

"Saint Shenoute is to be revered. Of utmost importance, he deserves all our prayers and hopes that he will, one day, soon, choose to find peace on a cloud of his own, where he can finally seek quiet contentment and spiritual satisfaction without interfence or interruption from any one. Do you understand?"

"I do, Chief Administrator," Theodore acknowledged wryly. "I understand completely."

"Excellent. Until then, we do what must be done, yes?"

"Quite, sir."

Raphael smiled. Theodore certainly had a bright future within the Heavenly Bureaucracy. "Now. What is it that you wanted of me?"

"I have the results of the investigation you requested."

Raphael frowned. "And?"

Theodore scratched his halo. "Wellll . . ."

Raphael sighed and rubbed the bridge of his nose. "There was an error."

Theodore nodded. "A failure to perform, if you get right down to it."

The Chief Administrator bit his lip. "The age of the document, the initiation date: Before I took over?"

Theodore shook his head.

Raphael stood. "Oh." He sighed. "Oh. Sheep poop."

The Novice nodded.

"Let's take a walk, Theodore. I feel I need some inspiration."

* * *

"Where *are* we going, sir?"

"Paradise."

The Novice was confused. "But, sir. This is it. Yes?"

Raphael shook his ahead. "I apologize for not being clear. I meant Jannah." He smiled ruefully. "I expect the data you've collected won't be pleasant. And that's more than I can take without some pleasant looking table service."

"Ah." Theodore snicked his teeth. "Never been myself."

The Chief Administrator smiled. "You'll enjoy it, I've no doubt."

* * *

"Peace, Brothers. Welcome, welcome. Table for two?"

"Unto to you, Peace. Yes, please," Raphael answered the host of Jannah.

"If you'd follow me," the host replied.

The Chief Administrator and his Novice were escorted to a small table. Flowers bloomed in a thousand colors, their combined scent a pleasure rather than a sneeze. Butterflies danced from bud to bud, bouyed by the soft breeze that caressed plant and angel alike. The sky, cloudless, was a intense blue peopled only by soaring falcons. The gentle chimes and tinkles and splashes of the small brook behind them soothed the ear, while the fish who darted about pleased the eye.

But not so much as the server who approached. "Refreshments?" she offered with a smile.

"White wine," Raphael answered. "If you would."

She winked. "I would."

"Good Lord," Theodore muttered breathlessly as she walked off. "I've never seen such raven hair go all the way down like that," he sighed.

"And legs that go *all* the way up. Like that." Raphael smiled. "Indeed, son. Women: One of His greatest and most enduring achievements."

"And those breasts." The Novice twitched uncomfortably in his seat. "I'm gonna need shriving," he murmured.

Raphael winked. "What happens in Jannah stays in Jannah, Theo." He sighed and straightened. "Tell me about it," he ordered flatly.

"Wha . . . oh. The admonishment order?"

"Yes."

As Theo explained, the Chief Administrator sank lower and lower into his seat. "My mistake, then," he summarized when the novice finished presenting his findings.

"Perhaps more of an unintentional oversight wrought by an unexpected spike in order volume," the Novice attempted, vainly trying to console his superior. "I checked the statistics, sir. The numbers may be useful."

Raphael chuckled mirthlessly. "How? As a defense?" He shook his head. "Our blessed leader—be thankful to He Who Shall Be Praised that the assignment is temporary—brooks nothing but holy perfection, especially when it's in the service of the Big Boss himself." He caught their server's eye. Her approach was a pleasing distraction, proof that the Man at the Top was an artist of the First Degree.

"Brother?" she asked with a smile, her perfect white teeth complemented by lips of a glistening cherry red.

"Two more glasses of wine," Raphael replied.

She winked as she bowed. "Your wish is my command." Her eyes sparked. "Would you care for something else? I've a wonderful assortment of treats that go well with the wine. I could show them to you, if you'd like."

The Chief Administrator laughed heartily, his immediate woe forgotten as his wings achieved a tumescence he'd last experienced—goodness—more than a millenia ago. "Thank you, my dear. Much as I'd like to see them, we must decline, to my eternal regret, I'm sure. Just the wine, please."

"Perhaps next time," she offered with a raised eyebrow and a saucy swish of her hips.

The Novice mopped heavenly dew from his forehead. "Oh. My. God."

Raphael good-naturedly slapped his assistant's knee. "Right in one." He took a breath and watched a pair of Painted Ladies weave a dance through the flowers. "Thank you for checking on this, Theodore. I'll take it from here."

"Sir. If I'm asked—"

"I doubt he will. But if he does, tell him I've taken care of it. After all, that's the truth. Or will be, once we get back to the office."

* * *

Raphael finished his weekly briefing. "In conclusion, sir, while order volume is up, this is an historical spike with which we're comfortably able to accomodate. As our response-to-order ratio clearly shows."

"What's this spike, eh?" Stenhoute growled.

"It's the autumn equinox season down below, sir. A traditional time for large gatherings of sinners; these are known as 'conventions.'" Raphael shrugged. "Admonishment orders are overwhelmingly issued for misdemeanors."

"What's this 'misdemeanor' nonsense? A sin's a sin!"

"Indeed, sir. I couldn't agree more."

"I don't like your tone, Chief Administrator," Saint Shenoute rasped. "I may only be here while your real boss is on vacation but, by all that's Holy, I'll run a tight ship while I'm in charge!" he declared righteously. "Speaking of tight ships, you've failed to report to me."

Raphael reared back, surprised by the harsh accusation. "Failure? Forgive me, sir! What failure?"

Shenoute's eyes narrowed and his wings flattened. "Are you mocking me? Your failure, Raphael. The one I had to bring to your attention. The incomplete admonishment order."

The Chief Administrator shrugged. "I appreciate your bringing the matter to my attention. And I've attended to it." He raised an eyebrow quizically. "I am cognizant of how busy you are, sir. It was a minor infraction to begin with and so long ago. I felt it so inconsequential, almost too trivial to waste any more of your time."

Saint Shenoute's eyes blazed. His lips trembled. His fingers clenched into fists. "You consider adulterous fornication trivial? Trivial?! Well! Do you?" he roared.

"I do not. But the matter was almost thirty years in the man's past. And with a female with whom he'd been affectionate before his marriage. It was a chance encounter; no premeditation and, as those things go, relatively little lust but quite a bit more than the usual tenderness.

"It was a reunion of boon companions, sir. They were—and remain—great friends. He's led an exemplary life since the event," Raphael replied bravely.

Shenoute's barking could be considered caustic laughter. "You take me for a fool, Chief Administrator," he replied with a cruel twist of his lip. "Let me guess: His admonishment was a stubbed toe in his morning shower."

"Nothing so mundane, sir! Certainly not. He was involved in a collision of his conveyance for which he was not only found at fault, but also suffered several painful injuries. This after a graded evaluation taking into consideration the severity of the original sin and the elapsed time since."

"'Graded evaluation.' That sounds like just the kind of spiritual sewage Maria would come up with," Shenoute noted acerbically. "Bureaucratic inanities such as this should rank right down there with lust, gluttony, and all the others." His eyes transfixed the Chief Administrator. "And the bureaucrats who connive to implement those inanties deserve nothing less than being spitted over the eternal roasting fires of Hell." He shot to his feet, his gnarled, bony hands planted on his hips. "I will not condone such laxity when it comes to implementing and enforcing His design, Chief Administrator. This is what you shall do. Immediately." Shenoute gave his orders.

The look of horror on Raphael's face grew as his wings wilted. "Sir," he began weakly. "That's . . . that's . . . with respect, sir; this course of action is inordinate and not in keeping with His guidance. Not to mention that admonishments are their most efficacious when occurring in temporal proximity to the sin warranting the admonishment."

"Indeed. That is why I've done *your* job and developed the action plan I've assigned to you. Besides, you forget yourself, Chief Administrator. I interpret policy; *you* implement my interpretation." Shenoute took his stool and dusted his hands. "When you've finished, you will report to me. Immediately. Do I make myself clear?"

Raphael rose shakily to his feet, his wings drooping like a Root of Evil in need of a pink pill. "Yes. You do. May I go?" he asked tiredly.

"Be off! And I want that report soonest!"

* * *

Shenoute, intent on drafting yet one more convenant for yet one more draft of inductees, took some time to notice Novice Theodore waiting politely on the edge of his cloud. "Eh? Who're you?" he growled.

"Novice Theodore, sir."

"Yeah? What do you want?"

"Chief Administrator Raphael asked me to deliver the report you requested."

"On?"

"The results of the admonishment order you ordered."

Shenoute slapped his quill down angrily. "And why is the Chief Administrator not delivering this report himself?"

Theodore gulped. "He felt in need of some quiet contemplation and spiritual renewal, sir. He entrusted me to deliver the report as soon as possible; he knows how important this is to you."

Shenoute intended fully to include the dereliction in his report to the Higher Ups when his assignment was complete. Not to mention his recommendation that important assignments such as Corporeal Admonishments needed a firm and harsh *male* hand in control. Graded approach: heretical poppycock! Something only a weak female would come up with. He made a side note to remind himself to have the Inquisitors run another background check on Saint Maria. "Get on with it, boy! Baal got your tongue?"

"No sir! Er. Well, sorry. Um. Yes, sir. As you instructed, the Sinner arrived home to find his spouse engaged in carnal activity with a perfect stranger. He fled the scene and sought comfort in an establishment conveying spiritous liquors. He overindulged and was later restrained by the forces of law and order. He was charged and convicted of said overindulgence while operating a motorized conveyance and, as a consequence, lost his job." Theodore cleared his throat. "His daughter became pregnant by a school companion. His son overdosed on opiods."

"Is that all?" Shenoute asked softly, so far pleased with the results of the Admonishment he'd ordered.

"No, sir."

"Well?"

"In abject despair, the Sinner took his life," Theodore answered softly.

Shenoute sighed happily. "Good! Good!" He shook his head. "Another sinner consigned to the eternal damnation he warrants!" He sighed with satisfaction. "Sinners, boy. We must root them out, excise the evil before it infects others. That's what we're called to do in His service."

"Yes, sir," Theodore sadly replied. A series of consequences that explained why Raphael was dead-drunk and naked in Jannah, being hand-fed grapes while bathing in a pool of wine, trying to decide if he should retire.

"Don't let it get to you, Novice. There's no greater Glory than purging away sin and corruption for Him."

Saint Shenoute clasped his hands behind his head and smiled beatifically. "His Will be done."

Collected Shorts

T he old man whistled as he pushed his dilapidated grocery cart down the cracked and crumbling sidewalk. His suit, a navy blue with magenta pinstripes, was threadbare. His white shirt was once button-down; safety pins held the collar points in place. The collar itself was buttoned but he wore no tie.

Half a block away, two cops watched from the shadows across the street. Despite the bulk and weight of their weapons, body armor, and equipment vests, their backpack environmental units kept them reasonably comfortable, temperature-wise, anyway. The combined weight of forty pounds of equipment on top of their Kevlar-padded and insulated tactical suits made chasing bad guys a pounding and thudding ordeal.

Fortunately, that didn't happen much anymore. Not up and out in the Burn, anyway.

The taller cop straightened as he raised his polarized face shield. "Who's the old guy across the street, Corporal?"

"Eh? Oh. That's Old Man Jenkins."

The taller of the two cops pulled out his ticket tablet. Corporal shook his head. "What's that for?"

"I'm gonna cite him for his multiple public safety violations."

"Are you kidding?"

"Not at all." The junior cop pointed. "It's day and he's out without a hat or eye protection. And I'm betting that outfit he's wearing ain't got no UV protection." He stepped off the curb.

His partner grabbed him by the shoulder. "Back off, rookie," he grumbled.

"What the fuck?"

"Leave him be. He's coming over, anyway. No need to step out of the shade."

"But—"

"Shut up, kid. Hey, Mr. Jenkins. What's with the feet?"

Jenkins smiled even as he struggled to free the front wheels of his shopping cart from the twisted grate of an old storm drain. "Well, poop," he sighed. Despite the temperature of just over one hundred five degrees—fairly average for a January morning in Iowa—the old man wasn't sweating overly much. He gave the cart a swift kick in the rear. It was enough to bust the front wheels loose and up onto the curb. "Thank you, Corporal Henderson," he said as the cop helped pull the cart onto to the sidewalk. "I had to find a pair of new shoes. Unfortunately, they're not quite my size. They're somewhat tight as I'm still breaking them in."

"Where'd you find them?" Henderson wondered.

The old man sighed as he mopped his brow with a red silk handkerchief, frayed on one edge and with a few holes. "In a pile of odds and ends tucked away in the corner of a basement." Despite its condition, he refolded the handkerchief gently and neatly before he returned it to the inside pocket of his suit coat.

"Looting, huh?"

Jenkins cocked his head. "I see you've a new partner." He leaned forward and squinted at the name tape velcroed to the front of the cop's tactical vest. "Welcome to Downtown, Officer Miller. To answer your question: No, not looting. The premises have been abandoned. As have all the buildings around us. With the exception of those seized by the state: I do not trespass."

Miller glared.

Henderson ignored the rookie. "You still haven't found a hat, eh?" he asked Jenkins. "Or sunglasses?"

The old man looked apologetic. "Regrettably, I have not."

"You know you're breaking the law," Miller said sourly.

Jenkins smiled. "I do not dignify the regulations promulgated by an overbearing, busybody nanny state as 'laws', Officer. Besides, this unusual heat will soon pass and such inane restrictions on my human rights will fade away."

"That kind of talk can get you cited for Failure to Respect the State."

The old man chuckled. "I haven't had a lick of respect for politicians and bureaucrats, or the meaningless mumbo-jumbo they generate, for over fifty years, Officer Miller." He raised his hands. "I ask nothing from the state, Officer, other than to be left in peace. In exchange, I do not avail myself of the services it provides." Jenkins lowered his hands and smiled. "I believe I get the better of the transaction."

Miller turned his glare to his partner. "Aren't you—"

"No. I'm not," Henderson replied curtly.

"What brings you gentlemen out into the morning sun?" Jenkins asked. "I'd think you'd have more to do Below as that is where everyone lives. There's little going up here on as you can see."

Henderson snicked his teeth. "I'm showing Miller the territory." He paused. "You know, the Goodwill can fix you up, Mr. Jenkins; that's what's it there for."

Jenkins looked horrified. "I'm in no need of charity, Corporal Henderson. While my cash reserves have been depleted, I'm still able to negotiate an exchange of goods. I've tried, multiple times. Yet the good people there insist I have nothing of value. Silly fools."

"Yeah? You have something worth trading? What would that be, Mr. Jenkins?"

"Why, my stock, Officer Miller," the old man answered as he patted one of the four black garbage bags in his cart.

"Of what?"

Jenkins eyes sparkled. "The largest part of my inventory can be called many things: undies, briefs, tighty-whities, drawers, knickers, skivvies, bloomers, panties, thongs. Over the years, I've added bermudas and gym and running and denim to the inventory."

Miller laughed. Even Henderson smiled a bit.

The old man nodded sagely. "I note your amusement. But it was not so long ago that they were essential items in everyone's wardrobe." His eyes twinkled. "And not-so-essential in many cases when it came to affairs of the heart. And of the libido." He winked. "That reminds me, Corporal Henderson. Your partner's birthday is just around the corner."

"It is."

"I hope she's doing well," Jenkins replied as he untwisted the piece of dirty yellow romex from around the top of one of the bags. "I found these the other day and thought she'd might appreciate such a gift from you."

Henderson took the small package. "What is it?"

Jenkins raised an eyebrow. "*It* is a pair of genuine silk lace panties; the style was known as a boyshort. They've never been worn. And, as you can see, still in the original packaging which trebles, perhaps even quadruples, their value." He took a breath. "And what makes them almost priceless is that they were produced in Vietnam," he declared reverently. "Before that poor nation got caught in the middle of the fight between us and China," Jenkins finished sadly. "Too bad, really. The product quality from that nation exceeded that of Bangladesh and India."

"I'm grateful, Mr. Jenkins. But I can't accept this."

"It's not a bribe, Corporal," Jenkins riposted gently.

"It's not that. It's just something I don't think she'd . . . appreciate, I guess. I mean, she doesn't have any now. Don't think anyone does given most everyone wears an elvis base layer twenty-four-seven."

The old man snorted. "Piffle. Those spaghetti suits are another example of the government getting into everyone's personal business. Nasa developed those Liquid-Ventilation Suits for astronauts to wander about in space, and on Mars and Venus. Demanding citizens don an elvis is another example of the government-industrial complex prying hard-earned wages from citizen's pockets."

Jenkins shook his head ruefully. "This meteorological unpleasantness will end one day and there'll be no need for such nonsense." He gently pushed the parcel away. "Keep it. She may not wear them but she'll have a memento of another, more pleasant time, an artifact produced by a people vaporized in nuclear fire. It's an antique garment; its value can only grow."

Henderson nodded. "Okay. Thanks, Mr. Jenkins. I appreciate it."

"My pleasure." Jenkins fell silent as he looked about. "It didn't use to be like this. There were always people outside, day and night." He pointed across the street. "It doesn't look like much now but that building was *the* place to live here in Downtown. This whole avenue, from the river to up north a mile or so, was lined with restaurants and bars. On Friday nights, the cars would be bumper-to-bumper. And there was a theater on every block. It was mag—"

"What's a theater?"

The old man blinked at the interruption. "Why, a place where people gathered to watch movies, Officer Miller."

"What's a movie?"

Jenkins shook his head. "Nowadays it would be a public health violation of the first degree. A movie was a form of entertainment. A theater was where everyone went to see movies."

Miller blinked. "At the same time? Together?"

The old man laughed. "Indeed. Hundreds." His smile faded. "Many closed during the first plague. Others held on grimly for as long as they could through the second and third torments. A few survived only to be shuttered permanently by law when Wuhan-Four swept the globe. That was when even the die-hard 'Don't Tread on Me' crazies realized the science types weren't making stuff up and that their recommendations were by and large sound." He paused. "Teenagers suffered the most when Wuhan-Three came here. With Four? I think it was having to bury so many infants and toddlers that the last of the whackos finally got a clue. Hmm. Or they finally died off. It's a shame it took so long and cost so dear for that to happen."

Henderson's face blanked. "Copy," he replied, responding to a comm received by the radio embedded in his helmet. "We gotta move on, Mr. Jenkins. You take care, okay? It's supposed to be another scorcher; expected to pop past one-thirty degrees by noon."

"Indeed. I have a shady little nest back behind my store. It's a good place to doze during the heat of the day. And somewhere safe for my inventory. It's already too warm to get the place ready for reopening. I work mostly during the cool of the night." He double-checked the twisted wire closures on his bags. "Good day, Officers. Stay safe."

"Oh! Almost forgot, sir."

"What's that, Corporal Henderson?" Jenkins asked.

"This is for you."

The old man frowned. "Now it's my turn to ask what is it. What is it?"

Henderson pressed a small plastic squeeze bottle into Jenkin's hand. "Oil. I figured those wheels could use a bit of lube."

"Oil," Jenkins croaked as tears puddled in his eyes. "From the ground?" he asked tremulously. "It's been such a long time," he murmured as he stared at the bottle cupped in the palms of his hands.

Henderson looked embarrassed. "Well. No. It's synthetic. But I didn't think your cart would mind the difference."

Jenkins shuddered as he fought back tears and chewed his lower lip. "God be with you, Corporal. Thank you." He pushed his cart back onto the empty street and limped off, struggling to keep the cart on an even keel and a straight path.

"What store?" Miller asked as he watched the old man move away.

Corporal Henderson sighed. "He and his wife had a clothing store down on First Street. It was flooded out in twenty-nine; that was a couple of years before the river dried up. He's been 'rebuilding inventory' for years. That collection of shorts he's pushing around began with what little he was able to salvage from the ruins."

Henderson looked grim. "My pappy always said the river knew it was dying and that flood was its last gasp." He stopped and looked back but Jenkins had already disappeared. "Mr. Jenkins believes things are going to get back to normal. That he'll be able to reopen his store. And that bag of underwear, and whatever else he's collected, will be his inventory, I guess."

Miller shook his head. "There's been no river for over thirty years. And there's been no recorded temp below ninety for at least that long. The man's crazy, huh?"

Henderson shrugged. "Probably. Doesn't matter. We gotta move it."

"One more thing: Who's God?" Miller asked.

"No one who lives around here. C'mon. We gotta go."

Henderson and Miller lowered their visors and stepped from the shade and into the Burn.

Will Lawrence lives in Aiken, South Carolina. He writes whenever the day job and the yard work don't get in the way.

Made in the USA
Columbia, SC
23 September 2023